those who need
e went on, "but
p to it, or might
do you suggest?"

"Why don't we team up, l
those I hear about who ar
in the evenings—unless th
of course. Or if no one has
around and talk to folks wh
or wagons. Why don't we go together!"

"Like
remem
wards with the physicians, noting their orders for the
patients.

"Exactly. I could pray with them while you treat them."

Her heart felt light as she smiled up at Elijah. She felt
strong and full of purpose. *Let's go together,* he'd said.
Was it wrong that the words made her think of feelings
she'd resolved to abandon in favor of independence?

* * *

**Bridegroom Brothers: True love awaits three siblings
in the Oklahoma Land Rush**

The Preacher's Bride Claim—Laurie Kingery,
April 2014

The Horseman's Frontier Family—Karen Kirst,
May 2014

The Lawman's Oklahoma Sweetheart—Allie Pleiter,
June 2014

Books by Laurie Kingery

Love Inspired Historical

Hill Country Christmas
The Outlaw's Lady
*Mail Order Cowboy
*The Doctor Takes a Wife
*The Sheriff's Sweetheart
*The Rancher's Courtship
*The Preacher's Bride
*Hill Country Cattleman
The Preacher's Bride Claim

*Brides of Simpson Creek

LAURIE KINGERY

makes her home in central Ohio, where she is a "Texan-in-exile." Formerly writing as Laurie Grant for the Harlequin Historical line and other publishers, she is the author of eighteen previous books and the 1994 winner of a Readers' Choice Award in the Short Historical category. She has also been nominated for Best First Medieval and Career Achievement in Western Historical Romance by *RT Book Reviews*. When not writing her historicals, she loves to travel, read, participate on Facebook and Shoutlife and write her blog at www.lauriekingery.com.

The Preacher's Bride Claim

LAURIE KINGERY

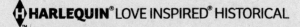

HARLEQUIN® LOVE INSPIRED® HISTORICAL

Special thanks and acknowledgment to Laurie Kingery for her contribution to the Bridegroom Brothers miniseries.

Recycling programs for this product may not exist in your area.

 LOVE INSPIRED BOOKS

ISBN-13: 978-0-373-28259-3

THE PREACHER'S BRIDE CLAIM

www.Harlequin.com

Printed in U.S.A.

And ye shall know the truth,
and the truth shall make you free.
—*John* 8:32

In memory of those lost in the tornadoes
that struck Moore and other communities
in central Oklahoma in May 2013

And as always, to Tom

Chapter One

⁓

April 1, 1889—Boomer Town, Oklahoma Territory

Alice Hawthorne sat down quietly on an empty bench in the back of the tent church. She'd waited until the little congregation was absorbed in singing "Shall We Gather at the River?" so she could steal in unnoticed. There was a family of six on the long bench ahead of her, but none of them paid any attention to her arrival—except for the shortest of the four stair-step boys. He looked over his shoulder at her, his face full of freckles, a cowlick at the back of his shaggy thatch of hair. When he noticed Alice was watching, he gave her a cheerful, gap-toothed grin. Despite the anxiety constricting her heart like a coiled snake, it was such a comical sight that she couldn't help but smile back.

"You turn around this instant, Otis Beauregard LeMaster," his mother hissed at him, without looking to see what or who had distracted her youngest. The boy obediently did so, and Alice was once again alone.

That suited Alice just fine. She hoped to continue to be overlooked among the inhabitants of the tent city as much as possible until the day of the Land Rush, after she had claimed her own 160-acre homestead. Her own and her mother's, she reminded herself.

It was the first of April. Just twenty-one days until the Unassigned Lands—the lands not claimed by one of the many Indian tribes that now called the Oklahoma Territory home—were opened for settlement by the Indian Appropriations Act signed by President Cleveland. His successor, Benjamin Harrison, had designated noon on April 22 as the moment the settlers could rush in, plant their stakes at the claims of their choice and become real homesteaders.

She'd be safe then, wouldn't she?

He shall cover thee with his feathers, and under his wings shalt thou trust... She remembered the verse from childhood, and it comforted her now when she felt like a terrified little bird fleeing from a hunter. Her fear was the reason she had come to the chapel service, to be reminded of God's love and protection.

As the hymn ended, so did her comfortable solitude. With a rustle of skirts, two women plopped themselves down to her left. Alice kept her gaze aimed at the front and hoped they would leave her alone. She had not been an unsociable person before she'd fled New York, but now, she feared each introduction.

The woman next to her didn't take the hint. "Hey, you're new here, ain't ya?" she asked, smiling in a friendly fashion, which revealed incisors that would have done a jackrabbit proud. "Don't believe we've met before. I'm Carrie Ferguson, and this here's my sister, Cordelia."

If she hadn't said they were sisters, Alice would have guessed it, for the two women at her left were so similar-looking with their sun-weathered long faces, noses so sharp they could slice cheese, the same teeth.

"N-nice to meet you," Alice managed to say. "I'm—" She thought about using an assumed name, but how could she lie—especially in a church, even one of canvas? "I'm Alice Hawthorne." Hopefully the two women would forget the name—easy to do in a temporary city populated by hundreds of people, with more coming every day.

"Been in Boomer Town long?" Cordelia asked.

If only the service would start, Alice fretted. She didn't want to answer a bunch of questions. But now that the hymn had concluded, the tall man who may be the preacher was talking to a middle-aged couple up front, and he seemed to be in no hurry.

Alice managed a small smile. "Just since yesterday."

"Where ya from? We hail from St. Louis."

"B-back East," Alice said and prayed they would let it go at that. She wasn't looking to make friends. Each person she gave her name to was one more person who could help Maxwell Peterson find her. And if he did, it would mean the end of her dreams.

"Looks like you've tripled attendance in the week you've been here, Reverend," Keith Gilbert, his deacon, exulted as he nodded toward the nearly full benches. "You must be doing something right."

"It's the Lord's doing," he told Keith. "I have such

plans for the church we'll build in the territory. I hope many of the folks here will be able to settle near us."

"Well, we're certainly planning to stake a claim near enough to help you build it, once you decide which way you'll head," Keith said, and added, "Lord willing."

"Glad to hear it, Keith," Elijah murmured. "I'm counting on your help."

Only one thing marred Elijah's joy in the growth of his congregation—his brothers weren't here. Wanting a fresh start as much as Elijah did, they had come to Oklahoma with him, but they wouldn't attend his chapel services. His middle-born brother, Gideon, wanted nothing more to do with God after he'd lost his wife and child in the influenza epidemic of '87, and since Elijah had also lost his fiancée, Marybelle Atkins, Gideon couldn't understand why Elijah didn't feel the same. Clint, the youngest of the brothers and still a bachelor, was at odds with the Lord, too, after so many losses of friends and family.

My brothers should be here, Elijah thought, with that old familiar ache. *Lord, please draw them back to You.*

"The Lord has blessed our work," he told the Gilberts. "Or perhaps folks come to the chapel because they need divine reassurance at this time of such big changes in their lives."

The Gilberts nodded in approving agreement, but Elijah knew Gideon would have said something. Like maybe they think the more they show up here in chapel, the more likely the Lord will grant them the 160-acre claim of their choice. Or they don't have anything else to do while they wait to claim their land.

Perhaps it was presumptuous to call the big tent that sheltered them from the blistering sun and spring rains a chapel—much less a church—but for now it was all the church they had, and Elijah was grateful for it. Hadn't the Hebrews worshipped God in the open desert air, all those years they wandered in the wilderness?

He was about to greet the congregation when Mr. Gilbert said, "Did you see the pretty lady sitting in the back? The one in the dark bonnet? She came in during the hymn. Can't remember seeing her before."

Elijah followed the direction of Gilbert's nod. Elijah couldn't see the woman's face at the moment, because her head was bowed and the bonnet she wore hid her features, but as if she had felt the scrutiny, she raised her head just then. He saw sky-blue eyes set in a heart-shaped face with a peaches-and-cream quality to it—she must be scrupulous about wearing a hat under the hot western sun. Her hair, what little of it he could see, was auburn. Her petite frame was clothed in serviceable calico.

Her blue eyes looked troubled, and he wondered why. *Who is she?* He thought he'd met everyone who came to his daily services, if not all the inhabitants of this tent city. But newcomers were arriving daily in anticipation of the Land Rush, so she must be a new arrival. He'd have to make it a point to introduce himself after the service, in case she was in need of assistance, as a woman alone very well might be. As the pastor of the freshly sprung-up encampment, his ministry consisted of helping the would-be homesteaders with their needs as much as it did with preaching. He was merely doing his duty.

Of course, she might not be alone after all, he reminded himself. Her husband might be buying supplies at one of the tent stores that had sprouted like weeds after a good rain. Or perhaps he was dealing with livestock or, like his brothers, was not a believer.

"Yessir, she sure is a pretty gal," Keith murmured, as if afraid Elijah wouldn't see that for himself.

Elijah wondered what Mrs. Gilbert must think of her husband noticing other ladies, but when Elijah darted a glance at her, Cassie was still smiling.

"We thought we should point her out to ya, Reverend," she said with a wink. "It isn't good for a man to be alone. You ought to go meet her, after the service."

Elijah sighed. At least they hadn't spoken loud enough for any of the other worshippers to hear. "The Lord calls some of us to singleness," he said. "I am one of them."

Neither of the Gilberts looked convinced, but he was thankful when they didn't press him on the point. He hadn't told anyone in the tent city about his lost fiancée, nor did he intend to. And in any case, there was no time to converse further.

He stepped to the makeshift pulpit someone had fashioned out of a long crate with a rectangular board nailed across the top to form a flat surface on which to lay his Bible.

"Good morning, congregation," he said, "and welcome, those of you who are new, to Boomer Town Chapel. I'm Elijah Thornton, and I'm glad you're here. I hope you gain encouragement from being among believers." He paused and looked around at the various members of his little flock, trying not to let his gaze stray to the back again. "I'd like to open our worship with a word of prayer."

He prayed that the Lord would bless them on this Monday. Three weeks from this day, they would race into the newly opened territory, each in hopes of claiming a homestead. He asked God to supply all their needs, physical and spiritual, to keep them free of greed and to remember to put others ahead of themselves—a tall order, he admitted, when they would soon be competing with one another for the best plots of land.

After his "Amen" had been echoed by those sitting on the benches, he raised his head and said, "While Mr. Gilbert leads us in 'Beneath the Cross of Jesus,' I'm going to ask his good wife to pass the collection sack. Now, no one here is wealthy, or I imagine you wouldn't be with us seeking free land from the United States government."

There was a chorus of answering chuckles from several of the flock, and even another "Amen" or two.

"So I don't want anyone to feel obligated to put anything in," Elijah continued. "But if you can spare a few pennies or a couple of bits, it will enable us to carry on the work of helping the sick and the needy among us."

It always humbled him to see how many dropped some coin or other into the drawstring sack as it passed from hand to hand down one row and up another. Apparently lack of wealth was no barrier to generous hearts.

Cassie Gilbert returned with the sack and sat down.

"Those of you who have been attending daily

know that I save my sermons for Sundays," he announced. "Instead, on weekdays, we've been praying for each other, knowing that wherever two or more are gathered in His name, the Lord is there, listening and wanting to satisfy our needs, and that the job of the church body is to build each other up."

"Amen," said the deacon.

"Are there any prayer requests? Let's hear them, and then we'll take our petitions to the heavenly throne, knowing He will answer us according to His will."

A tall, rawboned man with the droopy face of an old hound unfolded himself from the bench, his hat in his hands. "Reverend, I'd be obliged iffen you'd pray for my wife. She's feelin' poorly. The trip here was mighty hard on her."

"We'll do that, Asa," Elijah promised. "I'll come visit, too."

"Thank ya, Reverend. She'd like that."

A woman midway back stood then, her face creased with worry. "My son Billy slipped away over the line this morning. Left us a note sayin' he was going to stake us a claim while the pickin' was good. I'm so worried the federals are gonna catch 'im and kick 'im out for bein' a 'Too-Sooner,' and penalize the whole family for what he done."

Like everyone, Elijah knew the law dealt seriously with the "Too-Sooners," or just "Sooners" as they were called—those who sneaked over the line and thought to hide out on their claims till the opening shot, then hold their lands against all comers. Unlike the "Boomers," who were those living in the tent cities, waiting obediently for noon on April 22.

"Let's pray that Billy comes to his senses and re-
turns of his own accord," Elijah agreed. There were
other requests following the first two—anxieties
about whether they would be equal to the task of
wresting a living out of the prairie, concern over ailing livestock, squabbles among kin. He listened to
each one, wondering if the pretty stranger in the back
row might make a prayer request, but she did not. A
glance showed her still sitting on the back bench, her
face tense, her eyes watchful. What was she worried
about? *Please, Lord, comfort her.*

At last, when there were no more requests, he
bowed his head and began to pray aloud over each
one. Sometimes when he was done praying on a matter, others voiced their own prayers, expanding on his
requests or merely repeating them, but today no one
did. "And now," he concluded, "we'll just be silent
for a moment, knowing that there are often needs too
sensitive to say aloud, needs that You want to meet,
Father…" Perhaps the female newcomer's require-
ments were of that nature.

"Father, in closing, I pray that You will keep us as
one body united in purpose, with the goal of building a community united by faith. Bless these people
until we meet again."

It was his custom to shake hands with those who
had come, so while everyone was getting to their feet,
he moved to the back, hoping to meet the worried-
looking woman and find out what was troubling her.

Alice had hoped to leave the tent without meeting the preacher. His eyes—what color were they?
Brown? No, something lighter; hazel, she decided—

simply saw too much. They seemed to pierce through her carefully guarded exterior to her uneasy heart inside. But the garrulous sisters who'd sat next to her had started chattering to her the moment the reverend stopped praying, delaying Alice's escape.

She'd wanted an atmosphere of worship in which to make her appeal to God, so when she'd spotted the sign in front of the tent announcing services every day, it seemed to be a sign from Heaven. But it went against her resolve to stand and proclaim her prayer request boldly—and didn't everyone here have the same request anyway? So while Elijah Thornton prayed aloud, Alice prayed silently. *Please, Lord, let me win a good plot of land, so it won't matter if the bank takes our farm in New York, so I won't be forced to marry Maxwell Peterson to keep my mother from destitution...*

There was no polite way to evade shaking the preacher's hand, she saw that now—short of ducking under the rolled-up tent flaps on the side. The stair-step boys who'd sat in front of her lost no time in doing that, despite a call to halt from their mother. But a well-bred lady would not do such a thing, so Alice resigned herself to the encounter. She would keep it short and be polite but not reveal too much about herself. A person has a right to keep her worries between herself and the Lord, doesn't she?

The sisters had spotted someone they knew across the tent and had dashed over to greet them, so Alice was spared a further inquisition by the talkative twosome while she stood with the lined-up worshippers filing toward the preacher. Carrie and Cordelia's departure left Alice directly behind the parents of the boys, and while she awaited her chance to likewise escape, she had an opportunity to study the couple.

The husband radiated irritation. "If you can't keep the boys in line, Desdemona, maybe I'll have to start doing it—with my belt," he muttered to the fretful-looking woman next to him.

The woman was already pale, Alice saw, when the woman turned her face to look up at her husband, but she went a shade more so at the man's rumbling threat. "Now, Horace, that's a long time for young boys to sit still," she said with a timorous reasonability, but the man was not to be placated.

"It's the belt, if it happens again," he hissed.

Alice stiffened behind them. She should say something, Alice knew, but making a scene to protest the man's harsh threat would only bring her the very notice she was trying to avoid. Her view was not likely to be supported either and would probably result in LeMaster taking reprisal against his wife.

Desdemona's brow wrinkled in confusion. "But I thought you said we weren't—" She suddenly clamped her jaw shut and smoothed her features though as Reverend Thornton held out a hand to her husband.

Alice wondered what the woman had been about to ask.

"Good morning, sir," Elijah Thornton said to Horace LeMaster. "And is this your wife? Thanks for coming to the service. I hope you'll come back—"

LeMaster ignored the outstretched hand and the hint that he should introduce his wife. "We won't be comin' back," he said, his voice raised, his chin jutting forward at a pugnacious angle. "I just wanted to see if you were as big a hypocrite as the Chaucers said you were."

Everywhere in the tent, heads turned, and conversation ground to a halt. As Alice watched, Elijah Thornton's face flushed.

"You—you knew the Chaucers?" he asked, his voice suddenly hoarse.

"I *know* the Chaucers," LeMaster corrected him. "They're right here in the territory, waitin' to claim homesteads same as you. But unlike *you,* they didn't come here from a plantation. They didn't profit from the war, as you did, because they didn't turn traitor to the South. The war and the taxes levied against them by their Union conquerors and traitors, like yourself, left them destitute, and they lost their plantation. And you call yourself a Christian? Worse yet, a Christian *minister?* No, Thornton, we won't be back." Taking hold of his wife's elbow, he steered her around Thornton and out of the tent.

Being from the North, Alice didn't believe a Union sympathizer from the South was a bad man, but might Thornton be a hypocrite in other ways?

"Wait, sir! Please, can't we discuss this?" Thornton called after LeMaster, taking a few steps.

The man merely increased his pace.

Chapter Two

Thornton turned back, ashen now, his eyes stricken. Alice's heart went out to him. How very embarrassing, to be accused of hypocrisy in front of his congregation—or at least in front of the few who remained. Alice glanced around, and the faces of those who remained looked as shocked as Thornton himself—and uneasy, too, as if they wondered if LeMaster's accusations were true. They'd talk about what they had seen, Alice realized, and in short order those who had already left would know what had happened.

She watched as the preacher visibly pulled himself together and cleared his throat.

"I—I'm sorry for the unpleasantness, ma'am," he managed to say. "Such things normally don't happen at our services. It's your...your first visit, isn't it, Miss—Mrs.—?"

"Miss Alice Hawthorne," she said. She hadn't the heart to be evasive with him after what had just transpired. His eyes *were* hazel—a rich chocolate color mixed with rust and green, like a forest floor in autumn. His accent was Eastern, like her own, but with occasional tinges of a Southern drawl. His tone was deep, wrapping itself around her heart like a warm cloak.

"It's nice to meet you, Reverend Thornton. I...I enjoyed the service," she surprised herself by saying. She merely wanted to make him feel better after the awkward incident, she told herself.

"You're new to Boomer Town, aren't you?" he asked then. "And from the East, I think. New York?"

She nodded. "Upstate, originally. I grew up on a farm near Albany. More recently I've been nursing in New York City, at Bellevue Hospital." What was wrong with her? She hadn't meant to say anything more than her name before proceeding on into the sunlight. But there was something compelling about those hazel eyes set in an earnest, scholarly but masculine face that somehow rendered her as talkative as Carrie and Cordelia Ferguson.

His eyebrows rose, and those eyes warmed. "A nurse? You'll be much appreciated here, Miss Hawthorne."

"Thank you," she said. "But I've put my nursing career behind me. I—"

"The Lord must have sent you to us," Elijah Thornton went on, as if he hadn't heard what she had said. "We don't have any sort of doctor here. I go around and pray with people who are ill, but they need so much more than I can provide, Miss Hawthorne."

"But I've come to Oklahoma to farm," she told him firmly. "My mother is not young, and she'll need all my help, once we have our claim."

"Is she here now? In Boomer Town, I mean?"

Alice shook her head. "No, I'll send for her once I've managed to erect some sort of dwelling. And now I must be going, Reverend," she added firmly.

"Miss Hawthorne," Reverend Thornton continued, "please consider what I've said about nursing here. Pray about it, if you would. It's not that there's any great amount of sickness and injuries, but occasionally the need is great."

"I will, Reverend. Good day."

The man didn't know how to take no for an answer, Alice thought, as she entered the muddy main street of the tent city. And yet, Elijah Thornton was not the least bit overbearing. There was something very kind in his twinkling hazel eyes.

He was certainly nothing like Maxwell Peterson. If only she'd met a man like the reverend in New York....

Still, she'd made her decision, and there was no use dwelling on "if only." Marriage and family were not for her. She'd keep her independence and take care of her mother by working the land. No man was going to take over her life and divert her from that goal. Perhaps it was best if she did not return to the daily services at the Boomer Town Chapel, where she would have to listen to and look at Reverend Elijah Thornton—who did not wear a wedding ring, she'd noticed, nor had there been a wife hovering near him.

Yet the idea of not returning to the chapel sent a pang of regret through her. It *had* felt good to sing hymns with other Christians and to hear the preacher's deep, resonant voice praying for all of them. But could any threat to her independence be worth it? If she got to know people better at the chapel, they'd start nosing into her business. They'd want to know why a decent-appearing unmarried lady like herself was here in the territory all alone. They'd suspect she was running from something—and they'd be right.

Perhaps it was better to keep to herself. There were only three weeks to go till the Land Rush. Surely she could manage to lead a solitary existence among the crowded tent city until then, so that no one would suspect that a certain man in New York would pay highly to know where she was and what she was about to do, to make sure she never needed anything from him.

Normally Elijah joined his brothers for the noon meal, which was cooked over their campfire by Gideon, and usually consisted of beans and corn bread, or if Clint had hunted, rabbit, wild turkey or prairie chicken stew. Today, though, still feeling the sting of LeMaster's denunciation, he had gone to pay the promised visit to Asa Benton's ailing wife and had been invited to share dinner with them. The meal had been a simple soup and the last half of a loaf of bread, but Mrs. Benton seemed to take encouragement from his company and to keep inventing reasons for him to stay longer.

He paid several other calls around the tent city after that. It appeared the community was buzzing with reaction to Horace LeMaster's remarks, and Elijah spent a lot of time answering questions and easing their concerns as best as he could. Many would-be homesteaders came from the South, particularly Texas, and even these days—twenty-four years after General Lee had surrendered—the Civil War wounds had not completely healed between the North and the

South. Some folks felt as warmly toward him as ever, while others were definitely cooler.

Ah, well, he was not called to be popular but to preach the Gospel. Perhaps this would all blow over, perhaps it wouldn't, but he would be obedient to his calling.

Still he wondered where Miss Alice Hawthorne's campsite was and kept an eye out for it. But he never spotted her.

Before he knew it, the afternoon had passed and it was nearly time to meet up with his brothers for their nightly trip to Mrs. Murphy's dining tent for supper. The red-faced Irishwoman's meals were filling, cheap and quickly served, and if her beef was occasionally tough as boot leather, her desserts always made up for it. And it made a welcome change from Gideon's cooking.

Tonight, however, he arrived at their large tent only to be told they'd all been invited to take supper with a fellow Clint had met that day, one Lars Brinkerhoff.

"He's a Danish fellow, Lije," Clint said, using the name he'd called his eldest brother ever since he'd lisped his first words and couldn't quite manage *Elijah.* "He's been in this country a decade, he and his sister, and he's lived with the Cheyenne. They taught him tracking. You'll never believe how we met, but I think I'll save the story till we're there."

"How does it happen we wrangled a dinner invitation on such short acquaintance?" Elijah asked, though he was always happy to meet new people. Reaching out to others was his job as a preacher, after all.

Clint grinned. "That's part of the story. Let's just

say we went after the same antelope," he said with a wink.

"Neighborly of the fellow to invite us," Gideon remarked in his low, rumbling voice. "But I sure hope he doesn't plan on pairing us up with that sister of his—at least, not you or me, Elijah—since we're confirmed bachelors. Right, brother?"

Elijah knew Gideon's light remark was an attempt to conceal the ache that had resided in his middleborn brother's heart, losing both his wife and child to the influenza, and Elijah knew Gideon wasn't expecting a reply.

Precisely at six o'clock—Elijah checked the time on the silver pocket watch that, as the eldest, he had inherited from their father—the men walked down one row of tents and up another to where Lars had told them the Brinkerhoff tent was located. Since Lars's sister would be present, they'd washed, shaved and put on clean shirts—not that they didn't do such things regularly, but the prospect of being in the presence of a lady certainly gave them additional motivation.

Their noses told them before they reached the Brinkerhoff tent that they were in for a treat, for the air was redolent with the smell of cooking meat and baking bread and some sort of additional sweet scent.

A tall, well-built man arose from a hay bale on which he had been sitting and came forward. Dressed in fringed buckskin and knee-high leather boots, he had hair that fell to midshoulder and was so pale a yellow it was almost white. "*Velkommen*—welcome, gentlemen. I am Lars Brinkerhoff." He looked at Clint. "I am glad you and your brothers could come."

The men shook hands, and Elijah and Gideon introduced themselves.

"And this is my sister, Katrine," Lars said, gesturing. A young woman of middle height with the same sparkling blue eyes and flaxen hair—hers was confined in a long, thick braid down her back—straightened from where she had been bent over a cast-iron pot. When she smiled, dimples bloomed in each cheek, and Elijah supposed she could be considered beautiful, but he couldn't help wondering if Alice Hawthorne had anyone to dine with tonight, or if she had to eat her supper alone.

"Sister, may I present the Thornton brothers," Lars said, then pointed at each in turn, "Elijah, Gideon and Clint."

"I am very pleased to meet you," the young woman said, smiling at each. "I am happy that you could dine with us."

She had the same thick Danish accent, but coming from her, it sounded charming.

"Miss Brinkerhoff, it is our very great pleasure," Elijah said, stepping forward and bowing to her.

"Ah, but you won't really know that until you have tasted my cooking, will you?" she teased. "Perhaps you will not like it."

"But in such pleasant company, how could any food be less than wonderful?" Clint responded with a smile.

Elijah shared a look with Gideon, both of them clearly amused at their brother's unaccustomed gallantry.

"Well, let us put it to the test, shall we?" Lars said. "Gentlemen, will you have a seat?" He gestured to a low table made of a wide, flat board set atop bales of hay. They would have to sit on the ground, but provision had been made for that, with a folded blanket set at each place.

"It is not how I would like to serve guests," Katrine apologized, indicating the tin plates and eating utensils carved from wood, along with a crockery pitcher and wooden cups. "For now we travel light, yes? But Lars has promised me proper china and silverware once we build our house."

"Please don't worry about that, ma'am. Our eating utensils aren't fancy, either, but they get the job done," Gideon assured her politely, surprising Elijah that Gideon had spoken. He was quiet, even with his brothers, but usually talked much less when in the company of others.

"Mr. Elijah Thornton, since you are the *sogne-praest*—the minister—will you say the blessing, please?" Lars asked.

Elijah did so, thanking God for the privilege of dining with their new friends and for the delicious food of which they were about to partake.

Lars began to carve slabs off the savory antelope haunch that had been roasting on the spit and placed them on a tin platter, which he passed to the men, while Katrine lifted the lid from the thick pot and brought out a golden-brown loaf of bread.

"This is *kartoffelbrot,* potato bread, so it may taste a little different from what you are used to, gentlemen," she said as she sliced it. "I was fortunate to be able to trade for some fresh-churned butter, too," she added.

For the first few minutes, no one spoke except to

exclaim at the deliciousness of the food. The antelope had been done to a turn, and Elijah wondered about what herbs Lars's sister had used to give it such an exotic flavor. The potato bread was hearty and satisfying.

"So how did you and Lars meet?" Elijah asked Clint. "You promised to tell the tale when we got here. Something about an antelope you both shot at?"

A grin spread across Clint's tanned face. "Yes, and I was mighty upset at him for a couple of seconds for killing *my* antelope. I was out on the prairie east of here, lying on a bluff next to some rocks, drawing a bead on a prairie antelope down below. But before I could shoot, Lars, here, shot from the bluff across from me at the rocks right next to me.

"Well, I jumped up, mad as thunder, sure this fellow here was trying to murder me. But then he pointed below the rocks, and curled up amid them, there was the body of a rattlesnake, split right in two. I hadn't spotted it when I'd settled in there. If I'd shot at the antelope or maybe even moved the wrong way, that snake was close enough to strike me easy. I might've died!"

Clint's recital had been dramatic, but there was sobering truth in what he'd said. Clint might have been found on the prairie later, after he'd gone missing, dead of snakebite, but for the Dane's quick action.

Elijah had been sitting next to Lars, and now Elijah laid a hand on the other man's shoulder. "Mr. Brinkerhoff, we are most deeply in your debt. I can't thank you enough."

"Please, you must all call me Lars," the other man

said, grinning. "I was—" it came out *vas* "—happy to do it."

"Better yet," piped up Clint from across the table, "Brinkerhoff didn't let the antelope get away, either. While I was still gaping at the rattlesnake and pondering how I had almost died, this fellow shot the antelope that had run fifty yards away! Then after he had retrieved it, he was kind enough to offer to share the meat with us tonight," he said, pointing his fork at what remained on the spit.

"Why did you brothers decide to come to Oklahoma? If you do not mind that I ask, of course," Lars added.

"Of course it's all right," Elijah said. "We hail from Virginia, originally. Our parents had a plantation there before the war, Thornton Hall. You're familiar with our American Civil War?" he asked.

"The Northern states fought to free the slaves that the South held, *ja?*" Lars asked.

"Basically, yes, though there were other issues, as well," Elijah said. "Our pa sent us North to live with a cousin to avoid the unpleasantries of being loyal Unionists in the rebel South."

Elijah and Gideon were the only ones who clearly remembered leaving home. Clint had been only four, but Elijah and Gideon had told him stories of the middle-of-the-night flight from Thornton Hall, leaving behind all they knew, including their playmates, the Chaucer boys from the neighboring plantation. Elijah felt a twinge of pain as he always did when he thought of their former friends, but it seemed worse now because of the incident today.

Perhaps because Elijah had been lost in thought,

Clint now picked up the story. "Pa died in battle, so we went on living with Cousin Obadiah in Pennsylvania," Clint went on.

Elijah saw the involuntary twist of distaste on both Clint's and Gideon's mouths at the mention of their father's distant cousin, who'd hated all things Southern, including the innocent boys. He'd grudgingly allowed them space in his home, but not his heart.

"Then we sold the plantation for a good profit," Clint said, "since we were no longer welcome in Virginia, and bought a place in Kansas, where Elijah went to seminary, Gideon worked on a ranch and I became a sheriff. It was all right...but when we heard about the opportunity opening up in the territory, we knew we wanted to come here and start over on our own homesteads."

"You plan to start a church on your land, Reverend?" Lars asked Elijah.

Elijah nodded. "That is my purpose in coming to Oklahoma," he said. "God willing, and with the help of God's people, I mean to use my land to build a church in which our community of faith can be united in purpose. Together we can make Oklahoma a great state someday."

He felt that same inner certainty he'd been feeling for some time that his goal was in line with God's will for him as well as the territory. But once again, he said a quick prayer that if his feelings were in error, the Lord would show him—either by that still, small voice that He used, or by the way events unfolded.

Chapter Three

Had he sounded too pompous? Too stuffy? But a glance at Lars and Katrine showed only approval shining from their blue eyes.

"May the good Lord bless your efforts," Lars said fervently.

"Thank you," Elijah said. "And now, may I ask you the same question? Why did you leave your home? Clint tells me you have been in this country for ten years. What brought you to Oklahoma, from wherever you first settled?"

"America is the land of opportunity, is it not?" Lars said in reply. "When we arrived in America, we were not content for long in the East. We decided to journey to the West and see the 'wide open spaces,' as you Americans say. It was harder than we thought it would be. Perhaps we were naive, but the 'land of milk and honey' did not seem to be there for everyone."

"You mentioned living with the Indians, Lars," Clint said. "Miss Brinkerhoff, did you live with them, too?"

Katrine shook her head. "Lars did not want to expose me to danger and hardship, so I stayed in the city to work," she said, and then Elijah saw her duck her head.

Something had happened to Katrine while the siblings had been parted, Elijah thought. Something she did not want to talk about.

But Clint didn't seem to notice. "What kind of job did you take, Miss Brinkerhoff?"

She looked away. "I minded the children of a prosperous businessman and his wife for a time," she said, "but then I…left that and worked in some…ah, restaurants as a waitress…" Her voice trailed off as her eyes lost focus. "Then Lars returned from the Indians and told me of the Land Rush. We also thought it was a chance to make a fresh start, and—how do you say it?—wipe the slate clean. And here we are.

"I hope you have saved room for dessert, gentlemen," Katrine said brightly then. "I have made *ableskiver,* which is a kind of doughnut."

The brothers groaned when she uncovered a plateful of the Danish doughnuts, which were each topped with a dollop of blackberry jam. Elijah had thought his stomach couldn't possibly hold anything more, but he found himself reaching for one just as his brothers did. Lars and Katrine each took one, too. In seconds there wasn't so much as a crumb left.

The Brinkerhoffs answered their questions about life in Denmark, and Lars regaled them with tales of life among the Cheyenne until it grew dark. Then, full of good food and the pleasure of making congenial new friends, the Thornton brothers headed back to their tent. The sounds of the tent city settling in for the night were all around them—the faint tinkling of piano music from one of the many whiskey tents, the occasional nicker of a horse, the sleepy whine of a child who did not want to go to bed yet.

Elijah waited until they were back at their campfire, having a last cup of coffee, to discuss the unpleasant incident at the chapel this morning. He hadn't wanted to end the evening on a sour note, but he thought he'd better warn his brothers about the Chaucers.

Gideon looked up from the embers of the fire he'd just stirred up. "The Chaucers are *here?*"

Elijah nodded. "Figured I'd better tell you both, in case you run into them around Boomer Town, as we likely will."

Clint gave a disgusted snort. "Guess it was too much to hope that we'd left that problem back East. And they're already vilifying the Thornton name in Boomer Town?"

Again Elijah nodded. "So it seems."

"They better not be doing it when I'm in earshot," Gideon grumbled. "I know you've got to 'turn the other cheek' and all that nonsense, Lije, but I'm no preacher."

"Me neither," Clint said. "They start acting high-and-mighty 'round me, they'll wish they hadn't."

Elijah sighed. He couldn't blame his brothers for their reactions. They'd left Virginia because of the Chaucers and their kind, knowing the Thorntons would never be accepted and welcome in their old home. Now the Chaucers had come to Oklahoma, too, and had apparently brought their old enmity with them.

"Look, we've just got to be civil and get along

with folks until the twenty-second," Elijah told them. "The Chaucers—and others like Horace LeMaster whose minds they have swayed—probably just want the same thing we want. Free land. Chances are, once the Land Rush is over, they'll settle somewhere in the territory far away from us, and we won't ever set eyes on them."

Clint dug a groove in the dirt with the heel of his boot. "Hope you're right, Lije. Sorry that happened to you this morning. Did the rest of the service go well? Did more people come?"

Elijah was just going to tell his brothers about Alice Hawthorne and his hope that she would lend her nursing skills as needed, when he heard the sound of running footsteps heading toward them.

A heartbeat later a wild-eyed man burst into the circle of firelight. "Preacher, you got t' come! Deacon Gilbert's hurt bad—he's cut his leg and he's bleedin' somethin' terrible! I'm afeared he's gonna bleed t' death! His missus sent me to fetch you!"

"How did it happen?" Elijah demanded, as he strove to control the dread that threatened to swamp him. What could he do in the face of a serious injury but pray and try to comfort? Was he about to lose the man who'd been the very first to step forward and support Elijah's work?

"He cut hisself with his own ax—he was choppin' firewood. I—I gotta get back there!" the distraught man cried, already turning to run in the direction he'd come. "Miz Gilbert, she's carryin' on somethin' fierce!"

Elijah started to follow the messenger, but he had a sudden idea and turned back to his brothers. "I'll go to the Gilberts' and see what I can do for Keith. You two split up and see if you can find a Miss Alice Hawthorne in one of the tents. She came to chapel this morning, and she's a nurse. She has dark red hair and blue eyes, and I'd reckon she's in her mid-twenties. Ask if she'll come help. Tell her to bring bandages, and whatever else she thinks is needful, and come with you to help Mr. Gilbert."

Then he turned and ran toward the Gilberts' campsite, sending up a silent prayer that one of his brothers would be able to find Miss Hawthorne quickly among the maze of wagons and tents, and that she would be willing to follow his brother and help save a life.

The Gilberts' tent lay on the other side of Boomer Town, but it didn't take long for Elijah to reach it at a dead run, even though he had to weave through campsites, and dodge wagons and picket lines to which the horses were tied. Even from a distance, he could hear the sound of a woman's shrieks, and after hurdling the tongue of a freight wagon, he spotted the circle of men and women.

Half a dozen lanterns held by onlookers illuminated the scene, their lights bobbing and flickering. At the edge of the crowd, another woman held the wailing Mrs. Gilbert. Everyone was talking at once, some calling out advice to a kneeling man dabbing at the wound, others softly opining as to whether Keith Gilbert would bleed to death or die later of blood poisoning—assuming it was even possible to stop the bleeding. A handful of women joined the chorus of Mrs. Gilbert's wails, wringing their hands.

"Let him through, fellers. He's the preacher!" cried

the man who had come for Elijah. "Don't let Keith die without so much as a prayer said fer 'im!"

His words parted the crowd like a sword, and in the pale light of an upheld kerosene lantern, Elijah beheld Keith Gilbert, lying there pasty pale with wide, terrified eyes. Someone had rolled up a coat and put it under his head. A bloody-bladed ax lay amid an armload of kindling at his feet. But it was the crimson-stained left pants leg and the spreading pool of blood in the dirt that captured Elijah's attention.

"P-please, Preacher, d-don't let me die!" Keith Gilbert begged, panting and raising his arm in a feeble beckoning gesture. "It was my own fault—somethin' d-distracted me just as I swung my ax—a fool thing, to take my eye off an ax I'd just sharpened…"

Dear Lord, spare this man, Elijah prayed silently as he went forward and knelt by Keith. *Let Clint or Gideon find Miss Alice quickly, bring her here and give her the skill to save this man!*

"You're not going to die," Elijah reassured his deacon, though he had no idea if he was telling the truth. The man had already lost a good deal of blood, and he was pale as a shroud. "I've sent for a nurse, and I'm sure she can stop your bleeding." Someone had laid a towel over the wounded leg, and it was already saturated with blood.

Elijah aimed a look at Cassie Gilbert. Maybe giving her something to do would help her calm down. "Mrs. Gilbert, may I please have your apron?" he said. The apron was wrinkled and stained here and there, but it was better than nothing.

As he'd hoped, the deaconess untied it with shaking fingers and threw it to Elijah, who caught it and wadded it up. Elijah yanked off the blood-soaked towel, replaced it with the apron and leaned on the bleeding leg with all the force he could muster. When Alice got here—*if* his brothers could find her—he'd need to rip open the trouser leg so she could see the wound, but for now, trying to stop the bleeding was the first priority.

"Reverend," rasped Gilbert. "I know I'm a sinner, but the preacher at home said, if I gave my heart to the Lord, He'd take me straight into Heaven. That's right, isn't it? I'm a Christian, so He'll keep His promise, won't He?"

"Of course He will," Elijah assured him. "But we're going to do our best to save you. The nurse I spoke of will be here any second now," he said, and hoped it was true.

"Lord, in Jesus's name, please help Your servant Keith Gilbert so he can go on doing Your will on earth," Elijah prayed aloud. *Please, Lord, let Miss Alice get here in time.*

It seemed like an eternity that he leaned on the wound, not daring to let up on the pressure lest the scarlet stain spread farther on the trouser leg. Then he heard booted feet shifting in the circle of onlookers around him, and suddenly Gideon was leading Miss Hawthorne through the crowd.

Thank You, Lord.

Alice had barely been able to keep up with the big man who'd hastily identified himself as Elijah Thornton's brother Gideon.

She didn't want to do this. She knew if she tended to the wounded man, she would no longer pass unnoticed in the tent city. People would know her name and that she was a nurse, and the requests would never end.

And Maxwell Peterson might hear of it.

But how could she say no when a man's life hung in the balance? It wouldn't be right, even on a basic humanitarian level, and it certainly wouldn't be a Christian thing to do.

So she'd hastily gathered up her supplies. The kit she'd put together before her journey contained sturdy darning thread—which she'd boiled, then wrapped in an ironed handkerchief—similarly wrapped boiled needles, bandaging lint and a stoppered bottle of disinfectant.

She had hoped she'd never need those supplies, but now here she was, panting from her run and staring down at a man whose ghastly pallor told her that he would die if she didn't help him. Or maybe even if she did.

"Thanks for coming, Miss Hawthorne," said Elijah Thornton, who was kneeling over the man, leaning on a blood-stained wad of cloth on the man's left leg. "Mr. Gilbert accidentally gashed his leg with an ax. Obviously he's lost a lot of blood," he added, indicating the dark crimson puddle beneath the limb.

Alice took a deep breath, summoning the calm that had earned her a valued reputation with the doctors of Bellevue. She couldn't help a victim if she succumbed to the vapors, after all. "Let me see the wound," she said, carrying her bag over to the recumbent man.

"Very well, but I must warn you, each time I let up on the pressure, the blood starts flowing again,"

Elijah cautioned her. Splotches of dark scarlet on his sleeves confirmed what he said.

She nodded and said, "Give me one minute, please, before you release the pressure." She stared at the circle of gaping men and women around her. "Does anyone have a belt I can use? And a sturdy stick, or long-handled spoon, as well as a knife?"

Most of the men's trousers were held up by suspenders, but finally a skinny man at the back of the circle made his way through the throng, one hand holding a belt, the other one holding up his trousers; another man furnished a wicked-looking knife from his boot. A woman—Alice recognized her as the deaconess who'd passed the collection sack this morning—stopped wailing and rummaged in a crate fastened to the nearby wagon, coming up with a long-handled spoon, which she held out to Alice.

Kneeling beside the man, Alice did her best to smile down at him. "Mr. Gilbert, I'm Miss Hawthorne, a nurse, and first we're going to stop the bleeding with a tourniquet, so I can see your wound."

Mr. Gilbert swallowed with difficulty, but his wide eyes were trusting as he gazed up at her. "Thank ya, Miss H-Hawthorne…I don't wanna die. Please don't let me bleed t' death."

"I won't," she assured him, hoping and praying it would prove to be the truth. Lack of hope could kill a man as quickly as blood loss.

Quickly and efficiently, she slit the trouser leg up the seam and pushed it back from the wound. "Reverend, if you would apply pressure once more?" Then, trying to remember everything about the safe use of tourniquets—taught to her by a surgeon at Bellevue, who'd once treated soldiers in the Civil War—Alice drew one end of the belt under his upper leg, fastened the buckle, then began to twist the belt until she could twist it no more. Finally she stuck the spoon handle into the small remaining loop. Her eyes sought Gideon, who'd remained nearby. "Please hold this loop twisted tight as I have it," she instructed him. "Don't let it go unless I tell you."

He did so, keeping pale gray eyes trained on her.

"Now you can remove your hands," she told Elijah, and he eased away from the victim with a sigh of relief.

"Can you hold that lantern directly over his leg, please, so I can see what we're dealing with?" she asked another man who'd come into the circle, a man who looked so much like Elijah he had to be another of his brothers. Once the lantern light flickered over the temporary bandage, she gingerly lifted a corner of it and inspected the gash.

Thanks to the tourniquet, the blood flow had stopped, so she could see the wound on the inside of the left lower leg was about four inches long and at least an inch deep. It must have crossed a big blood vessel to have bled so much—not an artery, she thought, for the bleeding hadn't been spurting when pressure was loosened, just a steady, continuing crimson stream.

"I'm going to have to stitch up the wound," she told Gilbert and his wife. "It's going to hurt some."

He regarded her with eyes that were now calm. "You do whatever you have t' do, Miss Hawthorne. I'm in the Lord's hands as well as yours. Say, weren't you the newcomer at chapel this mornin'?"

She pretended not to hear the question but directed those with lanterns to come closer and hold the lanterns as steady as they could. Then, after cleaning the wound with carbolic, she started stitching.

Conversation died down as the men watched her work until all Alice could hear was the steady inhale and exhale of her own breathing, and the pounding pulse in her ears.

An hour later, Elijah watched Alice straighten after putting what was left of her supplies in an oilskin bag. Mr. Gilbert slept inside his wagon, having been lifted there by some of the men. His wife, who'd been profuse with her gratitude, sat beside him. His color was better, and a clean white bandage was wrapped around his newly sutured leg. Those who had been standing around watching the drama began to disperse to their own campsites.

"Thank you, Miss Hawthorne," Elijah said. "I am in awe of your ability." The words were so inadequate. Without a murmur of disgust or shrinking from such an awful sight as the ax wound had been, this woman had saved a man's life.

"Don't thank me yet," she said, her voice weary as she pushed back an errant curl that had strayed onto her perspiration-dampened forehead. "He could still develop septicemia—blood poisoning. What I wouldn't have given for a handful of catgut ligatures, instead of boiled darning thread," she said. "I'm glad now that I brought a jar of carbolic acid on my journey. There's nothing better to cleanse a wound."

"I thought we might have need of your skills but not so soon as it happened," Elijah commented.

"Once a nurse, always a nurse," she responded wryly.

"You met my brother Gideon, of course, but this is my other brother, Clint," Elijah said, when both men joined them.

"It's an honor to meet you, ma'am," the man who'd held the lantern said, and beside him, the big man who'd summoned Alice rumbled an agreement.

Elijah saw Alice staring dazedly at the wagon and around the campsite, as if she'd forgotten where she was.

"Come on, it's late," he said gently, wondering if she was a bit in shock herself, now that the emergency had passed. "We'll walk you back to your campsite."

"No, I must stay. Mr. Gilbert has to be watched," Alice protested. "His wife can't do it—you saw that she was exhausted. If he moves around in his sleep too much, the wound could reopen and bleed again. Or he could develop fever—"

Elijah hadn't thought about the need to watch Mr. Gilbert through the night, but it was plain Miss Hawthorne was dead on her feet and couldn't do it. Her cheeks were pale, and her eyes showed the strain of the past hour or so.

"I'll stay," Elijah said, "and my brothers will walk you home. I've sat up with the sick before," he added, when she opened her mouth with the obvious intent of objecting. "I'll come fetch you if he worsens during the night, I promise."

She stared at him, then her shoulders sagged in surrender and fatigue. "Now it's my turn to thank *you*, Reverend Thornton," she said. "I'll check on him in the morning. I'll have to keep an eye on him for several days and take the stitches out."

"Please, call me Elijah," he said, surprising himself. It just didn't seem right to stand on formality after such an event. He could see how fatigued she was by the dark shadows blooming under her eyes. "Get some rest, Miss Hawthorne. Gideon, Clint, please walk Miss Hawthorne back to her tent."

Gideon had told him that Miss Hawthorne's tent was five campsites to the left of theirs. Now Elijah knew where to find Alice, but he prayed he would not have to seek her out because of a medical crisis any time soon.

Chapter Four

"Good night, Miss Hawthorne. Thanks again for what you did," Clint Thornton said, tipping his hat to her.

"Good night, gentlemen." Alice watched Gideon and Clint Thornton walk away from her tent. Elijah Thornton was a good man, she thought. Apparently he was a true shepherd to his flock. His brothers seemed like good men, too, both the taciturn Gideon and the more talkative Clint, though very different from their preacher brother.

Alice stretched, feeling the muscles in her lower back and legs protest the long time she had knelt to suture the wound. She was more exhausted than she'd ever been, even after a double shift at the hospital or a difficult calving on the farm. The coppery, acrid stench of blood lingered in her nostrils.

Please, Lord, let Mr. Gilbert heal without infection, she prayed as she lay down on her cot a few minutes later. She'd have to go check on her patient first thing in the morning and hoped she could remember how to get back to the Gilberts' campsite. She'd been so intent on not losing sight of Gideon running ahead of her that she hadn't paid much attention to where they were heading.

She'd have to check and redress the wound every day, and make sure the patient and his wife knew the importance of keeping the wound clean and dry. Even sterilized silk suture was an irritant to the skin, compared to absorbable catgut, and she'd had to use coarse cotton darning thread. She'd go to the Gilberts' at sunrise, she decided, so that Elijah Thornton could return to his tent and prepare for his chapel service. Poor man, after sitting up with his deacon all night, he'd be even wearier than she expected to be come morning.

She'd offer to make some broth for Mr. Gilbert from the beef bone she'd been intending to make stew with tomorrow. With the blood loss, the man would be weak and perhaps feverish. Better take some dried willow bark to make into tea, she thought, in case the man's wife didn't have any. With the list of chores running through her head, she feared she wouldn't sleep.

But the heat and sunlight stirred her, apparently hours later. When she awakened, one glance at the watch she'd unpinned from her bodice and left lying on an upended crate by her bed told her that she'd overslept straight through to midmorning. She dressed quickly, then picked up her valise full of dressing supplies and medicaments, and headed in the direction she thought the Gilberts' tent lay.

Elijah would be conducting his prayer meeting at this hour, she thought, regretting that she had missed him, then assured herself it only mattered because she'd wanted to hear from him how his deacon had passed the night.

She managed to find her way to the tent with only one wrong turn. She found Mrs. Gilbert stirring a pot over the campfire, and Mr. Gilbert reclining in the shade of the wagon, propped up on pillows.

He was pale, but without the flush of fever Alice had been dreading. Nevertheless, as soon as she had greeted them both, she knelt at his side and felt her patient's forehead. She was pleased to find it no warmer than her hand.

"He had some fever during the night," Mrs. Gilbert volunteered, "but I brewed him some willow bark tea. I'm simmering some broth in this pot here, 'cause his appetite's still a little puny after all the blood he lost last night."

"Excellent," Alice said approvingly, silently commending the woman for her common sense.

There were only a few spots of dried blood on Mr. Gilbert's dressing, she noted, unwrapping it from his leg. She found the wound as she had hoped—a little pink around the edges, as was to be expected, but with no fresh bleeding and without the angry red appearance and purulent drainage she had feared. *Thank You, Lord,* she breathed.

After first anointing the wound with some salve from her bag, she applied a new dressing and a fresh bandage. "I'll be back to check on him this evening, Mrs. Gilbert. Keep an eye on his temperature, would you? Meanwhile, if you have need of me, I should be at my campsite most of the time—five tents to the east of the Thorntons'. If I'm not, please just leave me a note, and I'll come as soon as I find it."

"Not so fast, Miss Alice. Let me dish you up some breakfast," Mrs. Gilbert offered, pointing to a covered skillet.

Alice began to demur, not wanting to consume what might be the couple's limited resources, but the woman waved away her polite refusal. "Nonsense, it's the least we can do after what you did last night, and I'm guessing you hurried right here soon as you woke up, didn't you, poor lamb? You still look tuckered yourself, if you don't mind me sayin' so."

The woman's efficient kindness was a balm. Alice surrendered, and was given a plate heaped with scrambled eggs, bacon and biscuits. Afterward she felt as if she could take on the world or at least whatever challenges Boomer Town had to offer today. With a last admonition to her patient just to rest today and a promise from Mrs. Gilbert that she'd make sure he did so, Alice took her leave.

It might be a good day to look at saddle horses, she thought. There was a corral full of them at the end of one of the rows of tents that passed for streets in Boomer Town, watched over by a wiry man with the shifty, knowing eyes of a born horse trader. She'd strolled past the corral before, spotting a tall, handsome bay that looked as if he could run. But then there was that chestnut mare with the sweetest face...

Alice had taken the train as close as she could to the territory, then purchased a tent and camping supplies, a wagon and two stout horses to pull it the rest of the way to the border of the Unassigned Lands. She'd chosen Boomer Town—one of the many tent cities along the boundaries—more or less at random. The wagon horses were kept with others of their kind in a common corral, and she had paid a fee for their upkeep.

She'd initially planned to make the run in the wagon, but she hadn't expected there would be such hordes of would-be homesteaders waiting with her. More arrived every day. Now Alice thought the heavily laden wagon would hold her back, and only a fast horse would ensure her a good claim.

Alice figured it was probably best to buy her horse sooner rather than later to be sure of getting a good one. That would mean paying for its feed between now and the big day, but she'd have the advantage of getting to know her mount's temperament and ways in the meantime.

But if she wasn't driving her wagon into the Unassigned Lands, she'd have to leave it here in Boomer Town until after she had staked her claim. Already enterprising gents were offering to secure such wagons, stock and belongings for a fee until successful homesteaders could return for them, but could they be trusted? Alice reasoned it would be better to make friends with other settlers who were leaving their possessions in Boomer Town with family members and barter with them to watch over hers, too.

Before heading to the corral, Alice walked back to her tent and changed from her calico dress into a dark-colored blouse and the divided skirt she'd packed for riding, for she'd want to try out a horse's paces and manners before laying down any of her precious cash.

"Yes, ma'am," the horse trader said, when she arrived at the corral and told him that she wanted to buy a horse for the run. "I can give you your pick of this corral for four hundred dollars."

Shock rendered Alice momentarily speechless. "*Four hundred dollars?* B-But these look like *mustangs!*" she sputtered. The handsome bay and the sweet chestnut mare no longer paced the pen with the others. Four hundred dollars would be a considerable dent in the cash she had left that had to last until she had a dwelling built and crops in.

She closed her eyes for a moment in an attempt to stay calm. "I was told to expect a price more in the range of two hundred, and that was for a saddle-broken horse." These horses looked as if they'd been captured only yesterday after a lifetime of running loose over the prairie. If only she'd come yesterday, maybe she could have bought the bay or the chestnut…

"Horseflesh's in great demand, what with the Land Rush approachin'," he told her, his face smug. "Price is only goin' up in the future, so you'd be wise t' buy today."

"I assume that includes a saddle and bridle?" she asked stiffly, knowing the answer even as she asked.

The trader shook his head. "Bridle an' saddle are a hundred dollars extra," the man said with a smirk, nodding toward a pile of used cavalry saddles that looked much the worse for wear, with frayed stirrup leathers and girths, many with cracks and holes in the leather between the pommel and cantle. He seemed to be enjoying her distress, the scoundrel.

"Guess you could always use shank's mare," he added, with a meaningful glance toward her legs.

Alice willed herself not to take offense. Though she'd heard several were planning to do just that—walk—such a plan was the purest folly, a sure way to end up with nothing. She suspected the horse trader was trying to use her ignorance to sell her a nag at an exorbitant fee, but it was useless to accuse him of that. He'd likely only raise the price.

"Sir, you are no gentleman to try to take advantage of a lady like that," said a man's voice in a pronounced Southern drawl. "And with such inferior stock fit only for carrion."

"Who asked you?" the horse trader demanded angrily.

Alice ignored the trader, whirling to see a tall, distinguished-looking man who appeared to be in his forties, dressed in the dark blue uniform of a soldier.

"Private Bryson Reeves, ma'am," the man said, sweeping off a forage cap as he gave her a courtly bow. "I'm part of the Security Patrol tasked with assisting and protecting homesteaders before and after the Land Rush." He had ginger-colored hair, with eyes that might have been green or blue-green, she wasn't sure, for he squinted against the sun as he straightened again.

His manner was as charming as his face was well-favored, and she certainly welcomed his intervention. She hadn't heard anything about a Security Patrol, but maybe the officer could persuade the greedy horse trader to be more reasonable.

"Private Reeves, I am Miss Hawthorne," Alice said. "Am I correct in thinking that the price this man's asking for his stock is outrageous?"

"You are, Miss Hawthorne, ma'am," he agreed, flashing her a broad smile. "I'm honored to meet you. If you will allow me, I will show you a selection of much superior mounts, fit for a lady and fleet of foot. If you will follow me just a little ways?"

He offered her his arm, but since they'd only just met, she pretended not to see it and said, "Lead on, Private Reeves."

He took her to another pen at the other end of Boomer Town, one in which half a dozen tall, long-legged horses paced restlessly, snorting and showing the whites of their eyes. "Kentucky Thoroughbreds, ma'am, brought here especially for their speed. They will have no equal on the day of the run and will leave poorer specimens, such as the ones in the corral we just left, eating their dust. Am I not right, gentlemen?"

A trio of soldiers—dressed just as Private Reeves was, of about the same age and also bearing the insignia of privates—and a fourth man—dressed in denim trousers and a striped shirt and leather vest— separated themselves from the fence they had been leaning on at the far side of the corral and came toward her.

"My comrades-in-arms, Miss Hawthorne, Privates McGraw, Strafford and Wellington, and our friend, Lemuel Harkinson. It is he who had the brilliant idea of bringing Thoroughbreds from Kentucky to sell for the Land Rush to those smart enough to seize the advantage their proven speed can afford."

"Ma'am, I am enchanted to meet you," Harkinson said. "I would be delighted to put you in possession of one of my excellent Thoroughbreds."

Having a mount bred to race *would* give her an advantage, Alice thought, but her experience with the other trader had made her wary. "They're handsome animals," she agreed, for it was certainly the truth. "And what are *you* asking for one of your horses?"

"Five hundred dollars," he said, sinking her hopes

with those three words. "And worth every penny, when you consider the excellent homestead you'll be able to claim by riding one of them. Why, it'll be like riding the winged Pegasus of ancient mythology."

"No doubt," she agreed. Her body felt heavy with disappointment. "But I'm afraid it's beyond my means, sir. Good day. And thank you, Private Reeves."

She started to turn away, but Reeves put a gentle hand on her wrist, detaining her. "Miss Hawthorne, it would be my very great honor to buy one of Mr. Harkinson's horses for you," he said, bowing again.

She felt her jaw drop open. "Private Reeves, that's quite chivalrous of you, but it's out of the question. I could not possibly accept such an off—"

"Please, ma'am," he said, interrupting her with such a winning smile that she could not be offended. "Where my fellow soldiers and I come from," he said, his drawl thick as Georgia clay, "we were raised to protect ladies, especially ladies such as yourself who are…on your own, I take it? Please, let me know if I have mistaken the situation, but if you *are* without the protection of a husband or father or brother, my mother would have wanted me to assist you in any way I could. If you won't let me give the horse to you, consider it a loan. We can settle up later, once you're turning a profit on the land I'm sure one of these mounts can gain for you."

There was no way she could accept, even when the man invoked his mother and an atmosphere of Southern courtliness. The more sensible part of her questioned how a mere soldier could afford a gift such as the one he proposed, even if he was taken with Alice, as his expression suggested.

"As I said—"

"But just consider, dear lady—"

"You heard the lady," a firmly spoken masculine voice said behind her, a voice she'd heard before. A voice that was very welcome right at this moment. "She's not interested. Good day, gentlemen. Miss Hawthorne, I'll have Gideon find you the proper mount," Elijah Thornton said, "and at a reasonable price, too."

The other men's gazes felt like four sharp daggers between Elijah's shoulder blades as he escorted Alice away from them. Deciding to focus on Alice rather than worry that he'd just made enemies, he watched the lady beside him pull herself together.

"Thank you for coming along when you did," Alice said once they'd put more distance between themselves and the men lounging at the horse pen. "I knew to be wary of sharp horse traders, but Private Reeves was so insistent. I'm sure he was trying to be helpful, but…"

Elijah was fairly certain *helpful* wasn't at all what the private was trying to be. He hadn't heard clearly what the man was trying to talk Alice Hawthorne into, but he'd seen the other men gazing at her speculatively, like wolves eyeing a tethered lamb. A righteous, protective fury rose up in him as he imagined what the men had likely been thinking.

"I'm happy to be of assistance," he said, when he could trust himself to speak.

"I suppose there was no harm done," she said,

straightening her shoulders and elevating her chin a little. "I've dealt with overly gallant men before—doctors in the hospital and so forth. One just has to be firm, but Private Reeves wouldn't let me get a word in edgewise."

Alice must have seen concern in his eyes then, for she added, "I soon learned how to deal with such men at Bellevue, and by the time I finished my training, I was treated with respect." She took a breath. "These men said they're part of the 'Security Patrol' to ensure the safety of the homesteaders. Reverend, have you heard of such an organization?"

Elijah nodded. He had seen them riding around the camp, very proud and important in their blue uniforms, yet wearing only the privates' insignia. He'd overheard them with their distinctly Southern voices, conversing with a couple of Hungarian immigrants. It seemed to Elijah that they had been overly interested in the foreigners' circumstances. And why were men of mature years only privates, unless they had only recently joined the army? They'd bear watching, for sure.

"I—I had intended to relieve you at the Gilberts' this morning," she said, interrupting his thoughts. "I'm sorry, but I fear I overslept."

He smiled at her reassuringly. "I'm sure you needed it. I've never seen such calm and fortitude as you displayed last night, Miss Hawthorne."

The color rose in her cheeks, and she stared straight ahead as if embarrassed at his praise. "It's no more than was expected of me when I worked as a nurse, Reverend Thornton," she said. "A nurse cannot be of any help if she is wringing her hands and swooning, can she?" She went on without waiting for an answer. "In any case, I checked on Mr. Gilbert a little while ago, however, and I was very pleased with how he was progressing. The wound looked as good as I could have hoped for, and his wife had already seen to a slight fever he'd developed. I'll call on them again this evening."

"Excellent. I appreciate it, Miss Hawthorne." He cleared his throat. "I was actually out looking for you. I'm already in your debt for helping my deacon, I know, but there's a member of the congregation whose child is ailing, and I was wondering if I might ask you to visit them?"

He held his breath, wondering if she would agree. She'd said she'd left her nursing career behind, but after she'd performed so heroically last night, he dared to hope that she might have been so gratified by saving a life that she'd reconsider her stance against becoming a nurse again, and benefit Boomer Town.

Chapter Five

Alice was silent, remembering her reluctance to do anything that might make her stand out so it would be easy for Maxwell Peterson to find her. But really, what were the odds of him or his minions learning that she was here simply because she chose to help some inhabitants of a tent city hundreds of miles from New York?

She should not act like a frightened mouse the rest of her life, when there was something she could do to aid her fellow man. It had felt good, saving Keith Gilbert's life last night, and receiving his gratitude and that of his wife, Elijah Thornton and his brothers. A patient's appreciation, and his family's, had been what had kept her and so many other nurses enduring long hours and scant pay.

"I—I'll understand if this is something you no longer wish to do," Elijah said, before she could speak, "and remain grateful that you could aid my deacon last night. I know you said that you no longer wanted to pursue a nursing career."

He looked so apologetic that Alice realized how

long the silence had gone on and spoke quickly. "Oh, no, I'm sorry! I didn't mean to leave you waiting so long! That is— Yes, I will go see this sick child, if you will show me the way. I suppose we should stop back at my tent, though, so I can pick up my bag."

Within minutes, she had retrieved her bag and followed Elijah to a tent in the middle of Boomer Town. An anxious-looking father stood waiting for them at the entrance of the tent.

"Thank God you found her," he said, spotting Alice and the preacher. "It don't seem like my Nate's ever gonna stop throwin' up. I'm Jeremiah Kindell, miss, and I sure hope you can help him, like I hear you done with Keith Gilbert last night."

"I'll be happy to do what I can," she murmured, touched by the man's faith in her.

"Please, come inside," he said, lifting the tent flap. "My wife's in there with him."

As Alice's eyes adjusted to the dim light within the tent, she saw not only a wife and child within, but three other children, as well, all wide-eyed and fearful. She gave them an encouraging smile before focusing on the boy lying on a sheet in the middle of the tent, his head cradled in a worried-looking woman's lap.

The boy looked to be about seven or eight, and was pallid except for a spot of hectic color along each cheek. Alice could see pearls of sweat beaded on his forehead and damp hair plastered down at the edges. A cloth-covered bowl lay near his head, evidently at the ready in case he vomited again.

"What can you tell me about your son's illness, Mrs. Kindell?"

"We had this sack a' green apples I was gonna make into a pie, and Nate got into 'em when I wasn't lookin'. He musta et six of 'em at least afore I noticed," the tired-looking woman said. "Since then he's been crampin' and heavin' ever' few minutes, since last night."

Alice breathed an inward sigh of relief. A simple case of green-apple stomachache, a common ailment in active, ever-hungry boys. Nature would take its course and ease his symptoms in time. "I'm sure I can help him feel better," she said, and reached into her bag. "Do you have a pot I could use to make a tea for him to sip?"

After the woman rose and fetched one, Alice mixed ground ginger root, allspice, cinnamon and cloves, poured in some water fetched by the boy's father and encouraged the wan-looking boy to sip some.

"Give him a sip or two every few minutes," she advised the mother. "He'll feel better in a while, though he might have to visit the privy soon."

"Thank you so much," Mrs. Kindell breathed. "God bless you, Miss Hawthorne—"

"Hey, is that nurse still in there?" a man's voice called from outside the tent. "I got me this boil…"

And so it went. Word had spread that a nurse was seeing those with ailments over at the Kindells' tent, and before the afternoon was over, she had lanced the man's boil, seen a young man with quinsy throat, salved and bandaged a burn, treated a case of catarrh and pried a splinter out of a finger. And the afternoon was gone.

"I fear my simple request has ended up consuming the rest of your day, Miss Hawthorne," Elijah said after the patients finally stopped coming.

"That's all right," she told him, realizing that the time had seemed to fly for her because she'd felt productive and useful. "The only plan I had today was to look at horses. We're all of us just waiting for the twenty-second, aren't we?"

He nodded in acknowledgment. "You're a good and generous woman."

Her stomach rumbled just then, reminding her that she had never been able to start simmering the beef bone and the rest of the ingredients for her supper stew.

She wasn't sure if Elijah had heard it, but he said, "Why don't you join my brothers and me for supper? We usually go to Mrs. Murphy's tent. It'll be our treat. You can tell Gideon what you're looking for in a horse," he added, just as she opened her mouth to say she appreciated the invitation, but it wasn't necessary.

The truth was, it was so late in the day that she'd have to go to one of the supper tents, too, so she might as well accept. She *did* need a horse, after all, so it wouldn't look as if she was merely loathe to part with the preacher. The truth was, though, she had enjoyed Elijah's company and support this afternoon.

"No, you sure don't want a Thoroughbred for the run, Miss Hawthorne. Glad you didn't buy one," Gideon said, as the four of them sat at the end of one of the many long tables in Mrs. Murphy's tent restaurant. The place was full, so they were lucky to get enough space to eat together. The beef was—as the brothers had promised her—tough, but the buttered boiled potatoes, with yeast rolls and green beans, more than made up for it.

"Oh, there was no danger of me spending that much money on a horse," Alice assured Elijah's brother. "Not at the price they were asking. But why is a Thoroughbred a bad idea? They're faster than the average mount, aren't they?"

"For the first mile or so, sure—they'll leave all the other horses in the dust. But unless you're wantin' a claim just over the line, they can't keep up that speed. They'll be played out after that second mile. You want a horse with endurance, ma'am."

"Could you help her find one at a reasonable price, Gideon?" Elijah asked.

"I was already planning to."

"Is it possible to buy one that isn't still half-wild?" Alice asked, remembering the wild-eyed mustangs in the first horse trader's corral. "I don't think it would be wise to be struggling with a green-broke horse on the day of the run."

"I'll find you a good one, don't you fret, Miss Hawthorne," Gideon assured her.

"I think it's time you gentlemen called me Miss Alice," she said, and realized she was enjoying herself. It was so much more fun to eat supper with others.

"Then we're Elijah, Gideon and Clint. Have you ridden much before?" asked Elijah.

"I could give you lessons," offered Clint.

Alice laughed. It felt good to laugh, and she realized she hadn't done so in a long, long time. She felt she could relax and let down her guard somewhat around these men, and appreciate having friends. When one considered that they would all be competing for land, it was really quite amazing that everyone was so helpful.

"Bless you, but I grew up on a farm," she said. "I mostly rode bareback on our plow horses, though my mother said it wasn't ladylike. Goodness, that's been ages ago." It had been a decade or more since Hawthorne Farm had been a thriving, prosperous place, too, she thought, remembering how it had looked when she had come back as her father lay dying, had seen how the farm had fallen apart during his long illness, with all the good stock sold off to pay the doctor's bills and keep up the mortgage.

From there Alice steered the topic of conversation back to the brothers. She knew Elijah's goal in coming to Oklahoma was, of course, to build a church, but through skillful questions, she learned that Gideon wanted to start a horse ranch—not a big surprise, since Elijah had asked him to obtain a horse for her—and Clint hoped to be a town sheriff, as well as a homesteader.

None of these men were married, she mused. Why? Making a home out of nothing was hard without a wife to do the cooking and laundry while the husband tamed the land. And didn't any of them want children to pass the land on to? It was especially unusual for Elijah, a preacher, to be a bachelor. Every preacher she'd ever met before had had a wife and a handful of children.

It wasn't impossible that one or more of the brothers had been widowed, perhaps lost a wife in childbirth. Such things happened all too often. But perhaps the brothers were waiting till they were settled to go courting. It was none of her business, she reminded herself. She wasn't about to ask them about that area of their lives, for it might lead to similar questions aimed at her.

"Well, I suppose I'd better walk you over to the Gilberts' camp before it gets too much later," Elijah said to Alice, rising from his bench across from her.

She took a quick look at the watch she wore on her bodice. "Goodness! I hadn't realized so much time had passed," she said. It was the first evening that she hadn't watched the minute and hour hands crawl around the circle of her watch face with agonizing slowness until it was time to blow out her lantern. "Thank you, gentlemen, for supper and a most pleasant evening."

"It was our pleasure, ma'am," Clint said, sketching a bow. "Anytime you want company at supper, you can generally find us here of an evening."

Just as they were about to go their separate ways at the entrance to Mrs. Murphy's tent, a pair of men roughly shouldered past them, one of them clipping Clint's shoulder, then striding on as if unaware of the contact, but it had obviously been on purpose.

"Whoo-eee. Good thing they're leavin'," Alice heard one of them mutter. "I never did cotton to dinin' with snakes and traitors."

Clint pivoted and lunged in their direction, but Elijah reached out and restrained Clint with a quick hand on his arm.

"I know how you feel, but it's not worth it, Clint," Elijah said in a low, urgent voice.

"Yeah, they're not worth bruising our knuckles on—or getting ourselves thrown out of Mrs. Murphy's," Gideon growled, staring after the two men, his face as resentful as Clint's. "Reckon the trouble-making Chaucers have been talking again."

Clint shook off Elijah's hand, but Clint didn't follow after Elijah; Gideon standing still, too. "Lije, we'll meet you back at the tent." When Elijah gave Clint a searching look, he said, "Don't worry. We're not going back in there. I'm not going to do anything stupid. Night, Miss Alice."

Left alone with Elijah, Alice didn't know what to say. Her heart went out to the Thornton brothers, even though she didn't fully understand the reason for the hostility being shown to them.

Elijah sighed. "I feel I owe you an explanation, now that you've been witness to this sort of thing on two different occasions," he said. "Come. I'll explain as we walk."

"Please don't feel you must—it's none of my business," Alice murmured as she fell into step with him.

"Perhaps it's best if you know," Elijah said. "As Mr. LeMaster hinted at the other day, the Thorntons and the Chaucers both grew up on plantations in Virginia before the war. The Chaucer children were our closest friends."

"I see," she murmured. So that was the source of the drawl that occasionally crept into Elijah's otherwise Yankee voice.

"We spent the war years in Pennsylvania with a cousin of Papa's, while he went to fight for the Union. The plantation was left in the care of an overseer. Because of our father's loyalty to the Union, we kept possession of our plantation after the war, while our former friends, the Chaucers, lost theirs to taxes. But they made sure we were no longer welcome there," he said, bitterness edging into his voice, "so we sold Thornton Hall and moved to Kansas. We'd hoped to leave the past behind when we came to Oklahoma...." He sighed again and looked off into the distance.

Alice had the feeling "the past" included more than just their troubles in Virginia. "But this family, the Chaucers, make that impossible," she concluded for him. "Elijah, I—I'm sorry."

How much they had in common, she thought, though it wouldn't be wise to share her past with him. Both of them were trying to evade people who wished them ill—though Maxwell Peterson, she thought, with the same bitterness Elijah had voiced, insisted he only wanted to share his prosperous future with her.

Elijah met her gaze. "Thank you, Miss Alice," he said. "I'm only sorry I have to trouble you with it, but I thought, in case you heard anything more, you should be aware of what happened. We need say no more about it."

Keith Gilbert was sitting up on a camp chair with his wife when Alice and Elijah reached their campsite.

"I've been behavin', Nurse," he announced cheerfully, "though it's been infernal hard to watch my wife doin' all the work. Missed comin' to chapel this mornin', too, Reverend."

"I'll be glad when you're able to return, Keith, for I surely can't lead the singing the way you do," Elijah assured him, "but don't let me see you there till Miss Alice gives you the go-ahead."

Alice saw her patient and his wife exchange a wink. Were they reading something into the fact that

Elijah called her "Miss Alice" instead of "Miss Hawthorne"? Flustered, she focused on removing the old dressing. She could hardly correct their impression if they didn't voice it.

She found the wound was continuing to heal well, and his wife reported there'd been no recurrence of fever. *Thank God.* Alice quickly redressed the wound and bid them good-night.

After Elijah returned to the Thornton tent, he found his brothers preparing to retire. "I didn't want to ask in front of Miss Alice, but what do either of you know about these 'Security Patrol' officers riding around Boomer Town, proud as peacocks? One of them was the fellow who was trying to talk Miss Alice into buying that expensive Thoroughbred, but when I came upon him, there were three others."

"I heard they're former Confederate cavalry officers who've been allowed to rejoin the army," Gideon said. "Why?"

Elijah sat on the edge of his camp bed, rubbing his chin with his thumb and index finger. "Because it struck me that they all look to be in their forties or so, yet they're just privates."

"The word is that there were so many of 'em wanting to get back in the army after Reconstruction," Clint said, "that the federal government was afraid they'd take over and the war would start all over again. So they stripped them of their ranks before they'd let them rejoin."

"I see." Leave it to Clint to always have his ear to the ground, Elijah thought.

"What's your interest in this, Lije?" Gideon asked,

stretching his long legs out on his extralong cot. "Is it because that fellow was pressuring Miss Alice?"

"Yes, partly," Elijah began, feeling the protective streak rise up in him again as he'd felt when he had seen the way that ginger-haired fellow had looked at her earlier. "I didn't like the look in his eyes. I don't think she was quite aware of it, though she assures me that she's used to holding her own among pushy doctors and the like, but I'm not sure she's as worldly-wise as she makes out. And it got me thinking of how I'd seen these fellows talking to folks around Boomer Town. They were always with women on their own or foreign immigrants."

"Wouldn't hurt to keep our eye on these fellows," Clint said. "Anyone who looks crosswise at our Miss Alice will have all of us to tangle with."

"Agreed," murmured Gideon as he blew out the lamp.

Elijah's last waking thoughts were thankful ones. He was glad that his brothers were willing to help him watch out for Alice Hawthorne. He was blessed to have two solid, decent brothers who believed in protecting folks like Alice against those who would take advantage of them. Surely those character traits meant that, in time, they would return to the faith they'd been taught at their father's knee.

Chapter Six

It seemed to Alice, sitting in chapel the next morning, that most of the prayer requests that day had to do with various illnesses and injuries. And something Elijah said in his prayer about using one's talents in the Lord's service had her wanting to speak to him afterward.

She waited until nearly everyone else had left, passing the time by chatting with the talkative Ferguson sisters—or rather, Alice murmured "Hmm" and "I see" while they chattered. Then she approached Elijah.

She smiled as she held up her hands. "All right, I surrender, Reverend Thornton," she said, using his formal title since there were still a few others around. "You're right. I can see there *is* a continuing need for someone with medical training here. I'll do it until the Land Rush."

Elijah's smile lit up his serious face and warmed her inside. "Bless you, Miss Alice," he said, and took her hand between both of his. "You will be rewarded in Heaven, I know."

His hands felt so warm, as warm as the approval she saw in his eyes. "I'd be perfectly willing to have those who need care to come to my tent," she went on, "but some of them might not feel up to it or might have trouble finding me. What do you suggest?"

"Why don't we team up, Miss Alice? I've been visiting those I hear about who are ill or needing prayer, mostly in the evenings—unless they need me immediately, of course. Or if no one has made a request, I just walk around and talk to folks who are sitting by their tents or wagons. Why don't we go together?"

"Like making rounds in the hospital," she said, remembering the times she'd gone to the wards with the physicians, noting their orders for the patients.

"Exactly. I could pray with them while you treat them."

Her heart lightened as she smiled up at him. She felt strong and full of purpose. *Let's go together,* he'd said. Was it wrong that the words made her think of feelings she'd resolved to abandon in favor of independence?

"Shall we begin tonight, then?" he suggested. "I'll meet you after supper at your tent."

"Better yet, why don't you and your brothers come for an early supper? I'd intended to make stew yesterday, before you so kindly treated me to supper at Mrs. Murphy's. It'll just be a simple meal, but you're all more than welcome. Then we'll make our rounds."

The Thorntons brought more than their appetites when they came to supper. Gideon came leading a black horse whose rump was a blanket of white with black spots—an Appaloosa. When he placed the mare's lead rope in Alice's hand, he said, "I think she'll suit your needs, come the twenty-second, Miss Alice. I've tried her, and she's fast and agile. She can turn on a dime, and she has nice manners. I believe she'd be perfect for you for the Land Rush."

Alice felt her jaw drop. "Oh, she's beautiful!" she exclaimed, going to the mare and stroking her neck, and then her soft, velvety muzzle when the horse turned to snuffle her new mistress. "An Indian pony! Where did you get her? How much do I owe you? What's her name?"

The Thornton brothers laughed at the spate of questions. "I got her from Lars Brinkerhoff, a Danish fellow we've met."

"I've met him, too," she told him. "He and his sister, Katrine, were at the chapel this morning. He didn't mention the mare, though. He must not have wanted to spoil the surprise."

Gideon gave her a half smile and went on. "Lars lived with the Cheyenne for a time, and this mare was one of the string of ponies the Indians gave him when he left. He said you could have her for fifty dollars, and that includes a saddle and bridle, but you don't need to pay him until you decide she's the right horse for you. And he said her name, but it's some Cheyenne word, unpronounceable—at least to me—so I reckon you can give her a new name, Miss Alice."

Still stroking the mare and appreciating the kindness in her eyes, Alice said, "Then I'll call her Cheyenne. Thank you, Gideon."

The mare nickered as if she approved.

"You can leave her with our horses until the Land Rush, if you like," Elijah said. "Shall we ride out to the prairie tomorrow afternoon and try out her paces?"

She nodded, happy at the prospect of an afternoon of riding in Elijah's company. He was probably just being gentlemanly in offering to accompany her, she told herself, since it wouldn't be wise to go riding away from the tent city over unfamiliar ground on an untried horse. Keeping that in mind would help her to remember her own resolve, wouldn't it?

Their first stop was at the campsite of a man who'd asked for prayer for his daughter, because she had become weak and listless on the journey from Vermont.

After introductions, Alice sat and examined Beth Lambert. She was wan and pallid, just as her father had described. Alice found the mucous membranes around Beth's eyes and inside her mouth pale also, and her pulse was far too fast for a person at rest. Alice pulled her stethoscope—a gift from her mother when she had finished her training—out of her bag, then listened to the girl's heart and lungs. The heart rhythm, though rapid, was the regular *lub-dub* she had hoped for, rather than one with an extra beat that made the rhythm sound more like *Ken-tuck-y* or *Ten-nes-see,* as it would be with a heart murmur. The lungs were clear, free of the wet sounds or crackles that might signal consumption.

Nevertheless, she asked Beth if she'd been having night sweats or coughing. The girl shook her head.

"Chest pains?"

Again Beth shook her head.

"What have you been eating, Beth?" Alice asked. The girl wrinkled her nose. "Pretty much corn bread and biscuits, washed down with coffee, ever since we left the East. Don't have nothin' else."

"I see." Alice turned to the girl's parents, who were hovering anxiously nearby. Now that she'd spoken to their daughter, she saw the same pallor in her mother and father.

"I think your daughter is anemic—that is, her blood isn't carrying oxygen around as it should. She needs to eat more red meat, especially liver and eggs. In fact, I think those things would benefit all of you. Would you be able to get more of those in your diet?"

Thank You, Lord, for sending Alice to us, Elijah prayed. She was as tactful as she was skilled. She saw what needed to be done or said, and did and said it.

"Waal, I dunno," the father mumbled, scuffing a small rock out of the dirt and pushing it with his toe. "Beef's mighty costly."

"We left the East with not much more than the clothes on our backs," the mother said, and when the man next to her tried to shush her, she raised her voice more. "Jed, it's true, and our Beth is sick because of it." She turned back to Alice and Elijah. "By the time we bought the wagon and team, we didn't have much left for food on the trip, so we had to think cheap. We all et better back home."

While Alice hesitated, obviously trying to think of a solution, Elijah knew it was time to speak up. "The church has some money to help with such things," he told the man. "I'm going to give you twenty-five dollars, and I want you to buy a side of beef with it, and some liver, eggs and beans. Be sure and boil the bones to make soup, too. This money is only for nourishing food, mind you, so please use it wisely." He reached into his pocket and pulled out the money.

"Thank you, Reverend. Thank you, Nurse," the man said, shaking Elijah's hand, while the woman murmured, "God bless you folks for your kindness."

When they took their leave, they intended to stop at the Gilberts' campsite to check on the deacon's wound, since it was nearby, when a young boy ran up to them, his face white, his eyes terrified.

"Preacher, is she the nurse?" he said, pointing to Alice. "My pa needs her powerful bad! We found him behind some tents, all beat up. C'mon, I'll show you the way!"

They lost no time in following the boy and found the father, lying on a blanket by the wagon, just as the boy had said. One eye was swelling shut, his nose was bloodied and looked broken, and he had at least a dozen small cuts and as many scrapes.

"This is Miss Alice Hawthorne, and she's a nurse," Elijah told the man. "Miss Hawthorne, this is Abe McNally, and he attends our chapel meetings. Who attacked you?" Elijah inquired while Alice began to cleanse his wounds with a fresh cloth and some of that harsh-smelling disinfectant she'd used on Keith Gilbert's leg.

"Three or four men, all in black bandannas and dark clothes," McNally muttered, wincing as the carbolic acid stung a laceration on his hand. "I couldn't tell who they were. They pistol-whipped me, then took my pocket watch and Nancy's earbobs."

A whimper escaped from the woman standing nearby. "They was just colored glass, those earbobs, but Abe's pocket watch is gold. I told Abe he shouldn't

be flashin' it around this camp. There's too much
riffraff around Boomer Town, too many people t'
keep in line."

"I'm just glad young Tad was off playin', or they
might've hurt him, too," the man said, then let out a
groan. "Tarnation, Nurse. I appreciate what you're
doin', but that stuff *stings!*"

"I'll notify the Security Patrol about this incident,"
Elijah said, hoping he could speak to someone besides
the four who'd been ogling Alice yesterday. The Security Patrol was supposed to be watching out for
the settlers to keep this sort of thing from happening,
weren't they? Elijah would have preferred to speak
to someone from the army, but they were stretched
too thin along the border at present, keeping settlers
from entering too soon.

He was glad Clint planned to be the sheriff in the
town they would found. He didn't want their new
home to be a lawless place like Boomer Town.

Looking up just then, he spotted a dapper-looking
man in a derby hat watching Alice. The man held a
small notepad and seemed to be sketching her as she
tended the robbery victim.

What in the world? His hackles rose at the effron-
tery of what the man was doing and the avid, specu-
lative look in his eyes as he watched Alice. "May I
help you, sir?" he growled.

The man grinned and strode toward them, his air
brisk and confident. "Robert Millard Henderson, of
The New York Times. I was hoping to interview the
lady everyone's calling the 'Florence Nightingale of
the Oklahoma Territory.'" He grinned engagingly
at Alice.

Alice, kneeling by the man who'd been beaten up, went as white as the anemic girl they'd just left. "No!" she cried, and there was an anguished note in her voice that made Elijah peer at her carefully.

She swallowed, regaining her composure. "That is, no, thank you, sir. I—I'd rather not. I'm not doing anything that anyone with an ounce of decency wouldn't do, if they had the training."

"Very modest and commendable, miss," said the reporter. "However, our readers—and they include people throughout the whole country, you know—can't get enough of human-interest stories about the Oklahoma Land Rush. I've been hearing all over Boomer Town about the nurse who saved the life of a man who was bleeding to death. That was you, wasn't it?"

Elijah had never heard a man talk so fast. He was conscious of an urge to put himself between the reporter and Alice, and shove him all the way back to New York, if that was what Alice wanted.

"I'm sorry, Mr. Henderson. I'm busy here, and I don't want to talk to you." Alice went back to swabbing her patient's abrasions and cuts.

"But my readers would be fascinated with your story, Miss...?" Henderson let his voice trail off, inviting Alice to supply her name.

She ignored the unspoken request. "I said, I don't want to talk to you, sir. Please. Would you allow me to go on with what I'm doing, without your interference?"

"But, miss—" the reporter pleaded, coming a step closer.

Now Elijah did step between them. "You heard the

lady," he said firmly. "I'm Reverend Elijah Thornton, if you must have a name, and I'm asking you to respect this lady's privacy and that of her patient. Take yourself off, please."

Henderson scowled and drew himself up to his full height—which had to be almost a foot shorter than Elijah's. "It's a free country, Reverend Thornton," he huffed, "and one, moreover, with a free press. It's not against the law, as far as I know, for me to just move back a few paces and finish the sketch I was completing. That'll be for *Harper's Weekly*—I write articles for them, too, you see. I'll get this put on the cover, and the public will eat it up, this portrait of a heroic, self-effacing nurse serving the public."

Elijah felt his temper kindling at the man's self-important pushiness and his fulsome compliments, but Robert Henderson was well within his rights. Elijah felt Alice's urgent gaze on him, so he turned his back on the reporter and looked at her.

"Ignore him, Elijah," she whispered. "Let me just finish up here, and we'll move on."

Her movements quick and efficient, she bandaged the man's cuts and told him the signs of infection to watch for and advised cold compresses for his developing black eye. Then they left, heading for the Gilberts' as they'd originally planned.

The reporter had been an obnoxious popinjay, but Elijah was conscious, as they walked away from him, of an overwhelming curiosity to know why Henderson's request for her name had upset Alice so much. But now was not the time to ask her, not while she remained white-lipped and anxious. Her apprehensive expression, and the way she kept glancing over her shoulder until tents and wagons hid them from the reporter, made him ache with compassion for her and with that same desire to protect her that he had felt before.

Why was she so frightened? Was she hiding from someone? Had she committed a crime back East, so she was now running from the law? Or was she running from a husband?

It was best if the truth came from her. He had no right to demand it of her—that would make him no better than the pushy reporter. They were not courting sweethearts. Hadn't he resolved to commit himself to the work of the Lord, and remain unmarried? But since he'd met Alice, he'd begun to wonder if that resolve had been born out of grief and not the Lord's will.

Alice woke in a tangle of sheets in the middle of the night, knowing the scream that had awakened her had been her own. She sat up and lit the kerosene lantern, needing to banish the middle-of-night shadows within her tent.

She had been dreaming, she realized, as the warm light bathed the tent, illuminating the shape of her trunk and the camp chair on which she'd dropped her clothes last night after returning from her nursing rounds. Maxwell Peterson had been chasing her, his eyes red as burning embers, a ghastly smile curling his lips, revealing bright fangs for teeth. He waved a piece of paper written in blood, which she knew without seeing was her parents' mortgage.

"I'll tear it up!" he cried, his voice like the baying of a fantastical hound. "Just come to me, my pretty

Alice, and I'll tear it up! But if you don't, you'll have nothing! *Nothing!*" He bayed a maniacal laugh.

It didn't take much thinking, even in her shaky post-nightmare condition, to realize that her encounter with the nosy reporter had precipitated the dream. She poured herself a cup of water from the pitcher she kept on an upended crate by her cot.

It was silly to let the reporter's question worry her. She hadn't given the over-inquisitive fellow her name, so she had no reason to worry about Maxwell finding her here in the midst of the overcrowded tent city. He had no reason to suspect she'd even left New York, let alone come to this place in hopes of a homestead he couldn't touch.

A glance at her watch showed her it was yet hours till dawn. It was best to get some more sleep. She'd need her energy for the new day. She lay back down on her cot, pulled up the covers and closed her eyes again.

She and Elijah were going riding soon, Alice reminded herself. She was to try out her new mare to see if she could run, but all that came to her mind were images of Elijah—Elijah preaching; Elijah favoring a worried member of the congregation with a kind smile; Elijah laughing with his brothers, humor crinkling the corners of his twinkling hazel eyes. After a while, she fell back into sleep, this time a dreamless one.

Chapter Seven

They couldn't have picked a better afternoon to go riding, Alice thought. The sun beat down warmly on them, but the endless wind that seemed as much a part of central Oklahoma as its red soil prevented it from getting too hot.

The country was gently rolling, with flowers of every color dotted among the waving bluestem grasses. Alice recognized some of the flowers—wood sorrel, violets, fleabane, vetch—but others were unfamiliar to her. Trees—cottonwood, hickory and walnut—clustered near the occasional stream, along with clumps of blackberry bushes.

The Appaloosa mare was everything Elijah's brother had said she would be—good-natured, well-mannered and responsive, needing only a touch of Alice's heels to speed her from a sprightly trot to a smooth rocking-horse canter. But Alice sensed the mare was politely waiting for the command to go faster.

"Would you like to try a gallop? See if she's got

the speed Gideon promised?" Elijah asked, reining his bay gelding closer to her.

"I thought you'd never ask," Alice said with a smile. "Shall we make it a race? Say, to that rise over there?" She pointed to a bluff protruding from the prairie about half a mile away.

"Why not? It'll be good practice for the big day coming up," Elijah said. "Just be careful, and watch for gopher holes. Ready? *Hyaaah!*" He dug his heels into the bay, and the gelding rocketed out in front of the mare.

Alice touched her booted heels to Cheyenne's side. It was all the mare needed, and she took off like a shot, soon catching up with Elijah's gelding. She was glad she'd worn her divided skirt and had tied her bonnet on firmly, for there was no way she could have kept it on otherwise. Nor would she have wanted to try to cling to the pinto's back using a sidesaddle, even if there had been one available. She bent low over the mare's neck, savoring the rush of the wind in her face and the company of the man beside her.

Alice and Cheyenne reached the rise first. "I won!" she cried, swiveling in her saddle to see Elijah reach the finish line and rein his gelding in. "Though I suspect you were holding your horse back, weren't you?"

He smiled and raised his hands in mock surrender. "Guilty as charged, but in my defense, I wanted to be sure to see if the mare stumbled or gave you any trouble."

She smiled, touched by his consistent thoughtfulness. Elijah Thornton always considered others first.

"Well, I'm very impressed with Cheyenne so far," she said. "Gideon and Lars chose well. I'm sure she'll have enough speed to get me to a perfect claim." She wheeled the mare around so that they faced west and, holding her hand up to further shade her eyes, peered into the distance.

"I wish we could go look over the Unassigned Lands, figure out the best spots," she mused aloud. "How will we know which way to head, after the rifle shot sounds, and we're all running at once?"

"Lars has explored and hunted there, and knows the territory like the back of his hand," Elijah told her. "He said he had a map he made while he was with the Cheyenne that he'll show us and advise us where would be best for us, based on what we're wanting. I'm hoping everyone going to the tent chapel will be able to find a homestead in the same general area, if they wish."

His steady hazel eyes gazed down at her from his taller mount. Was there more to what he meant than what he said? Did he hope *she* would find a homestead near his? Did she *want* him to hope that? she wondered.

"Shall we ride back to that creek we passed about a hundred yards ago?" he suggested, pointing to it. "I'm thirsty, so I imagine these horses are, too."

They rode back to the stream at a walk, letting the sweaty horses cool down. Once there, Elijah assisted her to dismount, and they led their horses to drink. Then Elijah pulled a canteen from his saddlebag, knelt and filled it from the stream. Straightening, he handed it to her first, and she drank, enjoying the cold water.

"Shall we sit for a few minutes in the shade and

let the horses graze?" he said. "They won't go far—Gideon said your mare's been trained to ground-tie."

She nodded, knowing the term meant that once the reins were dropped, the horse wouldn't wander more than a few steps while she cropped the grass.

They sat in the grass in the shade of a cottonwood tree, and for a moment neither spoke, enjoying the quiet, which was broken only by the soft soughing of the breeze and the call of a mockingbird perched on a bough above them.

She'd missed this, Alice realized—the peace of being in the country, far away from the constant hustle and bustle of city traffic at all hours, with its streetcar bells, cries of newsboys calling out the big news stories, the ever-present noise outside that penetrated even the busy wards of Bellevue. All that time she'd spent in New York City, pursuing her dream of a nursing career, she'd missed this peace, she knew now. She should have left as soon as she had finished her nurse's training and sought employment with some country doctor near her parents' farm, she thought. Then she would have seen that her father was ill, and even if she couldn't have saved him, the place might not have fallen to rack and ruin.

But she wouldn't have come to this peaceful, beautiful countryside and been sitting here, the tall grass giving her and Elijah a pocket of privacy that made her feel as if it was their own world.

"We should have packed a picnic," Elijah said all of a sudden.

She was so surprised she dropped the sprig of bluestem grass she had been chewing.

Why had he said that? They weren't courting—

were they? Did he think they were? Oh, why had she gone on this ride alone with him? It had caused him to misconstrue their relationship, imagine their friend-ship was something more…. Yet she wanted it to be something more, she realized. But, no, it couldn't be. He would only turn into Maxwell and try to control her every move. Better to remain as she was, alone.

"Wouldn't that have been nice?" he murmured, apparently unaware of the tension that gripped her. "Fried chicken, fresh bread, cheese, pickles… Some-thing other than Gideon's endless corn bread and beans." He chuckled, then noticed that Alice was si-lent. "What's wrong, Miss Alice?"

She made a waving motion with her hands. "Noth-ing," she said with an airy assurance she didn't feel. "I—I didn't sleep well last night, that's all."

Elijah looked unconvinced. "You looked happy before I spoke."

Just as on the day they had met, she thought those hazel eyes saw too much. "It's nothing."

"Miss Alice, why did that reporter's request for your name make you afraid?"

It was eerie how he had keyed into what had pre-cipitated her nightmare. "Who says I was afraid?" she said quickly. "My name just wasn't any of that nervy fellow's business, that's all." Her words came out more sharply than she'd intended. "I'm sorry, Eli-jah. I—I just don't like the idea of my name being plastered all over some newspaper back East."

"You're not—and please believe me, I only want to help—in any trouble, are you? Back East, I mean?" His tone was gentle and uncondemning, but there was disappointment in his eyes.

Her throat felt thick with unshed tears and regret that she had spoiled the serene atmosphere of this place. And what he must be imagining...

"No, Elijah. I didn't rob a bank, or murder anyone," she said. "I've committed no crime. I just don't want my name in some newspaper, that's all. My mother always said a lady's name didn't belong in a newspaper except when she was married or when she died."

"All right, forgive me for asking," he said, his voice a little stiff.

The moment between them had been spoiled, and it felt as if there was now a wall between them.

He took a breath and looked away. "I suppose we should be getting back," he said, rising. He held out a hand to help her up, and she took it.

She couldn't leave things this way, not with this feeling of strain. "Elijah, there's nothing to forgive," she said softly, looking him in the eye.

Impulsively she laid a hand on his wrist, and the warmth of his skin gave her courage. "Please, I'm sorry if I sounded cross. I don't want anything to spoil our friendship—or the partnership we have to help the people of Boomer Town."

His stiff posture relaxed some, though his eyes still held a wary watchfulness. "I'm glad to hear you say it," he said at last. "In these few days I have come to value both things highly—and hold you in a position of great esteem."

So formal. So careful. But she supposed he was only trying to stay within the boundaries she had set for them. Friendship, not courtship.

She glanced upward at the position of the sun. "But you're right, we *should* be getting back. I—I need to do some mending before we go on our rounds tonight."

"Would you like to meet us at Mrs. Murphy's for supper?" he said. "Lars and Katrine are coming, and he's going to bring the map I mentioned."

She smiled, relieved that things would once again be more on an even keel between them. "That sounds good. The usual time?"

Full of hearty helpings of Mrs. Murphy's chicken stew—which was a lot tastier than her chewy beef, Elijah thought—they all stared down at the map Lars had spread out on the table. It was made of deer hide, tanned until it was amazingly supple. On it, in the flickering light of a pair of lanterns that hung over their table, Elijah could see undulating lines of rivers in the Unassigned Territories had been painted in some kind of blue dye. The hills were inverted brown vees. Stylized buffalo and deer dotted the area.

"This is the Canadian, that is the North Canadian and here is the Deep Fork," Lars said. Then he pointed to another river that ran north of the others. "This is the Cimarron, here."

"What does *Cimarron* mean?" Alice asked. "Is it an Indian word?"

Lars shook his head. "It is Spanish," he said. "It means 'wild' or 'untamed.'"

"Cimarron," she said again. "It's a beautiful name."

There was a bit of a poet in Alice Hawthorne, Elijah thought. It hadn't even occurred to him to ask the meaning of the word.

"And you think this spot here, on the south bank

of the Cimarron River, would be a good place for us to head to?" Elijah asked.

Lars nodded. "*Ja.* There is plentiful game here, and a number of tributaries run into the river, so the land is well watered. The land is gently rolling, with wooded areas breaking up the prairie. Right here," he said, pointing to a bend in the river, "a large boulder sticks out of the water. This would be ideal for your—our—town, I think."

"Then that's where we'll try to stake our claims on the twenty-second," Elijah said. "Agreeable to you, brothers?"

Gideon and Clint nodded.

"Just over two weeks from now," Katrine murmured, next to Lars.

"Will you folks be wantin' dessert? I made my ginger cake," Mrs. Murphy said, hands on her ample apron-covered hips as she stood by their table.

"Why not? We'll all take a piece," Clint said.

The Irishwoman was back in less than a minute, bearing a large round cake with brown sugar topping, still steaming from the oven.

"We'd better cut our pieces first, Alice," Katrine said with a chuckle, "or there'll be nothing but crumbs left for you and me."

Everyone laughed—everyone but Mrs. Murphy, who had been distracted by the map and was staring down at it with a wistful expression on her face. "Would that be where you're goin', then, the lot of you?" she asked in her lilting Irish accent, pointing at the bend of the river that Lars's hand still rested upon.

Elijah nodded. "God willing. Are you going to try for a homestead, Mrs. Murphy, or do you plan to return to where you came from?" There were a lot of entrepreneurs in Boomer Town, he knew, who were only here to make money satisfying the needs of the would-be homesteaders and would return home until the next section of Oklahoma was opened.

The big Irishwoman shrugged. "I'm going to try to get my own place. Mind ye, I don't really want to farm. I just want a lot in a town where I can build a café—a real café, I mean, not just a tent," she said, nodding at the canvas walls around them. "With tables, not crude benches."

"Do you have a wagon? Will you be driving it?" Elijah asked, realizing with some shame he had never spoken to the woman other than to order his food. He wondered if she had ever managed a team of horses.

"Yes, we have a wagon, Sean and I," Mrs. Murphy said. She jerked her head in the direction of a carrot-topped, freckled youth washing dishes in the corner of the tent. "That's my son, the only child Shamus gave me before he passed on, God rest his soul. Sean will be at the reins when the day comes."

"Then why don't you do your best to head to this bend in the Cimarron, too?" Elijah suggested. "I'm going to build a church on my homestead here, and I hope a town will spring up around it. There must be others who'd like lots in a town, so they can start businesses. I'm sure we'll need a café."

"And Gideon can supply your beef," Clint told her. "He's going to raise them on his ranch, aren't you, brother?"

Down the table, Gideon nodded his shaggy head and grinned.

"Then sure as my name is Molly Murphy, I'll be

there. *We'll* be there!" the woman cried, indicating her son and beaming.

Elijah gazed around the table, savoring the moment. All of them united in one purpose—and now Mrs. Murphy and her son, too. *Thank You, God. May these souls be the core of Your town and Your church in this settlement.* Hopefully the Gilberts, his deacon and deaconess, would be there, as well.

As if she could hear his prayer, Alice raised her head and returned his gaze, her blue eyes beautiful in the flickering overhead light. He saw her check the small gold watch she wore pinned on the bodice of her flower-sprigged calico dress. "Elijah, perhaps we'd better get going on our rounds," she murmured. "There were several who asked for prayer this morning for ailments, and I ought to check on the Lambert girl again and make sure she's getting the proper diet."

He nodded his assent and stood, waiting while she gathered her medical bag from beneath the table.

Lord, You've brought Alice Hawthorne into my life, and at the moment, Your purpose in doing so isn't clear. She's made it plain that she only wants to be my friend, and I'd already decided I wanted to serve You, not to marry. Yet why is there this growing warmth in my heart for her, Father?

Elijah only hoped God would show him what He wanted him to do.

Chapter Eight

It was late by the time Alice and Elijah finished their last visit, a stop at the Ferguson sisters' campsite. Cordelia was down with a head cold and a fever, and was so hoarse Alice had finally encouraged her not to speak while Alice brewed her some willow bark tea. But her talkative sister, Carrie, had more than made up for her sister's silence.

"I think instead of crying as soon as they were born, those two started talking," Alice remarked once she and Elijah had left the sisters.

Elijah chuckled. "I believe you're right—" Suddenly he stopped stock-still, holding up a hand. "Listen. Did you hear that?"

Alice stopped, and then she heard it—a child's frightened cries, interspersed with a man's angry shouts.

"Whatever can that be about? Come on, Elijah!" Alice cried, taking off at a run in the direction of the commotion. Was some parent going overboard in disciplining a child? But as they drew nearer, she realized that the child's shouted words were in some language she didn't recognize. A woman's voice pierced the night, adding to the cacophony. "Webster, stop! Just let him go!"

From behind her, Elijah cautioned her. "Miss Alice, please, let me go first. We don't know what sort of man—"

Heedless, she plunged ahead. No one was going to mistreat a child, even if he was his father.

When they came around a wagon, she saw them— a red-faced man holding a struggling child by the hair and boxing his ears. Even in the dancing light of the fire, Alice could see the child was filthy and disheveled. An Indian, she realized, seeing the boy's frightened obsidian eyes and darker skin. He was clad only in muddy rawhide leggings, his chest bare.

"Stop that! Stop that!" Alice shrieked, lunging at the man.

"Stop hitting that boy at once!" Elijah shouted, coming right behind her. "Miss Alice, be careful!!"

Startled, the other man let go of the boy.

Alice was sure the boy would rabbit away into the darkness. But to her astonishment, he ran straight to her, clutching her around the waist and trembling.

"There, there," she soothed, not knowing if the boy understood her as she ran a comforting hand down his shaking back.

"Mister, I'm within my rights," she heard the man protest. "I caught this little redskin thief stealin' our food."

"He's a *child*," she heard Elijah retort. "It's never all right to beat a child, no matter what race he belongs to."

"You're safe now," Alice murmured to the clinging boy. "Oh, Elijah, look at him—he's skinny as a rail! He's obviously starving."

"You're that Thornton preacher fellow the Chaucers were talkin' about," the man growled. "The one whose family stole their land, and now he wants everyone to think he didn't do nothin' wrong."

Alice groaned inwardly, while keeping a watchful eye on the man. *Another one who wants to hold the Thorntons accountable for long-ago wrongs and at the worst time.*

"I'm Elijah Thornton, yes, but—"

"Webster, you let that child have that food," called a woman—the man's wife, Alice assumed—from the wagon. "You weren't going to eat it, anyway. Now come to bed."

Webster turned back to Elijah. "He kin have the vittles, providin' you go away and leave us in peace, all right?"

Elijah picked up the tin plate, motioning for Alice and the boy to follow. The man and his wife disappeared back into the wagon.

When they were a few yards away, Elijah handed the plate to the child, who fell on it like a famished wolf, apparently confident enough in the presence of his protectors.

Alice looked at Elijah over the boy's bent shoulders. The boy was too busy shoving biscuits into his cheeks to care about anything else.

She thought the boy was about seven years old, but she couldn't be sure.

"Elijah, what are we going to do with him? Where are his parents?"

He shrugged, staring at the child. "He's obviously

an Indian—but not full-blooded, I think," he said, peering more closely. He knelt next to the boy, who had finished gulping down the food and was gazing at him with wary eyes. Obviously the child trusted Alice but wasn't sure if this white man was capable of being as brutal as the other one.

"Don't be afraid. I won't hurt you," Elijah told the boy, his tone gentle. "Do you speak English?"

The boy's shaking had stopped, but now that he had eaten, he once more clung to Alice's skirt. She could see from his expression that while he was curious about Elijah, he didn't understand what he was saying.

She touched him gently and knelt, too. "Alice," she said, pointing to herself. "Elijah," she said, pointing to him. Perhaps she should have said "Reverend Elijah," she thought, but that was a long name for a little boy to say.

The boy cocked his head, then said, *"Da-ko-ta,"* and pointed to his bare chest.

"Your name is Dakota?"

She wasn't sure if he understood, but he said, "Dakota," and pointed to himself again. Then he pointed at her. "Alss," he said, and then he indicated Elijah. "'Lijah."

"Your mama? Your papa?" Alice asked.

The boy stared back at her, his eyes blank with incomprehension, then leaned toward her and said, *"Cattan rechid lossin?"*

She must have looked as confused as he had, for he repeated the phrase again.

"I'm sorry, child. I don't know your language." Compassion flared in her for the boy. "Elijah," she said, "we have to take care of this child until we can find his parents."

"*If* we can find his parents," he countered, looking as worried as she felt, which touched her heart.

"Who knows when he ate last, and he's so dirty," she said, peering at his hair and hoping he didn't have lice. "Where did he come from, do you suppose? Was he left behind because of his mixed blood when the Indians left this territory?"

"Possibly," Elijah muttered. "I agree. We'll have to take care of him, see if we can find someone who speaks his language, so we can find out where he belongs. Poor boy."

Alice watched as Elijah reached out a careful hand and stroked Dakota's arm. The boy no longer seemed afraid of him. As she watched, Dakota's mouth opened into a big yawn.

"He must be tired. But the first thing he needs is a bath," Alice said. "Will you help me? I want to take him back to my tent, heat some water and give him a little scrubbing. I have a shirt that might fit him, if we roll up the sleeves."

"Of course I'll help you," Elijah said.

Dakota submitted with surprising equanimity to his washing, but perhaps it was because he was so exhausted by the events of the night—and by whatever he had endured before, Alice thought—so he was heavy-eyed and silent by the time she finished combing the tangles out of his shoulder-length hair. She'd been relieved to find that there was nothing living in it. Now that it was clean and drying, she could see that Dakota's hair was dark brown, not black, further proving Elijah's assertion that Dakota was of mixed blood.

While Alice had been washing the child, Elijah had spread out a pair of spare blankets and placed them on the ground near her cot, along with some folded towels for a pillow. Leaving the drowsy boy, she went to rummage through her trunk for the spare shirt she'd thought might fit him, but by the time she'd found it and turned around, Elijah was carrying the sleeping Dakota to the makeshift pallet.

The sight of the preacher laying the boy carefully down and smoothing a lock of hair away from his forehead did something to Alice's heart. *What a decent, kind man Elijah Thornton is,* she thought. Once more, she wondered why he hadn't married and had a flock of his own children. It was obvious he'd be a good father.

He could be carrying your son like that—yours and his, a voice within her whispered, a voice she resolutely ignored, but the longing that echoed in her heart refused to be silenced.

"I'll be going now," Elijah announced, breaking into her thoughts. "We'll talk tomorrow," he said, nodding toward the boy. He turned, and started to lower his head to clear the low tent entrance, then turned back. "You know, he may leave while you're asleep," he warned her gently. "I'm not sure what he's doing in Boomer Town, but he may be trying to find someone—his parents, for example—or some *thing.*"

Alice wrenched her gaze away from Elijah to stare at the sleeping child. "Oh, no," she whispered. "Oh, Elijah, I can't bear to think of him wandering and hungry again."

"I'm sorry," he said. "I didn't mean to distress you. I just didn't want you to be surprised if you wake and he's gone. You must rest yourself, Miss Alice, and leave this in God's hands while you sleep."

She knew he was right, but the idea of waking and finding that Dakota had left haunted her. "That's why we must find someone who can talk to him as soon as possible," she said. "Why, we don't even know what tribe he comes from. We need to find out who, or what, he's looking for. What happened to his parents—why he's alone."

"I believe the Lord will provide the answers," Elijah said. "I'll see you both tomorrow."

It was hard for Alice to settle down to sleep after that. Would they find the child's parents, or was he indeed abandoned because he was partly white? If no mother or father showed up to claim the boy, what would they do? It wasn't as if she could adopt Dakota, a single woman alone and, so far, without a permanent home to offer him. A child deserved to have a mother and a father, and both she and Elijah were unmarried—and she intended to stay that way.

At dawn, Elijah gave up pursuing a deep, restful sleep and got up. It had been almost midnight by the time he'd helped Alice settle Dakota for the evening, too late to discuss the boy with his brothers. When they woke up this morning, though, he had coffee ready, and he wasted no time in giving them a brief explanation of what had happened.

"Maybe Lars could help you talk to the boy," Clint said, stirring at least half a cup of sugar into the coffee. "At least he could tell you if the boy is Cheyenne.

And if he isn't, maybe he could use that sign language the tribes use to communicate with each other to figure out what tribe he comes from."

"Why didn't I think of that?" Elijah exclaimed, throwing his hands up in the air. He'd been right to think that answers would be easier to come by in the morning. "Perhaps I should go get Lars and take him to meet the boy."

"You could," Gideon said, "but not right now. He went hunting."

"How long will he be gone?" Impatience was a personal failing of his, Elijah knew.

Clint shrugged. "Depends on when he gets lucky. He's been pretty fidgety, just sitting around Boomer Town waiting for the Land Rush."

Elijah sighed. His brothers were both getting restless, too, being men of action. They didn't have the church and its growing congregation to keep them busy.

"I'm going to go hunt up some milk for Dakota before I go visit him," he said, remembering a member of his congregation who had a milk cow. As rail-thin as the boy was, some milk would be good for him.

But as he left their campsite, he suddenly realized he had no reason to be certain that Dakota was still there. Had the boy sneaked away during the night, as Elijah had told Alice Dakota might? Worse yet, what if he had stolen things from Alice, too? Elijah didn't think the boy would do that, after the way he had clung to Alice as his protector, but what had Elijah been thinking to leave the boy with Alice? He should have taken Dakota with him. Between him and his brothers, they could've kept an eye on the boy until they found a more permanent solution.

Maybe he'd better go check on Alice before he went and got milk for an Indian boy who might be miles away by now. He reversed his steps and headed for Alice's at a trot.

His fears proved to be groundless. When he reached the campfire, the first sight that greeted his eyes was that of Dakota, devouring a tin plate heaped with bacon and eggs, and a sugared doughnut. He spotted a tin cup half-full of milk beside him, too. Alice had already seen to the boy's needs.

"Good morning, Reverend Elijah," Alice said, catching sight of him as she reached into the frying pan with a long fork and pulled out four more freshly cooked doughnuts and dropped them into a bowl of sugar.

"Good morning. I see he's still here," he said, nodding toward the boy, not quite successful at hiding his relieved sigh. "Good morning, Dakota."

Dakota looked up from his plate long enough to give him a shy smile.

"No one leaves when there are doughnuts coming," Alice said with a wink, though something in her eyes told him that she was relieved, too.

She leaned over and whispered something to the boy, who swallowed his food, put his plate down and crowed, "Gute mor-nin', Preechah 'Lijah!" then gave a boyish belly laugh at Elijah's astonishment.

Elijah chuckled. "I see you've accomplished a lot already today, Miss Alice."

"Oh, he's just parroting sounds back, I think,"

Alice said. "I'm sure he understands it's a greeting, at least. But I wish we could find out more from him."

Elijah told her about Clint's suggestion of using Lars to try to communicate with the boy, and that Lars had gone hunting, the time of his return uncertain.

"Well, it seems we shall have to be patient," Alice said. "But what if it turns out he has no one?" she asked Elijah, unconsciously twisting a fold of her apron. "I mean, long-term…" Her voice trailed off.

Elijah knew what she meant. If Dakota was truly an orphan, what would they do then? A child needed a mother and a father.

"Why not bring him to chapel this morning, and we'll pray about it?" he suggested and saw her nod. He consulted his pocket watch. "Speaking of which, I'd better be going so I can prepare. I'll see both of you there."

But as he walked away, it was not of chapel or Dakota he thought, but of how appealing Alice Hawthorne always looked in the morning—fresh as the dew, her eyes kissed by sunshine, wearing her simple flower-sprigged calico as though it was the finest silk. Despite all his resolutions and her earlier declarations about her prized independence, he was starting to care for her more and more, he thought. Perhaps as they kept working together around the camp, she would learn to value independence less and a future with him more.

Chapter Nine

Alice wondered how Dakota would react to the chapel prayer service, whether he would get squirmy or try to leave. Arriving a little early, she picked a place near to the front so Dakota would be able to see Elijah easily. So far, though, Dakota seemed fascinated with the tent's rows of benches and the people filing in to sit down. *So far, so good.*

"Mornin', Miss Alice. Mind if we sit with you?" asked a familiar voice, and she looked up to see Keith Gilbert and his wife standing by the bench she and Dakota occupied. Mr. Gilbert leaned on a cane, but he appeared hale and hearty. Hard to believe he had lain at death's door just four nights ago, she marveled. *Thank You, Lord.*

"Please do. It's good to see you back in chapel, Mr. Gilbert. We've missed your song leading."

"Thanks. I've missed doing it. Thought I'd come just to listen today. Sunday will be soon enough to take up my duties again," Keith Gilbert said. "I've been following your instructions to the letter."

"Who's your friend?" Cassie Gilbert asked as she

sat down next to Dakota. She smiled down at the boy, and he smiled shyly back.

The deaconess's reaction, and that of the rest of the congregation, was a great deal nicer than a few of the residents of Boomer Town had given them as they'd walked to the chapel. Many had stared at the boy as she and Dakota had neared the entrance, their expressions as disapproving as if Alice had dared to enter church with a little piglet, fresh from a mud wallow in his pen. Alice had heard more than one person mutter "half-breed."

Why were people so hateful to those who were different? she wondered. Didn't they know this territory had been wholly assigned to the Indians, until the recent Indian Appropriations Act—or that everyone but the Indians were newcomers to America at one time?

"This is Dakota," she told the Gilberts, and explained what had happened last night.

"Dakota, it's nice to meet you. I'm Mrs. Gilbert, and this is my husband, Mr. Gilbert," Cassie said, even though Alice had explained the boy didn't know English. "Oh, Alice, he has such intelligent eyes! And such a sweet face." Impulsively she reached out a hand and cupped Dakota's cheek. The boy grinned up at her.

Amazing, Alice thought. Despite what he'd been through—and of course, she didn't know the half of it—he still responded positively to friendliness.

Not to be outdone, Keith Gilbert reached into his pocket and pulled out a small twisted bit of paper, and untwisted it, revealing a peppermint, which he held out to Dakota. "Here. See if you like this."

The boy eyed it curiously, then looked at Keith Gilbert, who pantomimed eating it. Dakota popped the peppermint into his mouth, and as Alice watched, an expression of delight spread over the boy's face. He'd clearly never had candy before. He pointed to Keith Gilbert's pocket, obviously hoping it contained more of the wonderful treat.

The Gilberts chuckled. "You've started something now, husband," Cassie Gilbert said.

"I'm sorry, I don't have any more," Mr. Gilbert told the boy.

Elijah arrived then, and as he strode down the aisle, he looked pleased to see Dakota sitting with Alice. "Welcome, Dakota. I see you've found new friends."

"*Haáahe,* 'Lijah!"

When it came time for the singing, Dakota responded enthusiastically, and no one seemed to mind that he sang a singsong chant with incomprehensible words while the others sang "Praise to the Lord, the Almighty."

We all praise the Lord in our own way, Alice thought.

"As we near the end of our second week in Boomer Town," Elijah said after the hymn was sung, "I'd like to greet our newest guest, Dakota." Briefly he told about finding the hungry boy the night before, leaving out the part about the man who'd been beating the boy. "So I'd like to take the opportunity to present a prayer request of my own, that the Lord will help us find Dakota's people, if at all possible. We're hopeful that Lars Brinkerhoff will be able to help us communicate with Dakota toward that end."

The usual assortment of other prayer requests followed, and when the service was over, Alice was pleased when Elijah, Dakota and she were invited to have supper at the Gilberts' campsite.

"It's to thank you for saving Keith and helping him heal, Alice," Cassie said, "and for all your prayin', Reverend. And we'd like to get to know this young man a little better, too," she said, beaming at Dakota. "I have a feeling he'll like fried chicken."

The Gilberts left before Elijah was finished greeting folks in order to prepare the meal.

"Ready to go?" Elijah asked, when the last member of the congregation had left.

"Should you let your brothers know that you won't be there for the meal?" Alice asked.

He laughed. "They're not there. I think they were envious of Lars going hunting, so they decided to do likewise, just as I was getting ready for chapel. Maybe they'll run across him and tell Lars we need a translator."

They had just stepped into the sunlight when Dakota spotted the four Security Patrol officers trotting past on their horses, evidently making their rounds. He pulled on the sleeve of Alice's blouse, then Elijah's shirtsleeve, and pointed.

"Cattan rechid lossin?"

It was the same phrase Dakota had said the night before, after they'd left the campsite where he'd been trying to steal food, Elijah realized.

"Cattan rechid lossin?" the boy said again, pulling urgently on Elijah's sleeve again. He pointed to the mounted privates.

"I think he wants us to follow them—maybe speak

to them," Elijah murmured. "Could he have met them before? Perhaps one of them can speak his language? Come on, it's worth a try," he said.

All three of them dashed after the four riders.

The privates were walking their horses down the dirt road, so it wasn't hard to catch them. Elijah ran up to the closest one.

"Excuse me," he said. "I'm Reverend Elijah Thornton. I wonder if I might trouble you with a question, Officer?" He knew very well the man was a private, and not entitled to be addressed as an officer, but he remembered what his brother had said about the Security Patrol being former Confederate officers. He didn't think they'd mind the added term of respect, especially if they remembered their encounter when Alice had been looking at their friend's horses. The man he was addressing was the very same ginger-haired fellow who'd been trying to talk Alice into buying that high-priced Thoroughbred.

Sure enough, the man didn't bother to correct him, but he caught the glint of recognition in his eyes—and the way those eyes narrowed when he spotted Dakota at Elijah's heels. "How may I help you, sir?" he drawled. "Ma'am," he added, fingering his hat brim as Alice caught up.

"We found this boy, here, and he speaks no English, but he seems to want to talk to you—"

"We don't have any responsibility toward the Indians," said another of the privates, one whose overlong blond hair and proud carriage reminded Elijah of a picture he'd seen of the late General Custer.

"Looks like a breed to me," another of the four muttered.

Elijah saw Alice stiffen at the term.

Dakota drew near and touched the man's stirrup to get his attention. *"Cattan rechid lossin?"* he asked, hope lighting his black eyes and high-cheekboned face.

"Do you know what he's trying to say?" Elijah asked hopefully.

"Yes, we think he may be of mixed race," he added, glancing at the one who'd made the remark. "Do any of you know any of the common Indian tongues or know how to do Indian signing?"

The four exchanged glances. Then the golden-haired one said, "Afraid not, Reverend. Maybe you should turn him over to the army, let them figure it out. Good day to you, sir, ma'am." Lifting his wide-brimmed hat in a gesture of polite dismissal, he nudged his horse into a trot, and the other three followed.

Alice stood staring after them. "Well, it didn't hurt to ask, I suppose," she said with a sigh, and they walked on to the Gilberts' campsite.

Dakota downed as much fried chicken as either Gideon or Clint could have, along with half a dozen biscuits and a helping of green beans—much to the delight of the Gilberts, who chuckled as the boy smacked his lips and rubbed his tummy in obvious appreciation of something he'd probably never eaten before. His black eyes lit up as Mrs. Gilbert sliced an apple pie and plopped the first piece onto his tin plate.

"Does my heart good to see a boy enjoy his food like he's doing, poor mite," Cassie Gilbert commented with a fond look.

Dakota lost no time in devouring the pie, also.

Then, apparently sated for the time being, he took great interest in Elijah's pocket watch, which Elijah obligingly handed over for his inspection. The boy opened and closed it and dangled it by its chain like a pendulum. Then he spotted a gray tiger kitten sitting under the wheels of the Gilberts' wagon and patted the grass, chuckling when the kitten ran out and pounced on his hand.

"That kitten seems to have adopted us," Keith Gilbert commented, as the boy picked it up. "Hungry little thing, just like the boy. Likes our scraps."

Satisfied that Dakota wasn't paying attention, Alice told the older couple about their encounter with the Security Patrol and the phrase the boy had repeated, doing a creditable rendition of the incomprehensible words.

"No tellin' what those words might mean," Keith said. "Hopefully that Lars fellow will have some idea."

His wife's eyes followed the child as he chased the playful kitten around the wagon. "We never got to raise children of our own, you know," she murmured. "Why, Keith, he's just about the age our boy would've been…" Her eyes grew misty, her face wistful, and she looked down at her own plate.

"Had a baby boy, but he only lived a few days," Keith Gilbert explained, his voice thick and gruff as he patted his wife's plump hand. "We never knew why. Then…well, the Lord didn't see fit to give us any others. 'Course, we married late in life…"

Elijah hadn't known about the lost son. Everyone had suffered losses, somewhere in the course of their lives, it seemed. Some losses were greater than oth-

ers. He'd lost a fiancée, while Gideon had lost both
a beloved wife and a daughter. He turned to study
Alice now, who was distracted by the antics of Dakota and the kitten. What had she lost? Why was the
pretty auburn-haired miss still unmarried? She professed not to need anything but her independence,
but had there been some man who'd loved her, whom
she'd lost to death? Or had the man—impossible to
imagine—preferred another girl?

She'd lost her peace of mind, at the very least,
Elijah thought, remembering the troubled look that
occasionally stole over her lovely features.

"That was a delicious lunch, Mrs. Gilbert," Alice
said. "Thank you for inviting all of us."

"Well, you're as welcome as can be, Alice dear.
Like I said, it's the least we could do after your skill
saved my Keith," Cassie said.

Alice smiled gently. "The Lord must not have
thought your husband was done with his earthly
tasks just yet."

Keith Gilbert grinned. "I believe you're right, Miss
Alice."

"Reverend… Alice…" Cassie began hesitantly,
glancing at Dakota, who was now sitting with the kitten in his lap, twirling a bit of straw and laughing as
the little gray tiger batted fiercely at it. "I was thinkin'
during the prayer service, and Keith and I discussed
it on the way back here… I mean, I don't know how
you'd feel about it, and please say no if you've gotten attached, Alice, but…what would you think about
Dakota stayin' with us? Least till you find his mama
and papa, that is," she added in a rush.

Alice blinked in surprise and looked at Elijah, whose face mirrored the same astonishment. How *did* she feel about it? She'd been pleased and relieved that she hadn't awoken to find Dakota gone this morning, but if she were honest with herself, she'd begun to worry about what would happen if his parents weren't found. What would she do with Dakota while she made her nursing rounds in the evenings? How would she look after the boy on the day of the Land Rush? And even supposing that problem could be solved, what sort of life would that be for Dakota, living on the homestead with a couple of women—her mother and herself?

And what if her past caught up with her and she had to run?

Elijah was silent, seemingly waiting on her to answer.

"I… Are you sure you want to do this, Mrs. Gilbert?" Alice asked. "I mean, we have no assurance that Dakota won't leave, now that he's not starving, especially when we can't communicate with him and know where he came from and how he came to be separated from his people."

"If he stays around white folks, he'll pick up English, I reckon," Keith Gilbert said. "He's obviously a smart boy."

"It might be the best solution, if he's willing to stay with them," Elijah said carefully.

Alice glanced at him. "Yes…if he's willing. If his people did abandon him, though, I don't want him to think I'm rejecting him, too. Could we…wait until Lars is back, to see if he can talk to Dakota and discover how he came to be in Boomer Town, stealing scraps? He can find out if Dakota would like to stay with the Gilberts then, too."

"That makes sense—" Mrs. Gilbert began, only to be interrupted when Elijah suddenly jumped up and began waving his arms at a man riding past the campsite at a trot. Tied on the back of the horse, Alice saw, was the carcass of a deer.

The big blond man's head turned as he heard his name called, and he halted his horse. *Lars!*

Elijah dashed over to meet him. "You couldn't have happened by at a better time, my friend," Elijah said, shaking his hand. "How fortunate that your tent happens to be right down the row from the Gilberts'. We're hoping you can clear up a mystery."

Lars smiled and dismounted. "Always happy to help you, my preacher friend. What's happened?" Then he spotted Dakota, who had seen his arrival and stood up to peer at him curiously. "Who's this?"

"This is Dakota," Alice said, coming forward with the boy.

"Come have a seat, Lars, and have some cold lemonade while you talk to the boy," Cassie Gilbert invited, beckoning him.

"Don't mind if I do, as you Americans say."

Once he was ensconced on a hay bale with the promised lemonade, Alice quickly caught Lars up on events. Dakota inched closer, staring with obvious fascination at the Indian beadwork hatband on the hat Lars had doffed.

"So you see, Lars," Alice concluded, "we were hoping you could tell us if Dakota is Cheyenne or not, and find out how he got here."

Lars turned to the boy. *"Tsitsistas?"* he asked, pointing directly at Dakota.

"Ótsêhámóe! Tsitsistas!" the boy cried, nodding his head excitedly and pointing to his chest.

"Yes, he *is* Cheyenne," Lars confirmed—unnecessarily, because everyone could see the truth written on the boy's face. "Though he's of a different band than the one I stayed with. Their land is southwest of here. And he is eight years old."

Eight, not seven, as she had thought, but she'd been close. Fear and hunger had a way of making a child look younger than he actually was.

Then Lars turned back to the boy and spoke to him in rapid-fire Cheyenne while the rest of them watched, excited that they would soon know the boy's story.

Lars lost his smile as the exchange went on. Dakota's face took on a tenseness, and his eyes looked dull with sadness. At one point, Alice thought she heard the boy utter that phrase again, *"Cattan rechid lossin."* Surely soon they would know what it meant.

At last, Lars turned back to the rest of them and reported, "Dakota's mother is dead. She died when he was a baby, and he was raised by an aunt. His father was an officer in the U.S. Cavalry, and he abandoned the baby who was born of the union between himself and Dakota's mother when Dakota was born. His name was Captain Richard Lawson."

"Cattan rechid lossin—Captain Richard Lawson!" Alice breathed. "Of course! He's been trying to tell us that name ever since we found him. That's why he wanted to talk to the Security Patrol privates—he saw their uniforms. His people must have told him

how the soldiers dressed, or perhaps this Lawson left some clothing behind."

"You said his name *was* Richard Lawson. Is he dead, too?" Elijah asked Lars.

Lars spoke to Dakota again.

A puzzled expression crossed over the boy's face. He shrugged, then uttered another spate of Cheyenne to Lars.

"He doesn't know," Lars translated. "His aunt told him only the man's name, and when Dakota heard that there were soldiers here guarding the borders of the territory, he ran away from the tribe to come and find his father."

"So he wasn't abandoned," Alice said. It was a relief to hear, but what were they to do about that? Help him find his father, who hadn't wanted him as a baby, or help him return to his home and his people?

Lars spoke to the boy again.

"No, he wasn't thrown out of the band, but he says he always felt as if he wasn't fully accepted because of his white blood. He wants to see if his father will let him stay with him now that he is almost grown to manhood."

Alice's heart ached for the boy. How hard it must have been, growing up a little different from the other boys in his village, abandoned by his own father, who'd apparently used his mother and then cast her aside. Her own childhood, in comparison, had been so full of love from both her parents.

"I could make inquiries of the army officers stationed along the border," Elijah said. "Surely someone will know if Lawson is still in the territory. I suppose he must be given the chance to step up and accept re-sponsibility for the boy."

From his voice, Alice could tell Elijah didn't think that was likely any more than she did.

"Please tell the boy I'll go to the army officers at the border and inquire tomorrow," Elijah said to Lars.

Dakota looked pleased when Lars relayed the news. And warily hopeful. Alice was all too afraid that anything Elijah was likely to find out would only crush that fragile hope. If Richard Lawson hadn't wanted his infant mixed-blood son, why would he want him now? She felt fiercely protective of this child, and resentful of the man who'd apparently care-lessly taken his pleasure and left when the situation became difficult.

More proof that men are not to be trusted.

Well, she shouldn't make assumptions, she sup-posed. They would have to wait for that answer.

"We have another question," she said to Lars. "I kept the boy last night, but the Gilberts have offered to take Dakota in, at least until his situation is made clear. Could you ask Dakota if that's all right with him?"

She could see Cassie and Keith Gilbert hold their breaths as the question was put to the child through Lars, but they needn't have. The boy's mercurial smile lit his face.

"Dakota says 'it is well,'" Lars reported. "He likes the Gilberts and is fond of Mrs. Gilbert's cooking, too. He says he hopes there will be more fried chicken."

Cassie Gilbert laughed. "You tell him, just as soon as Keith buys another at the butcher's tent!" Both Gil-berts looked happy enough to burst.

Alice was happy for the boy, of course, but she couldn't help feeling wistful, too. Even for such a brief time, she had felt good taking care of someone besides herself.

As if he read her mind, Dakota came to her then, and placed his hand softly on her cheek. *"Néá'eše, Alss."*

It was as clear a thank-you as she'd ever received. As she watched, her eyes stinging with tears, Dakota went to Elijah, too, laid a hand on his shoulder and said the same thing. Maybe independence wasn't to be prized as much as she had thought.

Chapter Ten

"They look so happy," Alice murmured later, as she cast a backward glance at the Gilberts and Dakota. Lars had already departed.

She looked a little melancholy, Elijah thought. Had Dakota filled a void in her life, even for that short period of time? This was a woman who should have children, and a husband, he thought, though he knew better than to say so. She'd already made her feelings clear on that score.

"The Lord is so good to us," he said, determined to share the thankfulness that had welled up in him when he'd first spotted Lars and even more when their friend was able to break down the language barrier between themselves and Dakota. Perhaps it would distract her from her sadness. "Just think—He sent Lars along right when we needed him as a translator, and He provided the Gilberts to watch over the boy, which will be a godsend for Dakota as much as for Keith and Cassie."

"Yes...." Alice murmured.

Her face was in profile to him as they walked

along, but he could see her expression was still pensive. "'All things work for good,' it says in Romans, and we have to believe He will work out Dakota's circumstances for good, too."

"I do," she said, a little too politely and lifelessly.

"There I go again, throwing Scripture verses at someone, just like a preacher."

That made her lips curve upward. "You *are* a preacher."

"Yes, but I try to avoid stepping over the line into sanctimoniousness."

"You do avoid it," she assured him. "Elijah, could I ride out with you to see the army officers tomorrow? Just for something to do," she added. "Before Dakota came along, I'd planned to ride Cheyenne some more...."

The thought that she would be with him made him happy, even though he supposed her request might be motivated more from a sense of being at loose ends now that she wouldn't be responsible for Dakota than a desire for his own company.

"Of course," he said. "Tomorrow being Saturday, there's no chapel service, so we can leave in the morning while it's still cool." It had grown steadily hotter as April wore on, so perhaps they could find out what they needed to know and return before the temperature climbed too high.

Her expression brightened somewhat. "I'll make us breakfast before we go."

Alice spent the rest of the day quietly. Before chapel this morning, she'd poured water over dried beans, and now she added vegetables she'd purchased at the greengrocer's tent and set the pot to simmering over a low fire. Vegetable soup would make a nourishing light dinner—if she ever got hungry after the delicious noontime feast with the Gilberts. At the moment, it didn't seem possible.

She had a lot to think about while the soup simmered. The past twenty-four hours had been eventful, to say the least—she and Elijah had found a starving Indian boy; fed and bathed him; found him a new, if temporary, home; and through an amazing combination of events, found out why he had come.

Elijah was right. The Lord *had* been good to them in sending Lars right when He did, so that they could leave Dakota with the Gilberts with a clear conscience, knowing Dakota would not feel rejected by the change. And through Lars's translation, they now had direction as to where to seek information about Dakota's father. She was fairly certain their inquiry would be fruitless. The U.S. Army was made up of thousands of soldiers—what was the likelihood that he'd still be in Oklahoma Territory and that any of those guarding the border would know Captain Richard Lawson? They could but try, she supposed, in the hopes of finding some answers for Dakota.

But if they weren't able to find Lawson, or Lawson no interest in the boy, were they honor bound to send word to Dakota's band of Cheyenne, in they wanted to take the boy back? Lars could message, she supposed, either before or after Rush, for he would be able to explain in their gue what had happened. She did not like to family members—hadn't Lars said that Dakota had been raised by an aunt?—worrying over the boy's disappearance, fearing he was dead.

What Alice wasn't so certain about were her feelings regarding Elijah. Yes, she'd indicated to him that her independence was her most prized possession. And he'd professed that he had felt called by God to remain celibate to serve Him. Neither one of them was looking to marry.

So if that was true, why was there such a definite *pull* between them? She couldn't ignore it, any more than she could ignore the fact of gravity. After all, she'd invited herself along on his errand tomorrow like a shameless hussy! Now she regretted having done so, even if she could claim it was because of her interest in Dakota.

It made her protestations of craving independence pretty unconvincing, didn't it? No one would believe she meant it, not when the preacher was single just as she was, and they spent so much time together. Yet she couldn't seem to help herself. The request to accompany him had just tumbled out of her mouth seemingly by its own volition.

She should write a letter to her mother, Alice thought. That had always had a way of sorting out her thoughts when she'd been at Bellevue for her nursing training, and afterward, when she took on the daily challenge of being a nurse in the busy wards of hospital.

She'd written her mother the evening she'd in Boomer Town, reassuring her of her safety scribing the setup of the tent city and the v "homestead hopefuls," as she had called th ages and nationalities, who populated it. Sh the letter from the temporary U.S. Post Office operating in—what else?—a tent.

This letter would be longer. She'd explain her decision to obtain a horse and describe the fine Appaloosa. She'd tell about her attendance at the daily chapel prayer meetings—which would please her mother, she knew.

Mary Margaret Hawthorne was a devout woman, despite the fact that her faith had been tested by the loss of her husband and the looming threat of the loss of the farm they'd worked together. She'd fretted about Alice's safety when she'd been in New York City, training and then working as a nurse. Mary had been even more anxious, Alice knew, when Alice had announced her plan to gain land in Oklahoma. Not only did it mean such a long journey alone for her only child, there was the danger of the Land Rush itself.

She'd describe her medical rounds in Boomer Town, which doubtless would surprise her mother, since Alice had been adamant that she had left nursing behind the moment she'd left Bellevue for her father's deathbed.

She'd describe the people she'd met in the camp, including the Thornton brothers, of course, and in particular, the eldest Thornton, the preacher—though she wouldn't tell her mother how conflicted she was about Elijah. Alice didn't want to give her mother a reason to think she might have found love at last when she hadn't decided how she felt about him herself yet. Did she love him, or was she going to bury that feeling and stick to her original plan? She hoped the very act of writing the letter would help her sort those feelings out.

She'd spent a good hour writing all these things and was resharpening her pencil with a paring knife when she heard the soft sound of footsteps approaching her tent.

"Alice? Are you within?" a voice asked diffidently, a voice that was female and heavily accented.

"Yes, Katrine, come in," she said, happy for the interruption.

The Danish girl ducked her head and entered. "I hope you're not busy. I won't stay if you are…."

"Of course not. I'm never too busy for a friend. What can I do for you?"

"I need nothing, thank you. Lars told me about the Indian boy you and Reverend Thornton found and all that happened with that."

"Yes. It was most fortunate Lars happened along when he did."

"The Gilberts are kind people. The boy will be blessed, whatever time he can pass with them. But I really came to invite you to supper with us. We will have venison steaks, now that Lars is back, but as soon as he eats, he will be at work salting the rest of the meat, tanning the hide and so forth long past dark. He will be like a man obsessed. I will have no one to talk to, so I thought if you came, we could make girl talk, *ja?* I am cutting out a new dress, and I want your o-pin-ion—" she pronounced the word very carefully "—about the trim for it."

Alice laughed, glad that Katrine's idea of "girl talk" didn't seem to include a discussion of men, as it always had back at Bellevue when she was a probationer nurse and the other probationers could only chatter about the handsome doctors on the ward. "Yes, some girl talk would be very good." No one at chapel had reported a need for nursing tonight, so she was happy to have something to fill her evening. "And I can contribute to the supper," she said, and told Katrine about the soup.

"Ah, so that's what I smelled simmering over your fire. *Ja,* that would be good."

"I'll just leave a note in case anyone comes looking for me," Alice said, putting away her letter to finish later. She was actually glad of the reprieve—she'd examine her feelings for Elijah more closely another time.

"Halt!" cried a cavalry officer, holding up his gloved hand and setting his horse into a trot. He unsheathed his saber and held it aloft, then used it to point to the west at a line apparently only he could see. "No prospective settlers are allowed to go past this point, not till noon on the twenty-second."

Elijah pulled up his reins and signaled for Alice to do the same. He thought the young soldier's manner rather officious—surely it would've been sufficient to use his finger to point out the boundary, rather than the saber. But with the troops spread so thin along the border in the attempt to keep back the Sooners, he could understand that the soldiers' tempers were getting a mite frayed.

"We weren't desiring to, I assure you, Lieutenant," Elijah assured the red-cheeked young officer, after taking note of his shoulder insignia. "I am Reverend Thornton, and this is Miss Hawthorne—" He gestured toward Alice, sitting her Appaloosa mare beside him.

The soldier touched the brim of his hat respectfully in Alice's direction. "Lieutenant George Marsh." His voice was brisk and no-nonsense, with a faint get-on-with-it edge.

"We were merely trying to locate a particular captain, known to be in Oklahoma—or at least he was. His name is Captain Richard Lawson."

Marsh shrugged. "Don't know him." The soldier's eyes were slits under the hand he held under his brim to shade them from the powerful sun. "That'd be like looking for a needle in a haystack, Reverend. Do you know how many troops are massed along the territory perimeter? Why, the Fifth Cavalry alone—"

"We understand the difficulty, Lieutenant," Alice interrupted smoothly, and so sweetly that Elijah thought Lieutenant Marsh didn't even realize he'd been interrupted. "But we have to start *somewhere*. Could you steer us to the officer in charge? He must have served some time in the army to be a ranking officer, am I right? He might know the man we're seeking, and if he doesn't, perhaps he could start an official inquiry?"

Bright spots of color had bloomed on the young officer's cheeks while Alice spoke. Elijah guessed it had been a good while since Lieutenant Marsh had spent any time with a lady. He seemed to melt in the face of Alice Hawthorne's smile. Elijah himself knew the feeling.

"Why are you looking for him, ma'am?" Marsh asked, visibly trying to keep that brisk, official tone, but failing miserably.

Elijah tensed. If she mentioned Dakota's name or his mixed blood, and said the boy was Lawson's son, they might be summarily dismissed. The cavalry had spent years battling Indians, and despite the fact that Oklahoma had once been given entirely to the Indians, many soldiers didn't think very much of them.

"We're searching for him on behalf of his son, Lieutenant, an eight-year-old boy."

Elijah smothered a sigh of relief. *Very wisely said, Alice.*

Marsh was silent for a moment, studying them, then he nodded to a small frame building surrounded by a cluster of tents some hundred yards up the line. "My commanding officer'd be Major Bliss, ma'am. You can find him in that guard shack, yonder."

"Thank you, Lieutenant. We appreciate your help," she said, smiling as if the young officer had actually produced Captain Richard Lawson on the spot. Elijah could imagine her using that smile on crusty, temperamental surgeons with amazing results.

Marsh fingered his hat brim again and wheeled his horse around with an unnecessary flourish. "Good day, Reverend, ma'am. I hope you find him."

They trotted their horses in the direction of the building. "Remind me to appoint you head of our future church fund-raising committee," Elijah said, letting his admiration show in his voice, once they were out of earshot.

"My mother always said you can catch more flies with honey than vinegar," Alice said with a wink.

Despite her success with the young lieutenant, Elijah realized Marsh was right. The chances of finding Captain Lawson with a simple inquiry at the border were abysmally small. Probably the best they could hope for was setting an inquiry in motion, *if* the commanding officer in the area could be persuaded the need of a small boy to find his father was important. Should the matter of Dakota's race became known, Elijah prayed this Major Bliss was free of anti-Indian bigotry.

They served an all-powerful God, Elijah reminded himself, who was capable of finding one particular grain of sand in a desert. One who had no prejudice, and who considered the needs of a small boy as important as the prayers of kings.

There were not one but two officers sitting at facing desks in the small frame building when they entered. Each had been bent over a stack of papers, but they rose immediately at the sight of a lady.

"We were told we could find the commanding officer for this sector here," Elijah said.

"I'm Major Bliss," said the older man. He had silver at his temples, but his military bearing was proud and erect. "And this is Captain Fairchild," he said, indicating the younger man. "And you are?"

Elijah made the introductions. Alice explained their mission, again avoiding any mention of Dakota's name.

"Captain Richard Lawson…" the major said, his eyes losing focus as he thought. He rubbed his chin and turned to the other officer. "Captain Fairchild, didn't Colonel Amboys mention a Captain Lawson one time?"

"I believe so, Major."

From the shared look in their eyes, Elijah suspected they knew something about Lawson, but he

couldn't be sure, and if they didn't volunteer anything, he could hardly accuse them of suppressing
information.

"Please, Major, any assistance you can give us will
be much appreciated," Alice said.

"Dunno if it's the same Captain Lawson you're
looking for, of course, but it's worth a try...."

"Where might we find this Colonel Amboys?"
Alice prompted with gentle directness.

"At the next guard station south, about five miles.
The farther south one goes, the more Texans are tryin'
to crowd into Oklahoma before the date, and they take
a lot of work to contain, I can tell you...."

Elijah sensed a barely leashed impatience rising
in Alice, but one had to know her to spot it, and the
major didn't know her. A telltale tightening of lips, a
straightening of her spine...

"So we can ride south five miles along the borderline and expect to find him?"

"Let me send a soldier to make inquiries, ma'am,"
Major Bliss offered. "Those Texans are a rowdy lot. I
wouldn't want— In the meantime, Miss Hawthorne, I
could offer you and the reverend some refreshments."

Was the major taken with Alice and trying to keep
her here? Or was he only trying to spare them a possible encounter with "rowdy Texans" and a long ride
in the hot sun?

"Oh, no," Alice said quickly. "I wouldn't dream of
inconveniencing you, Major. We have good horses.
We'll just ride south and find this Colonel Amboys.
Just straight down the borderline to the south?"

"Yes, ma'am," the major said with barely hidden
reluctance.

"Thank you, Major Bliss, Captain Fairchild," she said. "You've both been *very* helpful. Good day."

Swiftly they mounted up and headed their horses south. Elijah held up till Alice was beside him. "Again, my compliments on your diplomacy, Miss Alice," he said.

"Thank you. I can only imagine how long it would have taken to send a messenger there and back," Alice replied. "Besides, I think we're much better off speaking to the man directly so we can see his reaction." She turned to look at him. "Didn't it seem as if those men back there knew something and didn't want to say it?"

Elijah nodded. So Alice had seen the look passed between the major and the captain, too, and had interpreted it as Elijah had.

The reason became apparent when they reached the next guard shack in about an hour and a half, after a stop to water their horses along the way. Colonel Amboys, whose face had at least ten more years of weathering than the major's and was so barrel-chested his brass uniform buttons strained to stay fastened, looked dismayed as soon as Elijah said the name of the man they sought.

"Captain Lawson—that's Captain Richard Lawson, you say? Ironic. Those of us who are old hands with the Fifth Cavalry—not these pups still wet behind the ears, mind you—were just talking about him the other day when the officers had a sector meeting. Why don't you sit down, Miss Hawthorne?" he said, indicating the seat he had just vacated.

To Elijah's surprise, she did so without demur. Perhaps it was because they were finally going to get to the heart of the matter. Amboys gestured Elijah to one of two spare chairs along the wall and took the other for himself.

"What did you say your relationship to him was?" he asked Alice.

"Oh, we're not related," Alice assured him, and the colonel's expression lightened somewhat.

"Not a...special friend of his, were you?" the colonel persisted carefully.

Elijah's fists clenched involuntarily at his sides. Apparently the colonel thought Alice might be Lawson's sweetheart.

"No," Alice said, looking puzzled. "I've never met the man. His son has come looking for him, so we were trying to find him for the boy."

The colonel wiped his brow with a rumpled handkerchief. "That's good." He noisily cleared his throat. "I'm afraid the captain was...shall we say, a bit of a scoundrel? Toward females, I mean."

Alice blinked, and Elijah saw the moment when full understanding reached her. "So you thought I was perhaps an abandoned lady friend of his?" she said, and looked as if she was caught between a laugh and an outraged sniff.

Colonel Amboys grew a bit red in the face. "Yes. I—I'm sorry to offend a lady's sensibilities, but, yes, he was. Especially toward females among the tribes he was supposedly protecting."

Suddenly Alice stilled. "You said he *was* a scoundrel. What happened to him? Was he transferred elsewhere? Back East?"

Colonel Amboys pulled at his collar as if it were too tight. "Perhaps it would have been better for him if he had been sent back East," he began. "He was disciplined for his behavior among the Cheyenne, and transferred—but just to the next division, which supervised the Comanche reservation, which is just south of the Cheyenne's land. Unfortunately, he soon displayed the same predilection among the Comanches. One of the braves...ah, took exception, shall we say?"

"Please, sir, speak plainly," Alice said, her voice level.

The colonel raised weary eyes to Alice's while Elijah looked on, holding his breath.

"I'm saying Lawson is dead, Miss Hawthorne. The Comanche brave killed him for dishonoring his sister."

Chapter Eleven

Alice could only sit there for a moment, absorbing the enormity of what the colonel had told them. She'd assumed Dakota's father was either no longer in the army or had been transferred far away, and would be effectively out of their reach, but she hadn't imagined he'd be dead.

"Miss Hawthorne, are you all right? Can I get you some water? Perhaps a small glass of brandy?" the colonel asked, hovering over her and fluttering a piece of paper like a fan. It would have been comical if his news hadn't been so sad. "I can assure you the brave was dealt with and paid the penalty for his crime."

She saw Elijah come and stand beside her, and felt the warmth of his hand on her shoulder. Instantly the tears that had threatened to spill on Dakota's behalf stopped stinging, and she felt immeasurably stronger.

She waved away the fluttering paper. "Brandy won't be necessary, Colonel, thank you. I'm all right. Merely saddened on his son's behalf." She rose. "We appreciate the information, sir. We'll inform his son."

"But I'm sure word was sent to his widow back East—Ohio, I believe," the Colonel said, pouring her a glass of water and handing it to her. "Wouldn't his son have been notified...?" His voice trailed off and he cleared his throat again. "You're saying he had a child...other than his children by marriage?"

"Yes, Colonel," she heard Elijah say. "Born of that same predilection, as you called it. He's half Cheyenne."

"I see." The colonel's face was carefully blank. "Is there...anything else I can do for you, ma'am? Reverend?"

"I don't believe so. Thank you for your time, Colonel," Elijah said, and ushered her out to their waiting horses.

"You folks be careful, now. Looks like the summer heat's building up to a storm."

It was true, Alice saw. While they'd sat in the colonel's office, the blistering sun that had sent rivulets of sweat trickling down her back while she rode here had now gone behind lowering clouds. But Elijah didn't appear worried, and as often as not, she'd seen the clouds blown away by the ceaseless Oklahoma wind without loosing their damp load.

They were both silent until they were well away from the guard shack and riding again toward Boomer Town.

"Elijah, how are we going to tell Dakota?" she asked, breaking the silence that had been punctuated only by the chirping of birds and the occasional sound of voices as they passed more homesteaders camped at the border.

"We should pray about it, and ask the Lord to guide

us to the best way to tell Dakota," he began. "It won't be easy, no matter how we do it."

"Of course, but how will he take it? Will he want to run back to his tribe? That might be best, but some of them didn't accept him because of his white blood," she reminded him. "Poor little boy, trapped between two worlds." Before she could stop it, a tear slid down her cheek and then another.

Wordlessly Elijah handed her his handkerchief, and as she dabbed at her wet cheeks, she heard him sigh.

"We'll need to do it soon, so he's not tempted to leave on a search that we now know is futile," he said at last. "You know, it's likely for the best, as far as Dakota's concerned, that Captain Lawson is gone. Though it's tragic that Lawson never changed his ways, of course. With the character he had, though— or lack of it—it doesn't seem likely Lawson would have been a positive influence on Dakota, even if he'd been willing to have the boy."

"Yes, I know you're right," Alice said. "It's just so sad that he's lost all his family."

"He has the Gilberts," he reminded her. "They'll do their best to make up for the lack."

"Assuming he doesn't want to go back to his tribe. Elijah, when we reach Boomer Town, we need to warn the Gilberts about what we've learned so they can be prepared to comfort Dakota, and let Lars know that we'll need him to translate when we tell Dakota."

"I called on the Gilberts last evening to make sure he was settling in all right, and he seemed happy enough. He's certainly become the apple of their eyes in a short time. He seemed to be soaking up their love and attention like a parched wildflower after a rain."

She smiled at Elijah's apt comparison. "The Gilberts are good people." Alice felt a peace descending on her as Elijah finished speaking. She could believe things *would* turn out all right for Dakota. What a gift of encouragement Elijah had. She could not have imagined speaking to those soldiers without him at her side, a solid, comforting presence. With him there, she had felt brave as a lioness.

Why couldn't she have met him before Maxwell Peterson had tarnished any idea she had about a man being an equal, trustworthy partner? Was it possible they weren't all controlling tyrants like Peterson or womanizing scoundrels like the late Richard Lawson? Was Elijah a man who could see her as complementing his strengths, rather than someone to be subjugated?

She drew up the reins on those thoughts. It was too close to the Land Rush. She had to concentrate on securing a good claim and nothing else for the time being. She couldn't contemplate anything about her personal future until after April 22.

In the meantime, though, she'd cherish the sense of teamwork she had whenever she was with Elijah, working toward a common goal.

The first raindrop took her by surprise, landing with a wet plop on her nose. She looked up in surprise, just as the rain started falling all around them.

"We're still a good two miles away from Boomer Town!" Elijah shouted through the rain that had already become a torrent. "Can you ride hard?"

"Of course!" she called back. Just then lightning

cracked out on the prairie, and Cheyenne needed no further spur to lunge into a gallop.

They raced neck and neck over the rolling prairie, past low trees being lashed this way and that by the wind. By the time they glimpsed the first tents and wagons of Boomer Town ahead, both of them were already drenched to the skin. By tacit agreement, they rode to Alice's tent first, so she could dismount.

"I'll bring over some soup!" she called through the sheets of rain, as Elijah, still mounted and leading Cheyenne, started to head down the row to the Thornton tent.

"Don't worry about that. Get on some dry clothes before you catch a chill!" he called back, and then he was swallowed up in a curtain of water. "Drink something warm!"

Alice smiled as she ducked into her tent. *Silly man.* Did he really think she was going to remain in clothes that dripped on the ground a moment longer than necessary? But she knew he'd only said it out of concern for her.

She'd exchanged her wet riding clothes for a dry blouse and skirt, and hung them and the bonnet up to drip dry in one corner of the tent. It was still raining, and while she always kept some firewood dry inside the tent, the rain would have to stop before she could light a fire outside and brew hot tea, let alone heat soup to take to Elijah.

Alice lit the kerosene lamp within and undid her damp hair from its braid so it could dry. Then she settled down on her cot to read her Bible until the downpour stopped.

It was perhaps two hours later when she walked

down the muddy row to the Thorntons' tent. She wore
her still-damp boots rather than her other shoes, because the dirt "street" had become a sea of mud that
threatened to suck her boots off as she carried the
small pot of soup.

"Hallo, the Thorntons' tent!" Elijah heard her call.
He dropped the blanket he'd had wrapped around him
and laid aside the Bible that had been in his lap, but
Clint was nearer the entrance and lifted the tent flap
to let Alice in.

"Miss Alice, you're as good as your word," Elijah
said, seeing the pot she held. "Clint made me some
hot coffee soon as the rain stopped, but I'm sure that
soup will taste bet—" he stopped as a sneeze seized
him "—better. Thank you."

"Sounds like you caught the chill you warned me
against," she said, as Clint took the pot from her and
left the tent to set it over the fire.

"I'm fine."

His eyes drank her in. She'd changed from her
sodden blouse and divided skirt and was clad once
more in a simple calico-print dress. Her hair was a
riot of auburn curls held back with a narrow black
ribbon. He'd never seen her hair down and figured
she'd loosed it so it could dry. The sight of it was so
beautiful he could only stare.

Gideon, whittling on a piece of wood in the far
corner, looked up, greeted Alice and resumed goug-
ing at the wood.

Alice's color rose. "Uh…enjoy the soup. Perhaps
we should postpone our talk with Dakota so you ca
get some rest?" She turned as if to leave.

He realized how long he'd been silently looking at her. "I'm sorry. Maybe that would be best, since I'm rather embarrassed to admit I'd forgotten tomorrow is Sunday. There's been so much going on this week that I'd left my sermon preparation till this evening. A fine preacher, to have forgotten when the Sabbath is, eh?" Another sneeze erupted before he could catch it.

"God bless you," she said with a smile. "Perhaps I should brew some of my willow bark tea for you." A furrow of worry creased Alice's forehead beneath the tendrils that curled damply over it.

He shook his head and waved away her concern. "Thanks, but I'm sure I'll be fit as a fiddle after a good night's rest. I'll see you at chapel."

"That *was* a long ride we took. I know *I'm* tired— and sore in muscles I didn't even know I had." She chuckled. "Yes, I'll see you at chapel. We can talk then about when we want to speak with Dakota."

"That sounds good. Good evening, Miss Alice. Thanks again for the soup."

He *was* tired, he thought. Dog tired. How he was ever going to come up with something coherent to say to his congregation tomorrow, he didn't know. Perhaps, after he had some of Alice's soup, he'd be refreshed and able to pore over the passage on the Good Shepherd, who'd left his ninety-nine sheep and searched high and low for the one that was missing.

Later that evening, Elijah fell asleep with the lamp still burning, but before he did, he'd managed to cobble together what he considered a fairly good sermon for Sunday morning. With the Lord's help, he hoped it would touch the hearts of his congregation.

As he drifted off, he thought of sheep and their wandering, foolish ways. Certainly Dakota's father had followed a willful path to destruction. Gideon and Clint could be considered lost sheep, Elijah supposed, and he prayed the Lord would woo them back like the Good Shepherd He was. Ninety-*eight* sheep in the flock and at least two that'd gone wandering...

Had Dakota ever been exposed to the teaching of Christianity? he wondered. Now that it seemed the boy would be living among them, Elijah hoped he would be able to teach Dakota about Jesus and draw him into the Lord's flock. *One more lamb for You, Lord...*

Elijah dressed for chapel that morning with a head and chest thick with congestion. His throat felt raw and scratchy with each swallow of coffee, and his bones ached. He wasn't going to escape paying for the drenching he'd suffered the day before, unfortunately. He sneezed half a dozen times just while buttoning his shirt.

"Maybe you ought to beg off church this mornin' and spend the day on your cot, brother," Clint said after Elijah finished another paroxysm of sneezing. "I could take your sermon notes over to your deacon."

"Church starts in half an hour," Elijah said. "It's just a head cold, though it's awfully inconvenient that it chose today to plague me."

He made sure he stuck a fresh handkerchief in his frock coat pocket before he left for the chapel, already wondering if their talk with Dakota—his and Alice's—would have to be put off until another time.

But surely he'd feel better after conducting the Sunday service. It always energized him and raised his spirits.

Alice saw the patches of high color on each of Elijah's cheeks as soon as she had seated herself in the tent chapel. Still tired from their ride, she'd slept later than she'd intended to and, as a consequence, hadn't been able to speak to Elijah before the service. Now she sat with Dakota, while Keith and Cassie carried out their duties as deacon and deaconess, and was pleased to see for herself that the boy appeared to be thriving.

"Happee Sun-Day, Mees Alss," he greeted her, his black eyes shining. "Church, yes? Sing-ging?"

"Yes, Dakota, there will be singing," she agreed.

"Preechah 'Lijah talk, yes?"

"Yes." His vocabulary was increasing at a wondrous pace, she thought. He wore a new shirt, probably fashioned by Cassie Gilbert out of the material from one of her husband's old ones, along with his buckskin trousers.

"Preechah 'Lijah, *haáahe!*" the boy called out.

Alice turned her gaze away from the boy to see that Elijah had stepped up to his makeshift lectern.

"Hello, Dakota," Elijah said, as others smiled and chuckled. "Don't we love his enthusiasm, congregation? Did you know that the Lord longs for us to greet Him with that same childlike joy?"

"Amen!" Keith Gilbert cried, coming to the front to lead the singing.

Alice sang along with the rest, but she was hardly aware of the words. Elijah looked pale and tired, she thought. She'd have to insist he rest again today, and hoped he wouldn't be a typical stubborn male and try to resist her advice. She'd seen right through his assertion that he was "fine" yesterday, and now she knew she should have left some willow bark tea with his brothers despite Elijah's objection.

As the collection sack was being passed, she wondered why his brothers never came to chapel. Gideon and Clint Thornton were clearly good and decent men—surely they believed in God, didn't they? How hard that must be for Elijah, not to have his brothers here. Did it make him feel as if he had failed in some way?

Elijah stepped forward again. "Before I start into my sermon today, about the shepherd with a hundred sheep," he began, "I would ask your prayers for the Collins family. I was called to their campsite just at dawn for Mr. Collins's elderly mother, who'd been suddenly taken with a heart seizure."

Alice smothered a gasp. No wonder Elijah looked so worn. He hadn't been well himself, but he'd been awakened to minister to one of his flock. She tried to remember if she had ever met the deceased woman.

"I would have sent for our nurse, Miss Alice, to see if she could provide any relief for the lady," he went on with a glance at her, "but it was clear the elder Mrs. Collins had only moments left on this earth. As I sat at her bedside and prayed with her, she smiled and went Home to be with the Lord."

Murmurs of shock and sorrow rose around Alice.

"Jerusha Collins had been eager to start a new life with her family on their homestead not long from now," Elijah said. "Instead, she is starting a new life in eternity. In lieu of chapel tomorrow, I'll be conducting her funeral service for those who would like to attend and support the Collins family in their grief."

It had been like that when her father, also a believer, had died three months ago, Alice remembered. She'd arrived from New York City with only a few hours to spare before her father passed on. Though he had suffered greatly from the wasting illness that finally claimed his life, Hiram Hawthorne had smiled as he took his last breath.

Her attention returned to Elijah as she pictured the graveside service out on the prairie tomorrow. Again she noticed his pallor in contrast to his flushed cheeks. *Lord, please restore Elijah to health so he can minister to others.*

Elijah took a deep breath that was interrupted by a cough. "My sermon today…"

Just then Dakota tugged on her sleeve. "Preechah," he said, pointing. Then he uttered several incomprehensible Cheyenne words.

Alice bent to listen. "What about Preacher?" she asked softly, but of course the boy didn't have enough English words to tell her. As she watched, Elijah hesitated as if unsure of himself, then took a drink of water from a glass on his makeshift lectern. Beads of sweat dotted his forehead, which he wiped away with a handkerchief he pulled out of his pocket.

Was she imagining it, or did he sway slightly?

But others had noticed, too. "You all right, Reverend?" she heard Keith Gilbert ask.

Elijah seemed dazed as he turned toward the

sound of his deacon's voice. "I think…think I'm ill… Sorry…"

Without conscious thought, Alice jumped up and ran to the front. She and Keith Gilbert reached Elijah as he collapsed in a heap in the sawdust.

Chapter Twelve

Elijah passed out somewhere between the chapel and the Thornton tent as he was carried there by four men from the congregation.

Gideon, stirring something over the fire, stood as the little cavalcade approached. "What the—? Lije?"

"He collapsed at chapel, Gideon," Alice told him. "He's very ill. Help us get him into bed."

Clint appeared at the tent flap then and, staring, held it open as Alice ran ahead to pull down the coverlet on the cot. The men eased him onto it, and Alice stepped aside while Clint and Gideon helped remove their brother's trousers and shirt and pulled a sheet over him.

"I knew he was sick when Mr. Collins came and woke him up at dawn this morning," Clint muttered. "But of course Lije just went to do what he could."

Cassie Gilbert and Dakota had been part of the procession, and now Alice was distantly aware of Cassie Gilbert gently pulling Dakota away, murmuring reassurances he probably didn't understand. Keith remained, standing in a corner of the tent, his eyes closed—praying, Alice guessed.

Elijah's breathing rasped in her ears as Alice bent over and felt his forehead, and flinched at the burning heat. "He's spiking a fever," she told them. "I need cool water to bathe him." She couldn't give him the willow bark tea when he was too insensible to swallow.

"I just fetched some from the spring before you came," Gideon said. "I'll bring in a basinful."

Moments later, using a bit of towel Clint provided, she bathed Elijah's forehead, then his shoulders, arms and chest. She watched him start to shiver.

"Blankets…he needs blankets," Gideon said.

"Just one light one, please," Alice instructed, when Gideon had grabbed up the blankets on both his and Clint's cots. "Anything more and his fever will only go higher."

"I'm going to call a prayer meeting," Keith Gilbert said, as the afternoon faded into evening. "What shall I tell them?"

Alice looked up from her camp chair by the cot. Elijah was cooler now, but his breathing had an ominous moist sound to it that she didn't like, as if he breathed through water—*rales,* the doctors at Bellevue had called it. She didn't have to pull out her stethoscope from the medical bag she'd had Gideon fetch from her tent to know that there was congestion in his lungs.

"Tell them Reverend Thornton has pneumonia. Tell them to pray like they've never prayed before." She kept her tone matter-of-fact, not wanting to frighten the deacon or Elijah's brothers and reveal the fact she was afraid for Elijah. He had no medical care but what she could provide. It wasn't the first time she'd nursed someone so ill, of course, but it had always been with the guidance of a doctor and a head nurse.

Keith Gilbert closed his eyes for a moment. "I'll tell them," he said at last. "If the reverend comes around, you tell him that he's not to worry—I'll conduct that funeral service."

Alice blinked. In the past few hours she'd forgotten all about old Mrs. Collins's death. *Dear Lord, don't let Elijah die, too. Please spare him for all our sakes.* Without Elijah, the new church and the community he envisioned around it would not happen. *We need him—I need him,* she prayed, and was stunned by what she'd just prayed and had never dared to completely admit to herself.

Despite all her determination, a bond had grown between Elijah and her, a bond forged while seeing to the spiritual and medical needs of Boomer Town, and in their mutual caring for the half-Indian orphan, Dakota. Elijah was the most honorable, caring man she had ever met. He served his fellow man because he loved God, and because she knew Elijah, she wanted to be a better person.

She'd come here wanting to hide, to pass unnoticed, to leave her nursing skills behind and just live on her land with no one but her mother. She'd been afraid to share her name. In getting to know him, she'd shed the fear that had ruled her life of late and had learned to want to share her nursing skills again. The Lord had called her to be a nurse, after all.

Please, Lord, save Elijah.

* * *

Searing heat, alternating with a cold that was the worst he'd ever experienced, colder even than that first winter in Pennsylvania—when he'd been locked in the woodshed by Obadiah for some boyish infraction of his cousin's endless rules... Stabbing pain with each breath, like a dozen sharp needles sticking in his ribs...

Elijah groaned, but it sounded like someone else uttering the noise. Each breath was made harder by the sludge that seemed to have coated his lungs, inside and out. Parched throat. So thirsty. Had he become lost in the desert? But Oklahoma wasn't a desert...

He felt the presence of a darker shadow in the misty distance, a shadow that was pure evil. A voice inside him mocked, "You'll never live to build your church. Your congregation will be scattered and forget the ways of righteous men. Gideon and Clint won't ever find their way back to the Lord...."

No! He couldn't allow it! He had to survive, to get well! *God, save me!*

He felt the presence of warmth, and Scripture came to him. *My grace is sufficient... My power is made perfect in weakness.* The words encouraged him to let go and sleep.

I can't sleep, Lord! he protested. *I have to guard my flock against those who would tear it apart!*

Then he remembered that Jesus was the Good Shepherd, not him. Again he felt the presence of the Light encouraging him to let go and rest.

Elijah slept.

Even in his dreams he could feel cool, soft hands touching his forehead, bathing him with blessedly cool water. A soft, murmuring voice read the Psalms aloud near his ear. Was it Marybelle? Or Alice?

It was Alice. He could picture her, brisk and professional, but with a caring in those sky-blue eyes that had reassured everyone he'd seen her nurse. He could see her reaching down to check a pulse in a wrist, listen to breathing with that wood-and-metal contraption of hers...

He had to live...had to get better so he could tell her how important she was becoming to him....

"Alice, go get some rest. I'll watch over Reverend Elijah for a while."

Alice roused from her stupor at the gentle touch of Cassie Gilbert.

"Wh-what time is it?" she asked, even while her eyes flew to Elijah.

He was sleeping, his chest rising and falling. His respirations still rattled as he exhaled.

She reached out an unsteady hand and touched him. He was still hot but cooler than he had been.

"It's midnight, child—at least, according to your own timepiece on your dress," Cassie said with a soft chuckle, pointing to it.

"I can't leave. Not with Elijah like this." Five campsites away was too far if Elijah took a turn for the worse. Dazedly she looked around, expecting to see Clint and Gideon asleep in their beds, but the cots were vacant.

"I can watch him," the older woman insisted. "I've done some nursing—though not with formal training like you had. You can sleep right over there," the older woman insisted, pointing to one of the cots. "Clint put fresh sheets on it. He and Gideon are sleeping outside by the fire. Go get some rest, and I promise I'll call you if Reverend so much as twitches the wrong way."

"Dakota?"

"Sleeping, too, at our campsite. I didn't leave till Keith was back from the prayer meeting, of course. Just imagine—he says there'll be some keeping vigil in prayer all night for the reverend. Lars talked to Dakota, explained that you were a medicine woman and that 'Preechah 'Lijah' was in good hands."

A medicine woman, Alice thought, and couldn't help but smile a little.

"The boy's been chanting—I think that's how he prays." Cassie's smile was fond. "Now shoo, girl," she ordered, making swishing motions at Alice in the chair.

She'd just lie down for a few minutes, Alice told herself. She could listen to the quality of Elijah's breathing with her eyes shut so Cassie would think she was sleeping....

She woke at dawn, hearing birds beginning to chirp and the other two Thornton brothers talking softly outside the tent. How had she slept so long? How could she have slept at all, with Elijah in such danger?

Throwing her legs over the side of the cot, she sat up, her eyes going to Elijah's bed. Cassie. The older woman was bending over Elijah's forehead, but at the sound of Alice's cot creaking, she turned around.

"I was just about to rouse you," Cassie said. "I think his fever's starting to climb again."

"You shouldn't have let me sleep so long," Alice

you, Miss Alice, but I don't think anybody up there cares what happens here on earth."

Alice gazed at him, knowing this wasn't the time to argue. What had happened to this man to make him so cynical? Whom had he lost, despite his prayers? Was he speaking of the loss of their parents, in childhood, or was this a more recent raw wound of grief?

She turned to look at Clint. Did he feel the same way?

Apparently feeling her scrutiny, he said, "I believe there's a God, Miss Alice. I just don't know if we're on speaking terms, after what I've seen Him allow to happen."

She was too bone weary, despite the restless sleep she had gotten, to counter that in any convincing manner. She wanted to rail at them: Don't you know praying is all you can do? If there's even a chance it will work, why aren't you besieging Heaven with your prayers?

Elijah would have known what to say, but Elijah was lying insensible on the bed, balanced so precariously between life and death.

Cassie Gilbert might have known the right words, but she'd gone home to be with Dakota while her husband was conducting Mrs. Collins's funeral.

Clint reached out and touched his brother's forehead. "His fever's down. That's a good sign, right?"

She nodded. "But it will go up again. And can you hear his breathing?" It was impossible not to hear that harsh, wet rasping, she thought.

Slowly, Clint nodded, then asked, "Aren't you ever afraid for yourself, Miss Alice? Pneumonia's catching, isn't it?"

mumbled, then hoped her tone didn't sound accusatory.

"You needed it," Cassie said imperturbably. "And he didn't start getting hot till just a few minutes ago. I've been feelin' his forehead every little while through the night."

Alice flew to the bedside and confirmed Cassie's assertion with a shaking hand. Elijah's skin was fiery.

"Help me sponge him off again, Cassie," she said, and the older woman went to get some water.

Hot. So hot. How had he gotten trapped inside his cousin's furnace? Surely even Obadiah wasn't that cruel.... His brain felt as if it was on fire. If he looked hard enough, he could just see the flames....

Incredibly, he saw Marybelle Atkins, his lost fiancée, walking amid the fire, her eyes sad as she met his gaze. Her blond hair was loose, floating around her shoulders. She shook her head at him and walked away.

"Wait, Marybelle!" he called. "Wait, I want to talk to you!"

But his dead fiancée kept walking, the smoke—or was it mist?—swirling around her, hiding her...

"We've got to get this fever down," he heard Alice say. "If we don't, I'm afraid he'll have a seizure."

He heard his brothers' muttering voices, near but not as near as the soft voice. Talking about him—worried, fearful. *Gideon, Clint, I'm here! Don't give up on me!*

It was so hard to breathe. Each breath was such an effort and an agony....

The cold cloths landed on his skin again, but the touch wasn't soft and gentle as before.

"Come on, big brother," he heard Gideon say. "Don't give in. We all need you, Lije…" His strokes with the cold, wet cloth were insistent.

Then Clint's voice said, "Lije, come back from wherever you went. There's too much for you to do here, brother. Neither of us wants to run for those homesteads without you, and it's for sure neither of us can run a church. You've got the congregation scared witless, brother. Get better, please…"

I'm trying, Clint…

And then he was cold, colder even than before. The cold was so frigid it burned. It wasn't smoke that whisked around the evil darkness now, but snow.

Blankets! He needed blankets. Why was everyone letting him freeze like this? He reached out with flailing arms, desperate to grab at least the one blanket he always left rolled up at the foot of his cot.

"Easy, brother. Don't be striking out at Miss Alice, she's trying to help get your fever down, Lije!" he heard Gideon say.

Why were his own brothers telling lies? He didn't have enough breath, let alone the energy, to strike at her, even if he wanted to. And of course he didn't want to. He loved her!

"He's delirious," he heard Alice say. "He doesn't know what he's doing. He'll calm when the fever goes down." *If the fever goes down,* he heard her say within her mind.

And then he slept again.

He'd called for Marybelle. That had been the one sentence Alice could understand amid all his inco-

herent mumbling. *Who is she?* His voice had been anguished, the voice of a man who loved deeply, a man who loved only once. She'd been a fool to even begin to think she could matter to him the way Marybelle must have.

"How's he doing, Miss Alice? Is he any better?"

She hated to quash the hope she saw in his younger brother's eyes as he gazed down at Elijah, but it would be wrong to lie.

"No better, no," she said, avoiding Clint's gaze.

"But no worse?" Gideon asked, coming to stand by Clint at their brother's bedside.

"No worse." They didn't understand, Alice thought. To Gideon and Clint, if their brother was no worse, that was encouraging news. They didn't understand the toll that fever and congestion took on the body, drying it out and making it so hard to keep air flowing through, depriving the body of the ability to fight. And if nothing interrupted that, unconsciousness would progress to something deeper, to coma.

"Is he…is he…going to make it?" This came from Clint, and she heard the fear in the question, that even asking it was letting in the possibility that Elijah might not survive.

"I don't know," she said. "I'm doing everything I can."

"What can we do? Is there anything else we can do?"

"Pray."

Gideon uttered a smothered sound that might have been disgust, might have been despair. "I prayed once before, and it didn't do any good. Sorry if it offends

Alice blinked, surprised that he had voiced the question. It was rare for a family member to even spare a thought for the one taking care of their loved one.

"It can be," she told him. "But mostly pneumonia preys on the old and the young, and those who, like your brother, have caught a chill and are overtired."

"Then you'd best take care of yourself, right? I'm going to fix you some breakfast, Miss Alice, and you'd better sit outside and get some fresh air while you eat it. I'll sit with Elijah while you do that."

She wanted to weep at the kindness in his voice.

"I think," she began, taking care with her words, "Elijah will reach a crisis point tonight. Then he will either get better from there or..." She couldn't say the words.

"Or he won't," Gideon concluded for her and left the tent, as if he couldn't bear to remain in the same space as the words he'd just said.

Chapter Thirteen

Keith Gilbert came just before noon for an update on Elijah's condition. Alice spoke to him as frankly as she had to his brothers.

"I'll tell the church, and we'll be praying," he told her. "Mrs. Murphy said she'd be sending supper over for all of you," he said, including Gideon and Clint in his words. "Alice, Cassie will be coming to relieve you again tonight."

"I'll be grateful for her help," Alice said. "But I won't be sleeping." She wouldn't be leaving Elijah's side until the crisis had passed, and they had either won—or lost everything.

The deacon turned to go, but Alice reached out a hand to stop him. "Mr. Gilbert, how is Dakota? Is he… Does he seem content where he is or still restless?"

He sighed. "He seems to like Cassie and me, but before the reverend took sick, he kept saying his father's name and studying everyone who passed, especially those Security Patrol fellows. I hate to bring it up, since Elijah's so ill, but were you able to find out anything that day you went out and talked to those army officers?"

Alice took a deep breath. Their expedition to the border seemed like a decade ago, and yet it had been only two days ago.

She told him what Colonel Amboys had told them.

Keith Gilbert looked down at the ground for a long moment afterward. "I was afraid of something like that."

"Mr. Gilbert, I'm telling you so that you and your wife will be prepared. But if you're willing, perhaps it would be best to…wait a day or so before you tell Dakota? I know he'll have questions to ask…us—" she stumbled over the word, praying she wouldn't have to answer them alone "—through Lars, about what the officer said."

"That might be best," Gilbert said. "Honestly I don't think he's going to ask about it. Lars has stopped by a few times, in case the boy needed to talk, and he says Dakota's worried sick about Elijah. He'd be underfoot here now, but Cassie made him promise to wait until the reverend was better, so he wouldn't take sick, too."

Alice nodded. A child like Dakota, who had so recently undertaken a journey fraught with danger and hunger, might succumb easily to such a dangerous illness. The Gilberts would be devastated if anything happened to him.

Just as they'd all be devastated if Elijah didn't recover.

Hot again. And so tired, tired of the pain. The evil shadow was getting bolder now, closer…. His skin burned like fire—yet not fire. He burned as if there was ice coating his skin. So cold, but too exhausted to even shiver.

Perhaps he should get it over with, let the evil shadow overtake him. But whenever he would get this thought born of weariness, the presence of the Light grew stronger and held the evil in the shadow away.

A Voice in the Light murmured, "Not yet, Elijah. You have work to do yet."

Cool hands. A soft voice. Cool water on his skin that banished the fiery heat, if only for a while. A few drops of water on his tongue, not enough for him to choke on, but immediately absorbed into fever-seared dry tissues. Gentle hands turning him, placing cool, dry sheets under and over him when he had sweated the heat away.

Alice's voice. His brothers' voices. This time when he dreamed, he saw his mama and papa—but only from a distance, and only indistinctly. "Wait!" he called to them. "Have you seen Marybelle? Isn't she with you? I saw her yesterday…." But they didn't turn and answer, and then they, too, faded away.

She'd heard him call out for Marybelle again, and all at once, she had to know.

Clint sat on his cot watching his brother. They were alone in the tent, Gideon having taken refuge outside at the campfire again.

"Clint, who's Marybelle?" she asked, her gaze shifting to him.

Clint's eyes never left Elijah. "His fiancée. She died of influenza a month before the wedding, along with Gideon's wife and child."

So Elijah had loved before, only to lose his love to death. No wonder he'd devoted himself to serving God and building his church. And Gideon had lost a wife and a child. It was impossible for her to imagine surviving such losses.

If Elijah lived, was there ever going to be room in his heart again for the love of another woman?

At dusk Alice left the bedside, at Cassie's insistence, only long enough to nibble at the roasted chicken and mashed potatoes Molly Murphy had sent for their supper. She chewed mechanically, not really tasting the food, her gaze going constantly to Elijah's supine, sheet-covered form on the cot a few feet away.

She knew with everything in her that what she had said was true—tonight would be the turning point. She would use every bit of nursing skill she had ever possessed, every ounce of faith, to help him back away from the steep cliff he was heading for and to return him to health.

The sweet sound of two women singing "Rock of Ages" drifted inside the canvas from nearby. Curious, Alice lifted the tent flap and saw that the singers were Carrie and Cordelia Ferguson, the talkative sisters she'd met the first time she had gone to chapel. They stood at the edge of the firelight, holding a hymnal between them.

"We're just here to encourage the reverend," Cordelia told her. "Some of the other chapel folks are gonna join us in a while, and we're going to surround the tent all night with prayers. You don't have to pay us any mind—just let us know if there's news."

Alice felt tears sting her eyes. "Thank you," she murmured and let the tent flap fall.

Behind her, she heard Gideon groan. "I'll keep 'em supplied with coffee—I'm sure not going to refuse anything that might help my brother, but they'd better not expect me to talk to 'em when I go outside and sit by the fire."

Poor Gideon. He'll be like a caged wolf without his solitude.

But before she could spare another thought for Elijah's brother, Cassie called from the bedside. "He's starting to get restless, Alice. I think the fever's going up again."

This was it—the crisis was upon them.

Father God, if You have ever listened to me, please listen to me now, she prayed. *Please save Elijah, Lord. I know now that You never intended for me to lay aside my nursing skills, and I promise I never will. I pledge to You that I will nurse anyone who needs it from this day forward. Just please save Elijah, for all our sakes, and so he can go on to do the good I know he can do for You. I ask this in Jesus's name.*

She went to join Cassie at Elijah's cot. The battle was begun.

He flailed about for a while, and Alice felt the tears running down her cheeks as Gideon and Clint held him to keep him from turning over the cot. Then, when Elijah calmed, she and Cassie sponged him down.

They had a brief interval of peace before the bed creaked and shook from the force of his shivering. It was so fierce and prolonged that it seemed his bones must surely shatter and the teeth rattle from his mouth.

Earlier she had been aware of the voices raised softly in prayer outside, punctuated with the occasional hymn and the soft shuffle of feet walking around the tent. Now her world narrowed to the cot beside her and the man who lay on it, fighting for his life.

Lord, if You're not going to save Elijah, take him Home, she prayed at one point. *Just don't make him keep suffering. I can't bear this!*

The answer came back just as fast: *Alice, you can do all things because I have strengthened you. Be still, and know that I am here with you.*

She opened her eyes to see that Cassie's eyes were closed, her lips were moving in silent prayer.

All right, Lord, we are all asking in faith that You heal Elijah. You know the good Elijah can do in Oklahoma if he lives. But Your will be done.

Elijah had stopped shaking, and he lay sleeping. This had happened before—he would rest for a time after the chills, and then the fever would start to build again. In between, his breaths would come harshly, and his body would be racked with spasms of coughing.

Wait—was it her imagination or was his breathing easier now, free of that rasping wet sound? Didn't his color seem more normal, neither flushed nor with that icy pallor?

Alice watched for a long time, afraid to believe her eyes, while the older woman across the bed kept praying silently, her eyes closed.

Finally, when she could stand it no longer, she reached a hand over Elijah's chest and touched Cassie.

The old woman's eyes flew open.

"Is he—?"

"Look, Cassie, *look*. I think he's better. Listen."

Cassie's eyes widened, then she bent her head to listen. "He—he's breathing normally, isn't he? Oh, Alice…"

Shaking, Alice reached for her stethoscope. Both Clint and Gideon had gone outside to make more coffee, so she wouldn't alert them until she was sure. She placed the bell of the stethoscope over Elijah's chest and held her breath.

The blessed sound of normal in-and-out breathing, free of all but faint traces of the congestion, greeted her ears.

"Thank You, Lord," she whispered, and the tears flooded her eyes and ran down her cheeks.

Cassie cried, "Hallelujah!" which made it unnecessary to call Elijah's brothers. They came running in from outside, wild-eyed. One look at Alice's happy tears and Cassie's grin told them the news before they even looked at their brother.

"He's better?" they both asked at once, even as their eyes found the answer for themselves.

"Yes," said Alice in a tear-choked, shaking voice. "He's going to be weak for a long time but yes."

"Well, I'll be…" said Gideon.

"I'll tell the folks outside," Cassie said, and Alice saw Gideon give a surreptitious, relieved sigh.

"Tell them there'll be no visiting with the reverend till I give the word," Alice called after her. She knew how well-meaning folk could exhaust a fever-weakened convalescent. There were many in Boomer Town who loved Elijah Thornton, and she and his brothers would have to keep them at bay for a while. It was a blessed problem to have.

Cassie insisted Alice sleep for a while after that. Though Alice protested, she sank into a boneless slumber until dawn, when the older woman roused her to say she was going back to her campsite to sleep for a few hours.

"There's someone who wants to talk to you," she said with a smile broader than Alice had ever seen on anyone. She stood aside, so Alice could see Elijah. He was awake and gazing at her, his eyes tired but clear.

Alice wasn't even conscious of jumping to her feet and flying to the bedside. Clint and Gideon were there, too, beaming down at their brother.

"I hear I…have you to th-thank," Elijah said. His voice was but a shadow of its usual resonant, deep volume, and he had to pause to catch his breath, but she'd never heard a sweeter sound.

"Not me, the Lord," she said, again feeling the sting of happy tears. When had she turned into such a watering pot?

"Of…c-course," Elijah said. "But…thank you… for being His hands."

"Oh, Elijah…" she murmured, so happy she thought she might burst. In spite of her exhaustion, she felt like dancing through the dusty streets of Boomer Town. "Do you think you might be able to eat some broth?"

"S-sounds…good."

He drank a good bowlful, with Alice spooning it into his mouth, and his eyelids drifted shut right after the last drops. She continued to sit by his cot, so happy just to watch his chest rise and fall without the shuddering effort.

"Alice, go on back to your tent and get some rest," Clint said gently after a while. Somewhere during the crisis, he and Gideon had dropped the "Miss" attached to her name, and she didn't care.

"I'm all right..." She tried to protest, to point out she had slept some and her patient's condition was still too fragile for her to leave, but her fatigue-fogged brain couldn't even find the words.

"Gideon and I will take turns watching him, and I promise we'll call you if there's any change."

"All right," she said, "I'll be back in a few hours. But remember, no—"

He held up a hand. "No visitors, I know."

Elijah now knew the meaning of the phrase "weak as a kitten." He'd barely had strength enough to open his mouth to accept the sips of chicken broth Alice had offered. Now, Clint told him, she had departed for her own tent to rest awhile, and all he could do was lie on his cot in a sleepy haze and think about what had happened, and how the Lord had used her to save his life.

He remembered snatches of the past couple days— feeling the sudden blackness coming over him at the chapel and knowing he was powerless to stave it off. The racking chills and the bone-deep, agonizing aching all through him, the sensation of his lungs being clogged with something so thick he couldn't get a decent gulp of air, the stabbing chest pain every time he tried to. The spasms of coughing. Alice's cool hands, bathing the fire away, her beautiful face bent

low, furrowed with worry. The sound of her murmured prayers.

Sometimes in her ministrations, she was joined by
Cassie Gilbert. Other times, the faces of his brothers
hovered into view over him. But always he was conscious of Jesus in their midst.

He realized what a profoundly good woman Alice
was. Any man would be lucky to have her, but he
didn't want just any man to win her. He'd given up
the idea of marrying, but would the Lord release him
from that and let him court her? If He did, would she
consider giving up her prized self-sufficiency to become his wife?

Elijah's congregation was obedient to the no-
visitors rule, so they showed their love in the only
way they could. Covered dishes and pots of soup
began appearing that first morning after the crisis
had passed, left at the campfire, most of the time de-
posited when Clint and Gideon weren't even outside
to receive them and thank the givers.

And Alice brought her own offering later in the
day, a bowl of egg custard with nutmeg topping—"To
help you get stronger," she said. She must have been
to the Fairhavens' mercantile tent, and bought out
their supply of fresh eggs and sugar, and used Mrs.
Murphy's oven, he thought, but even the delicious
custard wasn't as sweet as the sight of her.

The first visitor permitted the next day, when Alice
deemed Elijah strong enough, was Dakota. He entered
the Thornton tent shyly, escorted by Cassie and Keith,
his dark eyes shining with excitement and joy. Alice
was already present.

"Preechah, you are better, yes?" he said, pronouncing each word with care. "I have cookies for you." He held out a dish piled high with them. It was obvious he had practiced the speech.

"Lars has started working with him, teaching him some English words," Cassie explained, with as much pride as if she were his mother.

"Yes," Elijah said. "I am much better. And I'm glad to see you, Dakota. Thank you for the cookies," he said, nodding toward them, not sure how much the boy understood.

"Cassie," the boy said, pointing to her, plainly wanting to give credit where it was due.

They didn't stay long, and afterward, Elijah insisted he felt strong enough to go sit outside for a while. With Gideon supporting him, Clint walking alongside in case more help was needed and Alice following, he made his way slowly beyond the canvas walls of the tent for the first time in four days.

They sat in the shade of the tent, but it was good to see the sun and feel its warmth. There had been times, during his shaking chills, when he'd have given an arm for its heat.

"I want to go to chapel tomorrow," he told Alice, who was seated on a camp chair opposite him. "Not to lead it," he said, holding up his hand when he sensed she was about to object. "Keith will do that, as he has been doing. I already spoke to him about it when you and Cassie were talking."

"I see my patient's getting ornery," Alice said with an amused smile. "A sure sign of recovery. All right, if you'll agree to return here for some rest right afterward. No lingering for one of the Ferguson sisters' endless stories."

"Yes, Nurse," he said meekly, but he let her see the twinkle in his eye.

Chapter Fourteen

Lars came to call on Elijah the next day, promising Alice as he took a chair that he would keep his visit brief.

"You are welcome, Lars," Alice said. "The visits from those Elijah is closest to seem to make him stronger—as does the fresh air," she added, for they were sitting under a length of canvas Elijah's brothers had erected so the sun wouldn't beat down too heavily on him.

"So what's your sister doing this afternoon?" Elijah asked him, after Lars had caught him up on the news around the camp.

"She is with Mrs. Murphy, teaching her how to make *kartoffelbrot* in exchange for slices of baked ham, potatoes and apple pie for our supper," the Dane said.

"That sounds like a good barter to me," Elijah said.

It had been an eventful day for Elijah, starting with his triumphant return to chapel that morning. He'd felt a little shaky as he had walked in, but he supposed that was normal. After all, he'd survived an illness that had killed many others. His spirits had been buoyed by the entire congregation's evident joy in seeing him.

"Preechah, Dakota comes!"

Elijah looked up and saw Dakota trotting toward him, with the Gilberts following at a slower pace. The boy's eyes were bright, his face full of the joy of living that he seemed to carry with him everywhere these days.

Elijah took a deep breath as he exchanged a look with Alice. It was time to tell Dakota about his father. *Give me the right words, Lord.*

Alice drew near and took a seat beside him while the Gilberts sat on a bench borrowed from the chapel. Dakota assumed a cross-legged position at Elijah's and Alice's feet.

"Dakota, Miss Alice and I want to tell you what we were able to learn about your father," he told the boy.

Dakota's face grew solemn, probably sensing from Elijah's tone that the news would not be happy. "Dakota listen."

Lars translated while Elijah and Alice gently and carefully told Dakota what they'd learned from the colonel who'd known his father, watching all the while for the boy's reaction. Elijah could see that the Gilberts were worried, too.

Dakota was unblinking and somber at the news of his father's fate. He paled beneath his light coppery skin, though, and Elijah saw the boy's hands clench at his sides.

"Lars," Alice whispered. "Tell him it's all right to cry."

"It's not the Cheyenne way to weep," Lars said. "I don't think he feels free to cry."

"But he's just a little boy, far from all that is familiar." Her blue eyes were full of compassion. "Tell him his father would understand."

Lars did so, and Dakota murmured something in Cheyenne. Lars then translated back to the others what he'd said. "I have no mother. I have no father. I am an orphan."

Cassie got up and knelt by the boy. Keith followed his wife and put his hand on Dakota's head. "You tell Dakota he's no orphan," he said, "not as long as he has us."

Dakota threw his arms around Cassie and gave way to his tears.

After a few minutes, when the boy's sobs had subsided, the Gilberts took him back to their campsite.

Lars, Elijah and Alice watched them go. "He'll be all right, I think," Lars said, "once he has time to adjust to the news."

Elijah agreed. Lawson had never taken an interest in the boy that he had fathered, so he was little more than an idea to Dakota in any case.

"But I probably ought to ride to the Cheyenne reservation in a day or so," Lars said, "to see if I can find the aunt who raised him."

Elijah and Alice exchanged another look, wondering if having to give the boy up would break the Gilberts' hearts.

"Dakota! Dakota!"

The three of them straightened in their chairs and listened. It was a female voice calling the Cheyenne boy, but then whoever was calling added some words in an unfamiliar tongue.

There it was again—"Dakota!"—but softly pitched, as if the caller did not want to call attention to herself. And then they saw her, skirting the alleyway behind their tent—a Cheyenne woman, leading a paint pony, her hand cupped around her mouth to project the voice, but not its volume.

The woman spotted them a heartbeat later and leaped onto her mount, clearly intending to flee. She was quick, but Lars was quicker and caught hold of the paint's reins before she could drum her heels into the horse's flank.

Elijah heard him say some quick words in Cheyenne, clearly a reassurance by tone. At the sound of her language in his mouth—a startling thing, Elijah imagined, given Lars's most un-Cheyenne pale blond hair and light eyes—her eyes grew large as silver dollars. She stared from Lars to Elijah and Alice and back at Lars again.

Lars spoke to her again, his voice calm, as if he were speaking to a wild creature. "I told her I spent much time among the *Tsitsistas,* learning to track, learning their ways," he translated for Elijah and Alice.

The woman wore a long buckskin dress, and her feet were shod with fringed leather boots—typical clothing for a Cheyenne woman. She was perhaps a few years younger than Lars—not newly a woman grown but certainly at the height of her attractiveness, with long, loose hair black as the deepest hour of the night and eyes to match, her high cheekbones proclaiming her proud heritage.

"I told her my name is Lars, or Gaurang, as a band of her people called me," Lars went on, after he spoke to the Cheyenne woman again. "She will know it means 'Man of Fair Skin.' I won't tell her the other name they called me, 'Corn Hair,'" he added with a grin. He didn't bother with his surname, as his was too complicated and cumbersome.

The woman pointed to herself and spoke. "I am Winona Eaglefeather," Lars translated for her. "She named a band of Cheyenne that I knew of from the reservation but that had lived at some distance from the one I stayed with. She says she seeks Dakota, her nephew, who has run away from her village."

Alice gasped.

Lars allowed his smile to broaden as he nodded. "I will tell her that he is here in this tent city."

Her relief was obvious, but unlike a white woman, she did not weep or cry out with joy. Her eyes shone like polished obsidian as she spoke.

"She says her heart rejoices," Lars translated, "and begs that we will take her to him."

Alice jumped up. "Please, may I fetch the Gilberts back here?"

Elijah knew she wanted to spare him the quick walk to the Gilberts' campsite. He *was* tired, he admitted to himself.

As Alice dashed away, Lars explained to Winona what was happening. He told her Dakota had been caught stealing food by one of the townspeople.

Elijah saw the Cheyenne woman's eyes flash with fury at being told that the man had struck Dakota, but Lars assured her that Elijah and Alice had quickly intervened to stop the beating.

Winona flashed Elijah a look of gratitude and said something.

"She says some whites are good to the Indian, but some are not," Lars explained. "I will tell her about the Gilberts and that Dakota has been staying with them, and how the older couple loves him. And I will tell her about Dakota's father's fate."

Elijah watched a succession of emotions flash across Winona's eyes, and when Lars had finished explaining, she spoke again, her tone angry.

"She says the earth has lost nothing without Richard Lawson walking in it," he said.

Inwardly Elijah had to agree, though he regretted the man's wasted life.

"Lars, please tell Winona that Dakota will need her now more than ever and that he will be very glad to see her."

They heard footsteps, and looked up to see Alice and the Gilberts returning, with Dakota leading the way, a curious expression on his face.

Recognition between the woman and the boy was instantaneous. He dashed into her embrace.

Her eyes tightly shut, Winona ran her fingers over the boy's skinny back and stroked his hair, speaking in a voice hoarse with emotion.

"She says 'Dakota, where have you been?'" Lars said. "'I have been searching everywhere for you! I was so worried. Why did you leave, saying nothing to me?'"

Dakota uttered a spate of words.

"He said, 'I'm sorry, Aunt Winona, I did not mean to distress you. I had to find my father! Four Bears taunted me that I had no father—at least not one who would claim me—that my father was nothing but a white smoke that floated wherever the wind blew. I thought I must prove him wrong.'"

Elijah saw the boy shudder and bury his face against her waist as he said something more.

"He is telling her that he found out today that Captain Richard Lawson is dead."

Winona bent low, murmuring something comforting to the boy.

The boy's face cleared a moment later, and he caressed Winona's cheek as he spoke again.

"He assures her that he is well, though, because the preacher placed him with these people he calls Aunt Cassie and Uncle Keith, and they are very nice to him," Lars said, pointing to the older couple. "He is telling Winona that Aunt Cassie made the shirt he wears." The boy, obviously proud, showed it off. "He said, 'They feed me so I am not hungered as I was when I found my way here. I have good shelter.'"

Elijah looked above the embracing Cheyenne woman and boy, and saw the confusion and distress in the Gilberts' faces. Elijah knew this was the very thing they had feared, that someone would arrive to claim the boy they had come to care for so much in just a few days.

Winona raised her head then and spoke, and a moment later, Lars translated, "Please tell this man and his wife I appreciate their care for my nephew until I could arrive. I am in their debt. I will take him home now."

As soon as her words were spoken, though, Dakota erupted like a young cougar suddenly let out of a small box, his voice angry and passionate.

"He says he will not go," Lars translated. "He says he will never return to the village where they despise him."

Elijah heard the Dane give Dakota a terse command, and guessed he was commanding that Dakota hold his tongue.

Even with the language barrier, Elijah could tell that Lars was speaking to the boy as if he were an elder male of the boy's tribe, whom Dakota would automatically respect. He was counting on the strength of the relationship he had built with the boy thus far.

Obediently Dakota hushed, and Lars spoke to Winona in low, urgent Cheyenne.

"I asked her to give the boy a few days," he said. "He's had some very bad news today, and he's still adjusting. Mr. and Mrs. Gilbert, I hope it's all right, but I told her that you would let her stay with you while she decides what would be the best course and that you're very good people."

"Of course we will let her," Cassie Gilbert said.

Winona crossed her arms and spoke again.

"She says she will sleep by the campfire with Dakota, and she will decide what should be done. She says she would like to talk to the Black Robe and the medicine woman also—she means you, Elijah, and you, Alice."

Elijah knew *Black Robe* was a term Indians used to refer to any Christian minister or priest. Alice looked bemused, he saw, at being called a "medicine woman."

He saw the tension leave Cassie's face. "Please tell Winona she is very welcome," Cassie told Lars. "We have food left from lunch, if she is hungry. I imagine she is, since she's been traveling."

Lars repeated Cassie's words to Winona, and Elijah saw a bit of the wariness fade from the Cheyenne woman's features. Dakota relaxed, too, now that he knew he wouldn't be wrenched away from the Gilberts—for now, at least.

Keith Gilbert spoke to Lars. "Elijah's nearly ready to start to lead the service again. Maybe you and the boy could talk Winona into coming? If she sees that Dakota has landed among good people, maybe she'd be more apt to stay with the boy here, instead of taking him back where he's looked at as something 'less.'"

Lars nodded. "I'll see if she's willing."

Saturday morning there was no chapel service, but Elijah sneaked out of the Thornton tent and walked to the chapel tent for a bit of exercise—and to review the past few days and take stock of what had happened. It was the first time he'd been alone since the lung fever had struck him down.

How You have blessed me, Father, Elijah thought as he looked out over the empty benches. *Thank You for restoring my health.* Oh, he still tired easily, and Alice continued to watch over him like a hen with one chick, but he could practically feel strength trickling back into his muscles. *I am more grateful than I can ever express. I only hope I can bring many others into Your kingdom, since You have left me here to serve You.*

He was thankful, too, that the Lord had reunited Dakota and his aunt, just when the boy had needed her the most. Surely only God could have helped Winona find her way to the right tent camp and caused Lars, the only man in Boomer Town who could speak both English and Cheyenne, to be the one to hear her calling her nephew.

God is so good.

Winona had come to the Friday chapel service, with Lars sitting by her to translate Elijah's words. The Cheyenne woman wasn't a Christian, and she had told Lars that she was willing to come to the chapel only because her nephew wanted to. But she seemed to enjoy the singing just as Dakota did. Truly music was the universal language, even if the tunes were very different from what Winona must be used to.

He and Lars had devised a plan whereby the two of them would teach Winona and Dakota English in the afternoons, for both had expressed an eagerness to learn. This afternoon was to be the first lesson. It was a good sign that Winona was thinking of staying, wasn't it, if she wanted to learn their tongue?

Elijah had great hopes that, by learning English, Dakota's aunt would come to feel at home among the inhabitants of Boomer Town and decide to stay with the Gilberts after the Land Rush. And if the book Winona used to read English was the Bible, so much the better. Perhaps in discussing the meaning of what she read, she would come to share their beliefs, too. He would plant the seeds, and God willing, they would grow and prosper into faith.

More and more inhabitants were pouring into Boomer Town every day, now that the Land Rush was only nine days away. With nothing to confine it, the tent town was expanding. Soon it would blur into the next tent cities north and south of them. Elijah rejoiced that there had been a dozen or more newcomers in the service yesterday.

He and Alice had recommenced their medical and pastoral calls last evening. Fortunately there had been little serious illness after old Mrs. Collins had died, and he had come down with pneumonia—just a few lacerations, an upset stomach or two, a toothache and a few folks who felt increasing anxiety about how they'd fare on the day of the Rush.

Of course, he couldn't promise any of them they'd be able to stake a prime piece of land with water and excellent land for grazing and putting in crops, but he prayed with each one and urged them to "cast your cares upon Him, for He careth for you," as the Good Book said. He did assure them that, whatever happened, if they kept close to the Lord, He would bless them according to His will.

Everyone who'd been attending his chapel services assured him that they were going to try to end up near the south bank of the Cimarron where Elijah and his brothers were heading, for they wanted to settle near him and help him build the church.

It occurred to Elijah to wonder about the Chaucers. Hadn't Horace LeMaster, that fellow who'd denounced him as a hypocrite after the service over a week ago, said the Chaucers were in the territory? He hadn't run into them around Boomer Town, and neither had Gideon or Clint, so they must be in some other tent city along the border—perhaps the next one in either direction.

Bless them, Father. Help them to let go of the grudge they apparently still nurse toward Gideon,

Clint and me, and help them find good claims. But if it's all the same to You, let them settle somewhere far from us.

Perhaps he'd better get going, he thought, after consulting his pocket watch. Alice had invited him and his brothers to lunch, and he couldn't wait to see her.

Full from their noonday meal, they'd agreed to make their rounds first and meet up with Gideon and Clint at Mrs. Murphy's tent for supper. A talkative old man had kept them later than they'd intended, and now it was almost eight. They'd have to hurry or they'd be too late to get a meal. As they walked, Elijah had been entertaining her with an account of Winona and Dakota's first English lesson.

"They're both very quick to pick up words," he said. "Winona, especially. I'm guessing she's already had considerable exposure to English when soldiers such as Dakota's father visited their camp. And where one of them doesn't understand, the other often does and can help. Dakota can name all of the things around the tent. I'm sure it won't seem like any time at all until they're fluent—"

His voice trailed off, and Alice looked up to see what had interrupted him as they approached the tent diner.

Folks were milling around outside the tent, talking, while others walked away. From inside the tent came the sound of a woman keening.

"No supper tonight, Reverend," a man told them as they drew near. "Mrs. Murphy was robbed just before she was to open. Both she an' her boy got knocked

out and all their money from the day before taken—
plus a goodly bit of the supper she was goin' t' serve."

"In broad daylight?" Elijah asked, incredulous.
"Did anyone see anything?"

"One couple who'd lined up early for supper said
they heard a commotion inside, then the sound a' runnin' feet away from th' far side a' the tent. The man
ran around the side of the tent, but all's he saw was
several men runnin' away with black bandannas on
their faces an' hats pulled down low. He gave chase,
but he lost 'em among all the wagons and tents and
whatnot. Your brother's in there, Reverend, talkin' to
Mrs. Murphy and her son."

"What about the Security Patrol?" Alice asked.
"Did anyone report this to them? Are they searching
for the men responsible?"

"They come and took a report, said they'd go
lookin' for anyone matchin' the description of those
men that done the robbin', Miss Hawthorne. But land
sakes, once those fellows took their bandannas off, no
one would know they were the culprits. It coulda been
anyone. Maybe you oughta go on in and see what you
can do for Mrs. Murphy, ma'am," he told her. "I just
caught a glimpse, but she's got a right wicked cut on
her forehead."

"I'll do that," Alice said, a sinking feeling swamp-
ing her. Everything had been going so well...

Elijah followed her. Inside the tent, all was chaos,
with tables and benches overturned, tin plates and silverware scattered amid the sawdust shavings on the
ground. In the cooking area, pots lay on their sides,
with what might have been stew congealed on the

sawdust and the sides of the pan. Mrs. Murphy sat in one of the chairs, her son, Sean, holding a cloth to her head and trying to console her, but it was doubtless she could hear her son over her wails of despair.

Clint stood nearby, his face grim. When he spotted Elijah and Alice making their way through the wreckage toward him, he came forward.

"Glad you've come," he said. "Mrs. Murphy's pretty upset, as you can hear."

Alice had gone straight to her, and Elijah could hear her murmuring softly to the woman as she peeked underneath the cold cloth. He caught a glimpse of a jagged cut that was still oozing when the wet towel was lifted and felt an immediate queasiness churning in his stomach, just as he had on the night Keith Gilbert had cut his leg so grievously. How could this slender woman beside him look at the things he'd seen her face so calmly and not turn a hair? She'd been given the gift of healing, all right. He sent a silent prayer of thanksgiving for Alice Hawthorne.

"This is the thanks I get for tryin' to fill people's stomachs with good, honest home-cooked foods," Mrs. Murphy cried when she saw Elijah. "Robbed, we were! They took every penny I had in th' till! Threatened t' shoot my Sean if I wouldn't tell 'em where I'd put yesterday's profits. I knew I should have put them away where I keep them hidden, but I needed to be able to make change…" Her voice escalated into another wail. "Sure and I shoulda gone back to the Ould Sod when I was widowed!" Her Irish brogue was thicker now in her distress.

"Ma, it'll be all right," her son insisted. "It's only

two days' profits that were taken. We'll be all right....
See, Miss Hawthorne's here, and she can tend to ye."

"'Tis the idea of it, boyo—that someone could be
so wicked," Molly Murphy told her son. "But I should
shut me trap—sure, and you were clobbered worse
than me."

"No, Ma, I got a hard head," Sean said, but even
from here Elijah could see the goose-egg-size swelling at the boy's temple.

Alice raised her head and looked at Elijah. Guessing that she wanted something, he left Clint's side and
went to her, though he was careful not to look at the
red-stained cloth on Mrs. Murphy's forehead.

"Do you think you could fetch my medical bag
from my tent, Elijah? It'll be right on top of my trunk.
I need to stay with Mrs. Murphy," she said.

"Of course."

By the time he returned, Clint and a couple men
from outside were righting the tables. A pair of
women who attended chapel cleaned the mess from
the preparation table. Molly Murphy lay on another
of her long tables, a tablecloth covering her legs. Sean
sat on a bench by his mother, holding her hand, his
other hand holding a wet cloth over the lump on his
forehead.

"Ah, thanks for being so quick," Alice praised,
hearing Elijah's footsteps. "I just need some disinfectant and bandaging for Mrs. Murphy's laceration—
fortunately it doesn't need stitches—and some willow
bark to brew tea for the headache she and Sean have
been too brave to complain about."

The boy had been brave, certainly—he'd been
man enough to forget his own pain in comforting

his mother. In Elijah's absence, he saw that Alice, too, had worked wonders on the Irishwoman's composure, for she was now calm and quiet.

He set the bag down on the table close to Alice, and she reached inside for the jar of carbolic acid, soaking a small square of linen in it.

"This is going to sting for a moment, Mrs. Murphy. Keep being brave, now—"

The woman gasped and clapped a hand over her mouth to stifle the squeal she couldn't help but utter.

"That's it, all over. You were very courageous, Mrs. Murphy," Alice crooned as she began to wrap a length of lint around the woman's forehead. "I just wanted to make sure you didn't get a nasty infection in that wound."

"Do you have any idea what you were hit with?" The question came from Clint, who'd come closer now that he'd seen Alice was nearly done.

"They broke a bottle a' vinegar over my noggin' 'cause I jumped at them for knockin' me boy down," Mrs. Murphy said. "They threatened t' go after my Sean with the jagged end of it, even though he was just lyin' there, dazed and not fightin' them anymore," the woman said. She pointed to the offending bottle, which was in the sawdust nearby, broken off at the neck. "Aye, but they were wicked men, the *spalpeens*."

Elijah's eyes sought Clint's. Who could be behind all these attacks? Why couldn't the Security Patrol's presence prevent them? And what could they do to keep their fledgling community safe?

Chapter Fifteen

After they returned from Mrs. Murphy's diner, Clint told Elijah he was of the opinion that the diner robbery could be blamed on the same ruffians who had assaulted Abe McNally, that member of the congregation whom Alice had tended a week or so back. Many other such robberies and assaults had come to light, too—not all of them on members of Elijah's congregation. Some of them had happened while Elijah had been ill.

"It's got to be all the same men, Lije. There's always four men doing the robbing or attacking, and they're always wearing black bandannas."

Elijah rubbed his chin thoughtfully. "Have you talked to the men on the Security Patrol? What do they say?"

Clint gave a snort. "They've duly investigated each one, but they say they haven't got a single lead. The four men just seem to melt into the maze of tents and wagons when they're pursued." He shrugged. "I don't know…maybe I'm being too hard on the patrol, Lije."

"What can we do about it?" Elijah asked, suspecting his younger brother had a plan. Clint always had ideas when it came to law enforcement.

"The incidents always seem to take place at dusk or after dark. Private McGraw says two of them patrol every night, but maybe Gideon and I should add our efforts. You know we're wakeful at odd hours anyway."

Elijah nodded. "Go on."

"So Gideon and I decided we're going to start doing a little night patrolling of our own—see if we can't catch these four outlaws in the act, or at least help to serve as a deterrent. We've only got a few more days to have to do it, after all."

Elijah had to admit it was a good idea—and typical of Clint and Gideon to think of how they could help the town in the way they were best suited. "Well, just be careful. You're always going to ride out together, not either of you alone, right? We've had enough excitement in this family for a while."

By a unanimous vote, the Sunday morning congregation decided to give the week's donations to Mrs. Murphy to replace the money that had been stolen from her Saturday night. Elijah would take it to her after the service, since the Irishwoman was never able to attend the chapel services as she was busy either serving or preparing food.

"Why do they give this woman this money?" Winona, who was sitting with Alice, Dakota and Katrine, asked, with the help of Lars on her other side. "I know her money was taken, but she does not come to chapel."

"Yes, but many of us have eaten her food, and

Molly Murphy is a good woman who did not deserve this bad thing that happened to her, the robbery," Alice explained. "We give her this gift out of Christian love, showing her the same love God shows us."

Something flickered in the depths of Winona's black eyes as Lars translated. "Us—you mean the Great Spirit loves all Christians?"

"Not just Christians," Alice said. "Everyone. God loves you, just as He loves me, Winona." Elijah had told her that he hoped to help Winona know Jesus through her English lessons. Maybe she could help with this, too.

"It is surprising. The Great Spirit—" Winona paused, clearly trying to express the vastness of the Deity "—is over all things. You say the Great Spirit loves me, too? Winona, a Cheyenne woman?"

It sounded as if Winona found the idea impossible to fathom.

"I do, Winona. I believe it with all my heart."

Winona sat back, looking thoughtful.

They decided to share potluck that night—the Thornton brothers, Alice, the Brinkerhoffs, the Gilberts, Winona and Dakota, each bringing something to eat at a communal dinner at the Thornton campsite. Gideon and Clint had gone hunting that morning, so the Thornton brothers contributed a side of beef that had been roasting over a spit all afternoon, and the Brinkerhoffs brought *flødekartofler,* scalloped potatoes, and *Dansk rødkål,* which was pickled cabbage. Alice brought yeast rolls and freshly churned butter. The Gilberts came bearing a chocolate cake, which Dakota proudly proclaimed he had helped to frost under Cassie's direction, but he confessed he had eaten a good bit of the frosting, too.

The evening breeze was balmy, a welcome relief from the heat of the day.

"We are so blessed," Elijah said, as he stood to say grace over the food, "to have come so far and made such good friends—a solid foundation for the town we're going to build, with God's help. Just think, all of you—in just over a week we'll race to stake claims in the Land Rush, God willing, and be setting up homes on our claims within days afterward. I pray that the Lord will bless this food and keep us close together." *And that I will find a way to speak to Alice about a shared future,* he added to himself.

"Hear, hear!" cried Clint, raising his glass of cider.

"Amen," murmured Keith Gilbert.

"Amen," said Lars and Katrine, for it was the same word in Danish.

"'Amen' mean is okay to eat?" Dakota asked, pointing at the bounty that had been laid out in front of them.

Everyone laughed except Winona, who looked embarrassed for her nephew, and said something in Cheyenne in a reproving tone.

"Yes, it is okay to eat," Elijah told the boy, as everyone began to dish food onto their tin plates. He noticed Dakota hung back until the adults had served themselves, though—waiting for one's elders must have been part of his aunt's admonitions.

Later, as everyone leaned back, their stomachs full to bursting, Keith pointed to yet another heavily laden wagon making its way down the narrow dirt road between the rows of tents and wagons. "Good thing the run's going to be over pretty soon, Reverend. If Boomer Town got any bigger, we'd be able to elect our own representatives to Congress."

"Yes, we're certainly bursting at the seams," Elijah agreed.

"If there are so many tent towns just like this all around the perimeter of the territory, there can't possibly be enough land for everyone who has come wanting a hundred and sixty acres," Alice fretted.

Elijah wanted to say that, if she wasn't able to stake a claim, she could share his homestead, but he sensed how much it mattered to her to have land of her own. And of course he knew better than to make such an offer in front of the others when he had come to no understanding with her privately. Instead, he murmured, "There's a verse in Psalms that says that the Lord will give us the desires of our hearts."

"We will all help each other to get our claims," Lars assured her. "Remember, Katrine is going to stay with the wagons, so we are not encumbered by them. Afterward, we'll take turns getting back to our wagons and driving them to our claims."

Lars had been translating the conversation to Winona, and now, through him, she said, "It is the white-eyes way to think of 'claiming' pieces of land. The Cheyenne—and all of our red brothers—believe the land belongs to everyone and is not a thing that can be owned. Once we roamed the plains and prairies freely. Now we must live on the reservation, the White Father in the East says."

It was something to ponder, Elijah thought, the way the Indians looked at things differently. "It is my hope, Winona, that the red man and the white man—

men of all colors—will live side by side some day in peace, as the Lord wants us to," he said.

Winona studied him for the longest time. "It is what I wish, too, Reverend Elijah."

"You Thorntons always did keep odd company," drawled a voice behind them, and Elijah looked up to see three men on horseback in the road, looking down on them. They were brothers, judging by a similarity of features—the exotic slant of their eyes and an olive tone underneath their weathered faces—and somehow he knew he'd met them before. The man who'd spoken had a Southern accent—a Virginian, if he didn't miss his guess. The man jerked his head toward Winona and Dakota, and then at Lars, whose long blond hair was in contrast to his Indian-style fringed buckskin trousers.

"Everyone here is our guest," Elijah told him, trying not to sound defensive. He wanted to tell the newcomers it was none of their business with whom he broke bread. "But I fear you have the advantage over me, gentlemen."

It was a polite invitation for the strangers to introduce themselves, but it didn't garner a polite response. "I *wish* we'd ever had the 'advantage' over you cheatin', Yankee-lovin', traitorous Thorntons," one of the other mounted men sneered, his drawl as Virginian as the first man's.

"Chaucers," growled Gideon beside him, and suddenly he and Clint were standing protectively, fists clenched, in front of the women.

Chaucers. Of course. Elijah recognized them now—Theo, Brett and Reid. He hadn't seen them since he and his brothers had made their abortive attempt to move back to their plantation in Virginia, only to be rebuffed by the hostility they had encountered there, stirred up by these three men. It had been Brett who'd just called them names.

"Yep," said Reid. "I reckon it was too much to expect we could move some place and not have to be reminded of how y'all prospered and caused us to lose our home. Now you're takin' up with redskins, I see." He pointed a long finger at Winona and Dakota. "And outlandish foreigners," he added, jabbing his finger in Lars's direction.

Elijah saw Winona put a protective arm around Dakota. The boy huddled against her, not understanding much of what the Chaucers said, but comprehending the hostile tone perfectly.

"Get off your horse and say that, Chaucer," Gideon ground out, rigid with fury as he took a couple steps toward the trio on horseback.

"Gideon, no, that's not the answer." Elijah said, aware that Clint was just as angry. *Lord, help me. I can't hold back both of them and my own temper, too.* He turned back to the Chaucers. "If you can't be civil, I'll have to ask you to ride on—"

But he was interrupted by Alice, who had moved around Gideon and Clint and now stood facing the horsemen, bristling with indignation. "How *dare* you say such things?" she cried. "No one here asked for your opinion, let alone your rude remarks about these people who've never offered you any offense."

"Thornton, you got yourself a spitfire, I see," Brett responded with a smirk. "Good for you." He tipped his hat to Alice. "Brothers, we've got better things to do. Let's go."

To Elijah's immense relief, the Chaucer brothers kneed their mounts into a trot and disappeared around a corner.

What could he possibly say after what had just happened? Elijah stood there for a moment, staring in the direction the Chaucers had gone, shaking with the emotions rocketing through his body—fury, embarrassment, regret. He'd already told Alice about the feud, but now Brett Chaucer had compounded the problem by verbally assuming Alice was Elijah's woman. Had the idiot ruined his chances of making that true?

"Just so you know, brother, I'm not ever gonna back down from them again if they challenge me," Gideon muttered.

"Me, either," Clint said. "If they're smart, they won't try it a second time."

Elijah made a gesture to indicate he'd heard them. They could talk about it later, but for now he was more concerned with those who had been the main targets of the Chaucers' gibes.

"I'm sorry you had to witness all of that," he said at last, addressing their guests. "There aren't words to express how much I regret that. Obviously ill will has followed us here to Oklahoma. I regret that those men let their hatred spill over to you."

"I did not understand the words he said, but the tone made the meaning clear," Winona said wearily. "The day of harmony between all whites and red men seems a long journey away."

"It's not your fault, Reverend," Keith chimed in stoutly. "I've learned fools will be fools." His wife nodded their agreement.

"There is a Danish saying," Lars began, "*Han skal have meget smör, som skall stope var mans mund*—it means, 'Pigs grunt about everything and nothing.'"

Elijah heard chuckles, but the buoyant mood of the evening had been spoiled, and soon everyone said good-night and gathered up their dishes.

"I—I'll walk you back to your tent," Elijah said to Alice, who'd been quiet since her outburst.

"It's not necessary," she said quickly. "It's just a short distance."

"Nevertheless." After what had just happened, and after his earlier talk with Clint about the assaults and robberies around Boomer Town, he wasn't about to let her—or any woman—walk by herself. And he wanted to say something about Brett Chaucer's disrespectful remark.

"All right," she said, and they headed down the road.

"I'm sorry about what Brett Chaucer said. He had no right to make such an assumption," he said.

"I think Lars's proverb pretty much summed up what I think about what he said," Alice murmured, with a weak attempt at a smile. "I certainly don't hold you responsible."

Thornton, you've got yourself a spitfire. Good for you.

What if he *wanted* Alice to be his, in truth? Now probably wasn't the time, though, to let her know he'd been giving serious consideration to deepening their relationship past friendship—if she was willing, of course. "I—I appreciate that."

"Gideon and Clint seemed pretty angry," she commented then. "I thought for a moment there was going to be fisticuffs." She gave him a wry look.

He sighed. "They've both got hot tempers," he said. "Especially Gideon. I worry about him sometimes. He…he holds too much inside."

"You're afraid the cauldron will boil over one day," she observed.

What a wise, insightful woman she was, to put a voice to his inner fears. "Yes. Though I was rather angry myself tonight, I must admit."

"It's understandable. You're human, after all, Elijah."

He nodded. "But what kind of 'man of the cloth' would I be if I gave way to an impulse to yank that smirking Chaucer off his horse and rub his face in the dirt?"

"You had the impulse, but you didn't give way to it. You're the most honorable man I know, Elijah."

"Thank you."

Their gazes met and held for a long moment. Should he say what he'd been thinking about saying? Or had this night been too tainted by negative emotions to have a chance of succeeding?

But he'd waited too long, and Alice was already turning to go inside.

"Good night, Elijah. I'll see you at chapel tomorrow."

Chapter Sixteen

❧

Excitement buzzed inside the chapel tent Monday morning as Alice took her place on a bench. Over and over she heard folks say "One more week" and "A week from today, we'll be there." Anticipation was colored by a tinge of wistfulness and uncertainty, though, for with the Land Rush this close, members of the congregation realized they wouldn't always be together like this in a canvas tent-chapel in Boomer Town. Though they longed to be settled in their new homes, there was no guarantee of being able to settle near one another, or even that they would be able to stake a claim at all.

How far she had come in two weeks, Alice thought, from a timid mouse afraid to give anyone her real name to a woman with friends sitting all around her—the Gilberts, Winona and Dakota, the Ferguson sisters; and the men, women and children she had met while nursing them who had become her friends, too.

And there was Elijah, of course, who at this moment was stepping up to his makeshift lectern. Her life had certainly become richer after meeting him, Alice mused. He had influenced her in so many ways. He'd encouraged her to give of herself, and now she couldn't imagine why she'd wanted to leave nursing totally behind. She'd no longer tread a hospital's halls, but she gained so much more than those she helped. It was a gift to be needed.

Through Elijah's example, she had learned to trust God to calm her fears. She no longer looked over her shoulder, fearing Maxwell Peterson was right behind her. How silly it had been to think he'd given her a thought after she'd fled New York. He had always wanted power and influence, so it had been a mystery why he had wanted her. No doubt he was pursuing some heiress by now.

She'd only received one letter from her mother—postmarked during the time Alice had been traveling to Oklahoma—but her mother hadn't written anything to make her think Peterson had gone ahead with foreclosure on their farm, despite the farm's ongoing shortfall. His threat to do so had apparently been a figurative saber to rattle over Alice's head, and once she had disappeared, he'd lost interest.

But the most important impact Elijah had had on her life was simply that she was no longer able to imagine her life without him in it. Her independence no longer seemed like such a thing to be prized. She'd begun to think a life without this man's love would be a lonely, gray void, even when her mother came to join her.

And she was realistic enough to know that, as much as she loved her mother, Mary Margaret Hawthorne would not be with her forever. Then there would be nothing to give life joy, nothing to make life more than a hardscrabble existence just to scratch a living from the prairie.

Last night's confrontation with the Chaucers had been painful for everyone who'd been there but especially for Elijah, she thought. She hoped what she'd said to him outside her tent had helped soothe his lacerated spirit. But she could tell that Elijah had more on his mind than just their enemies' ugly jeers. She'd sensed he had wanted to say something that had nothing to do with the Chaucers and everything to do with the two of them. She'd waited, and finally bid him good-night in hopes it would spur him to speak and reveal what was in his heart.

But he hadn't. No doubt he was wearied by the incident and thought another time would be better. That was all right—they would have time, and maybe what he had to say was better said without a cloud hanging over it. Perhaps tonight he would tell her.

"Friends, it is our final week here in Boomer Town!" Elijah said, lifting his arms jubilantly, and the whole congregation cheered.

"Amen, Reverend!" someone cried.

"In seven days we'll be in the Promised Land!" another shouted.

Elijah grinned at their enthusiasm. "Just think—in a week, God made something from nothing. He created the earth and all that is in it, the land, the water, the animals that creep on the earth, fly through the sky and swim in the rivers and oceans. And He created mankind to rule over it all."

He paused and took a sip of water. "Yes, in a week, our lives will all be changed, one way or another.

For some of us, it will be the first time in our lives we have a plot of land to call our own. Others have owned land but simply need a new start in life in a new land. And yet God is always willing to give us a new start in life, and it's not dependent on a government somewhere opening up a territory, or some specific time and date. It's there for the asking, whenever we want it."

After the service, Alice was just as surprised as Elijah when Horace LeMaster, followed by his wife and all four of their stair-step boys, stood in line to shake his hand.

"I've been watchin' you, Reverend, the way you conduct yourself around Boom Town and all, and I'd just about decided I was wrong about what I said to you. But then I heard how you responded to those Chaucer boys last night, and I became one hundred percent convinced. I was wrong, Reverend, and I hope you'll forgive what I said a coupla weeks ago to you."

"Of course, Horace," Elijah said, beaming. "I'm happy to see you back."

Rounds had taken a long time this evening—not because there were a lot of new illnesses or injuries, for other than a child who'd developed a nasty chest cold, there was no illness to speak of. It was as if the population of Boomer Town was buoyed by anticipation of what was to come and had no time for sickness. Mainly folks just wanted Elijah to pray with them individually for their success on the day of the Land Rush and in the future.

They'd stopped by to check on Beth Lambert, the girl who'd been weak and pale from anemia, and found her blooming with health—rosy-cheeked, happy and energetic.

"We're so grateful for the advice you gave us, Nurse Hawthorne," her mother said. "To see our Beth bloomin' again—why, I just can't thank you enough. I don't mind saying me and her father feel better, too. I'm glad you stopped by. I made you somethin' to thank you."

Mrs. Lambert climbed inside the wagon, and in a moment she was back, holding out two folded pieces of cloth.

Alice took it and unfolded one of the cloths, and saw that a beautiful design had been embroidered into the plain cotton, that of the medical caduceus—twin serpents twining around a staff, next to a woman who had clearly been made to look like her, down to her auburn hair and blue eyes. The woman wore a navy blue cloak with a red cross on one shoulder. The other towel depicted a little house at the end of an enormous flower-sprigged field, with a sun rising behind it. Underneath the design, she'd stitched the words *Best of luck in Oklahoma.*

Alice felt tears stinging her eyes. "These are beautiful," she breathed. "Mrs. Lambert, thank you so much." Impulsively she gathered the woman into a hug.

The woman was flushed with pleasure. "Aw, they're just dish towels, Miss Alice. It was somethin' to work on of an evenin'. Think of us when you use them."

"Oh, but they're too pretty to be used. I'm going to frame them and hang them in my new house," Alice told her, her heart full because of this woman's gift, and all the thanks and smiles she'd garnered because she'd agreed to help Elijah with the medical needs of Boomer Town.

They headed for her tent not long after that. Perhaps now Elijah would sit outside with her and share what he'd been so obviously wanting to say the night before.

"Say, Reverend," a voice called out, and Alice saw Mr. Johnston, one of the older men in the congregation, with his son, a young farmer, sitting on bales of hay outside their tent. "Me an' my son were just discussin' a bit of Scripture, and we were disagreein' on the meanin' of it. S'pose you could sit a spell and explain it to us? It's in Second Thessalonians, and it's about the Second Comin'…"

Elijah gave Alice a rueful glance. "This is probably going to take a while," he said in a low voice. "I'll walk you back to your tent and then come back, all right?"

"Nonsense. It's not far," she told him, and wished she was bold enough to ask that he stop by afterward. But dusk was already deepening, and here and there lantern lights were blooming. She knew Elijah was too careful of both their reputations to be observed coming to her tent after dark. "Good night, Elijah."

Their conversation would have to wait for yet another day, Alice thought as she walked briskly on.

Her tent was illuminated by lantern light, too. Had she left it burning when she went to accompany Elijah on rounds? She didn't think so; she hadn't needed its light then. Perhaps Gideon or Clint had come and lit it, so that she wouldn't have to enter a dark tent?

How thoughtful, if that was the case. They'd all been more vigilant lately….

To reassure herself, she reached into her medical bag to touch the knife she'd placed there the other night after Mrs. Murphy had been robbed. Was it one of the criminals with the black bandannas lurking inside, waiting to pounce on her?

No, she was being ridiculous. No sound came from within the tent. There was no one inside. She'd lift the tent flap and see that everything was just as she had left it. "The Lord is my light and my salvation, whom shall I fear?" she murmured aloud, and lifted the tent flap.

"Hello, Alice," said a voice she'd hoped never to hear again, coming from the last person she had ever wanted to see. She froze in her tracks, dropping the medical bag with the knife still inside it. Suddenly, despite the warmth of the Oklahoma April night, she was as cold as if she had swallowed snowballs. Her pulse took off like a jackrabbit scurrying across the prairie.

"You always did like to talk to yourself," Maxwell Peterson said. "I heard you murmuring to yourself outside." He sat in the camp chair across from her cot, like a figment in her nightmares, dressed in the same sort of fancy pin-striped suit he always wore, his soulless pale blue eyes gleaming in the lamplight. His derby hat was perched on top of her Bible on the upended packing crate by her cot.

He stood. "Come on, how about a hug for the man who's followed you hundreds of miles from civilized New York to the wilds of Oklahoma Territory?" Maxwell said, and before she could refuse or step back, he'd enveloped her in his arms.

He was a tall man and powerfully built, so it was like being embraced by a grizzly bear. Alice tried not to flinch or pull away as those massive arms went around her and threatened to squeeze the breath from her body. She always thought he'd liked it all the more when she struggled, so she reminded herself to be still.

He released her at last. "I was wondering if you were ever coming back to your tent. I'd begun to think these yokels had led me astray about which was your tent," he said, making an airy gesture in the direction of her nearest neighbors. "So where were you, Alice, my dear? Out painting the town?" He threw his head back and gave a hearty laugh. "As if there was anything in this hole of a place worth painting!"

"I—I was visiting some of the townspeople," she said, trying to stifle the tremor that threatened to creep into her voice. It wouldn't do to show fear, just as it didn't when facing a cougar.

"Visiting? What could you possibly have in common with the hicks I've seen here?" he demanded, as if asking to be let in on some joke.

"I—I've been…nursing the sick, Maxwell. And a lot of the people here have become friends," she said and was sorry she'd let defensiveness into her voice—yet another weakness one dared not reveal to this ruthless man.

He ignored the last half of her statement as if she hadn't said it. "'Nursing the sick,'" he echoed. "I thought you'd hung up that ugly uniform and those thick, hideous shoes you wore at Bellevue forever,

Alice. I told you that you'd never have to work a day in your life ever again, my dear, once you were mine. Still, I suppose you had to do *something* to pass the time, didn't you?"

"What are you doing here, Maxwell? How did you find me?" she asked, wondering if she was fast enough to back out of the tent and run screaming to the Thorntons.

It was too late. Of course it was. It had been too late the moment Maxwell Peterson arrived in Boomer Town. She just hadn't known it until she had trustingly lifted that tent flap.

"You…you didn't go terrorize my mother, did you?" she asked suddenly, sick to think of him wringing her whereabouts out of her frail, aged mother with the mixture of intimidation and threats of which Maxwell Peterson was a past master. "If you harmed her—"

"You'd what? No, silly one, I didn't bother your old *mater*. Alice, when you have the assets I do, it's no problem to hire a detective—or a herd of them, for that matter," he said with a grin, sitting down again. "Sit down, Alice," he said, pointing to her cot, the only other place in the tent for her to sit—as if she'd come to his dwelling, not her own. "You've got to be dead on your feet, tending to the poor unwashed and all that. I don't know how you stand it."

She complied, keeping her eyes on him all the time.

"But it wasn't all my well-paid detectives, but my new best friend from *The New York Times* that did the trick, in the end."

She could only stare at him.

"Yes, Robert Millard Henderson. I believe you met him almost two weeks ago, when he interviewed you about your nursing? 'Florence Nightingale of the Oklahoma Territory,' he called you. It was most impressive. And you were so modest, not wanting to give your name. Commendable—but the people you'd been ministering to were only too happy to share that bit of information."

Alice remembered it now—the impertinent, pushy newspaperman and Abe and Nancy McNally. She'd looked back as she and Elijah had walked away, and had seen Henderson lingering with the McNallys and hadn't thought about it past the next day. She felt the blood draining from her face as she realized how neatly she had stepped into the trap.

"You just happened to see a *newspaper* article?" she asked.

"No, he was among the many I've paid to look for you, Alice, my dear. He was merely the lucky fellow who hit pay dirt. He's been handsomely rewarded, of course." Maxwell was smug as a cat that had just drunk a whole pitcherful of cream.

She'd known she shouldn't give her name! But the McNallys had given it for her, sure that she was only being self-effacing. It was all she could do to smother a groan.

She was going to die tonight—or at best, suffer a beating. Maxwell didn't accept rejection well and hadn't ever since he'd first tried to court her when they'd grown up together. *Lord, help me! If You ever cared what happened to me, save me now!*

"So how does it feel to be the face that launched a thousand queries, my clever, beautiful Alice?" he said. Chuckling, he suddenly leaned forward and kissed her forehead.

His mercurial change of mood left her dizzy. "Cl-clever?" she stammered. She'd feared his fists would clench at any moment and make her pay for escaping him, and now he was calling her *clever?*

"Yes, clever. I had no idea you had such spunk, or such enterprise, either—to come all the way to Oklahoma to surprise me with a wonderful new future for us."

"For *us?*" she parroted, feeling as if she was lost in a maze. *What on earth does he mean?*

"Yes, for us. You weren't content to be a rich New York City aristocrat—too confining a role for you. I should have seen that," Peterson mused aloud. "You always did like a challenge—though you would have wanted for nothing as my wife, you know. But, no, you came here instead to make this wonderful surprise for me."

"Surprise..." Could she do nothing but parrot his words and stare at him? she thought, angry with herself.

"Yes, my spirited darling. You wanted to surprise me by getting us a homestead—not that a hundred and sixty acres would ever be enough, but it would be a start—a base of operations, while we bought up land around us and eventually owned a prairie empire, right? It was going to be your wedding present to me, wasn't it? Please don't mind that I've guessed what you were up to, Alice. It only makes me prouder of you."

Clearly, she marveled as she stared at him, it had

never entered his mind that she had come all this way to avoid him.

He'd grown a beard and mustache since she'd last seen him, and he fingered it now, vainglorious as ever. It only made him look more ruthless, she thought.

"So if any of these friends you've been making are gentlemen admirers, Alice, you'll just have to tell them your sweetheart is here now, so they'll have to go nurse their broken hearts, won't you?" he said, grinning as if *he* was letting *her* in on the joke now. "Because I don't share."

The last four words hung on the air as if the threat they represented was a palpable thing.

Elijah. His image rose up before Alice suddenly—his earnest, handsome face, his kind eyes, his gentle smile—a smile that would never be aimed at her again. She could never tell Maxwell she had begun to care for this man, not if she wanted Elijah and his brothers to live.

Men who had crossed Maxwell before had been made sorry they'd done so. Alice had guessed he'd been responsible, though he'd probably only hired others to mete out the punishment. Naturally there'd never been anything to tie the retaliation to him. One man who'd resisted selling a choice property Maxwell coveted had been found riddled with bullets—and his grieving widow had been only too glad to sell it to Maxwell for a greatly reduced price. Others had disappeared, their bodies never found.

No, she could never mention Elijah's name, or associate with any of her former friends, because she'd rather die right now than to bring any harm to him and his family.

"Where…where are you staying?" she said at last. "You can't stay here, of course," she added, gesturing at the tent that seemed even tinier with him inside it. "My reputation—"

"Shall remain unsullied, of course," he finished for her. "No, it's too small for the two of us, even if it was proper, and Caesar's future wife must be above reproach," he said in that grandiose way that had always set her teeth on edge. "No, I've got a much larger tent—I suppose you'd call it a pavilion, really—in back of your campsite, close enough for togetherness, but not close enough that tongues will wag," he concluded, merrily waving a finger.

"In back of my campsite?" she repeated. "But there were already people in back of me, Maxwell. The Carters, the Weisheimers, the Santinis," she said, ticking the names off. "What did you do with them?"

"They've been paid well to relocate," he said, as careless as if he spoke of flies being swatted.

He'd thought of everything, she thought, as hope died within her.

"And don't worry about Race Day—or the Land Rush, or whatever they're calling it," he said with another airy wave. "There's a general down here who owes me a favor—I was able to wangle his son out of some trouble he found himself in. We'll have to get up early, of course, but we'll be let through at the crack of dawn, so we can find just the piece of land that suits us—adjoining plots. Three hundred and twenty acres, not a hundred sixty, since we won't be married then.

"Of course, it won't be but a patch on the amount of land we'll end up with, eh? And then we can be married shortly after the big day. The King and Queen of Oklahoma, that's what they'll call us, won't they?" He chucked her under the chin. "How'd you like that, eh? Or maybe Senator and Mrs. Peterson—or even President Peterson and his First Lady. Mrs. Maxwell Peterson—has a nice ring to it, doesn't it?"

Chapter Seventeen

Maxwell had finally left her tent around midnight, after talking endlessly about "their" plans. Not only was he confident he could buy up all the land around their joined homesteads, but he planned to start a bank in the town he would found nearby, which would in a short time become the largest bank in Oklahoma.

From there he would progress to being mayor, then senator. By that time she would have given him four or five children at the least—three boys, the oldest of which they'd name Maxwell Junior, of course. He would inherit the banking business, or if he wanted to join his father in his political aspirations, he might be the Peterson to become president of the United States if Maxwell Senior did not.

They'd have a couple girls, too, little red-haired copies of their lovely mother, daughters who would make brilliant marriages some day that would enlarge the Peterson empire. Meanwhile Alice would be the social leader of Oklahoma womanhood, the jewel of his home.

Alice had listened numbly, and he didn't seem to

notice that she said nothing, since he took silent admiration as his due. At last, when she began to sway with weariness, he finally glanced at his ornately designed gold pocket watch.

"Sorry, m'dear. I've enjoyed our reunion so much I hadn't noticed the time. I'll depart for my pavilion and let you get your beauty sleep. Don't worry about cooking me a big breakfast in the morning— I've brought Horst with me to double as my cook and valet. He'll fix breakfast for both of us—though I hope you don't insist on rising with the birds, do you? My other men are waiting back in Wichita, of course, with wagonloads of materials for our new home. Didn't want too many of my personnel here. Figured we'd want our privacy, eh?"

He'd kissed her full on the mouth then, and it had been all she could do not to suffer at the touch of his cold, fleshy lips. But he didn't seem to mind her lack of response.

"Still the shy little maiden, aren't you? Good to see that these hayseeds haven't corrupted you. After breakfast we'll have the whole day to spend together. You can show me the sights." He'd laughed hugely then, tickled at his own joke. "I've brought you a saddle horse and your riding habit, Alice, my sweet. We can go explore the prairies, eh?"

"Good night, Maxwell." Maybe if he wasn't expecting her to rise till late, she could sneak out of her tent and run to the Thorntons, and explain to Elijah what had happened, so he would not make the mistake of coming to look for her and bringing Maxwell's wrath down on his head.

If only she hadn't held back her heart from Elijah, prating about "independence." Her insistence on independence had only left her free to have Maxwell wrap his chains around her. If she'd given Elijah the slightest encouragement, hinted that she couldn't imagine life without him at her side, he'd have declared himself by now.

Or maybe it was best that she hadn't surrendered to her feelings after all, she thought, staring up at the faint light of the full moon filtering into her tent. Maxwell wouldn't have been deterred from his goals even if she'd been engaged to marry Elijah Thornton, and the Thornton brothers might all have paid the price then. It was better for everyone she'd met in Boomer Town if she just quietly went and told Elijah why she had to step out of his life.

How would she get out of showing Maxwell around Boomer Town? She hadn't the least desire to parade through the narrow dirt "streets," and listen to his scornful remarks about the crude tents and its salt-of-the-earth, hope-filled populace. She didn't want to encounter anyone she knew and see the puzzlement in their eyes as they beheld her with this stranger, and learned who he was to her. And Maxwell wouldn't hold back, she knew. He'd be crowing to anyone who would listen as a way of marking his territory.

It would be better to proclaim herself as bored with Boomer Town as he would be and go on endless horseback rides with him away from town. She didn't think it likely that he'd try to take advantage of her when they were alone—for a ruthless man, he was curiously inconsistent in his desire for above-question respectability. Their rides would be the only thing to alleviate a week of stifling days with him at his campsite, playing endless games of chess with the marble chess set he always traveled with, eating the gourmet meals Horst would cook.

Alice slept fitfully at last, only to wake with a start when someone's rooster crowed the dawn. Hollow-eyed, she'd dressed, stowed the medical bag she'd dropped in the middle of the dirt floor and slipped out of her tent, only to find Horst sitting in a camp chair at the entrance.

He stood and gave her a punctilious bow, pretending not to see how he'd startled her. "Good morning, Miss Hawthorne," he said in his perfect Bavarian-accented English. "A pleasure to see you again. Let me brew you some coffee, yes? I will wake Mr. Peterson and tell him you have arisen."

"Oh, no, that's not necessary. I was just—" she began, already knowing she would not be walking down to see Elijah now.

"But those are his instructions, Miss Hawthorne." He was perfectly polite but inexorable.

"No, don't do that. I—I wouldn't want you to disturb him since he went to bed so late," she said and faked a huge yawn. "I—I'm actually still rather tired myself. I think I'll go back in and doze a little longer."

Horst bowed again. "Very good, Miss Hawthorne."

Letting the tent flap fall behind her, she lay down on the cot, fully clothed. Holding the sheet up to her face to stifle the sound, she wept.

Odd that Alice hadn't come to chapel, Elijah thought, but perhaps she hadn't slept well that night and decided to sleep in that morning. Perhaps he could give Winona and Dakota their English lesson a little early, leaving him time to ask Alice if she'd like to go riding out on the prairie with him this afternoon. They hadn't taken the horses for a gallop since he'd been ill, and though it was still sunny, a cool wind had blown away the summerlike heat. Perhaps out there among the tall grass and rolling countryside, they'd have enough privacy that he could ask Alice if he could court her.

But she wasn't there when he went to her tent at two o'clock, either, and she had left him no note. A prickle of unease slid down his spine, but nothing was disturbed in the tent, as far as he could tell.

There was a new tent, huge and fancy-looking, behind Alice's, that hadn't been there before, almost like something a medieval king would hold court in. He didn't care. More and more people were coming into Boomer Town each day, and perhaps those whose tents had been behind hers had shifted elsewhere.

He left her a note on the top of the crate by her cot, saying he'd been here to see if she wanted to go riding. They could still go this evening, he supposed. It might even be nicer when they could watch the sun setting behind the hills to the west.

Probably she'd left because she'd learned of someone needing her nursing. He hadn't thought to look for her medical bag when he'd been inside her tent. Yes, that had to be it. She'd find his note and come over to their campsite, and all would be well. He'd just take a stroll around town and see if he could run across her.

But he didn't spot her familiar figure in the flower-sprigged calico dresses she favored, nor had anyone he inquired of seen her. Returning to their tent, he asked his brothers if she'd come while he had been out walking around, only to have both of them shake their heads.

"You have any reason to be worried, Lije?" Gideon asked.

Elijah shook his head and told him how he'd found everything in order at her campsite—but that he hadn't found her tending some homesteader around Boomer Town, either.

"Maybe she's just gone out for a walk past town," Clint offered. "Sometimes ladies get a notion to go gather wildflowers, don't they? Or maybe, being as it's Alice we're talking about, healing herbs or some such."

"I don't think she'd go out there on foot, alone." Elijah shook his head. "Not after what happened to Mrs. Murphy, right here in town." During his walk, he'd seen Cheyenne, Alice's Appaloosa, in the corral with the rest of their horses, so he knew she hadn't gone on a solitary ride.

Gideon looked thoughtful. "Come to think of it, Lije, I saw some woman riding out this morning 'round about the time you'd have been finishing up at your chapel. She was a ways away, going down that side road that leads out of Boomer Town, yonder," he said, pointing in that direction, "and I caught a glimpse of dark red hair as she went past."

Elijah leaned forward.

"But it couldn't've been her," Gideon said. "This woman was riding sidesaddle in a fancy riding habit, not a split skirt like Alice wears when she rides, and she was sitting on this high-stepping liver-colored chestnut with a bobbed mane. There was some Eastern dude riding beside her."

"Doesn't sound like Alice, then," Clint said.

"No," Elijah murmured, but he wouldn't feel at peace until he saw her. He shifted his gaze to the entrance of the tent, as if he could will her presence.

"Think we oughta speak to the Security Patrol and ask if they've seen her around town?" Clint said.

"No." They hadn't been of any help before. "I think I'll just go down to her tent and wait for her," he said and headed outside.

"Invite her to join us for supper at Mrs. Murphy's, why don't you?" Clint called after him. "I saw Mrs. M earlier, and she said she's making that tasty ginger cake for dessert."

Elijah had walked past four campsites, spurred on by an apprehension he couldn't put a name to, when he spotted Alice, sitting outside in the shade of her tent. She was looking in the other direction. But before relief could seize him and cause him to call out a greeting, he saw that she wasn't alone.

A big, richly dressed gent with light brown closely cropped hair, mustache and beard sat in a camp chair beside her—*too* close beside her—dressed in a hacking jacket, jodhpurs and high two-toned leather boots—the sort of gentleman's riding apparel he hadn't seen since they'd left the East. He had a folded newspaper in one hand and was idly flicking a riding crop at his boots with the other. Hovering nearby, between Alice's tent and the new, large one behind her, stood a middle-aged man dressed in a servant's livery.

Elijah stopped stock-still in the narrow roadway, staring. There had to be an explanation. Perhaps he was a brother or some cousin from New York. She'd never spoken of such—in fact he'd believed she was alone in the world but for her mother—yet it had to be the case.

Almost as if she sensed his presence, Alice looked in his direction then and went still, like a fawn who'd spotted a wolf. Her eyes widened, then went blank. The man had looked up, too, and slowly, almost negligently, leaned closer to her so that they were touching from shoulder to elbow, his almost-colorless pale eyes narrowing into slits as he studied Elijah.

Elijah came to stand by the path that led to her tent. "Miss Alice, I see you have a visitor," he commented, straining to sound normal. *Who is this man, Alice?* he wanted to demand. *Why is he sitting so close to you?*

She'd gone pale as paper. "Yes…h-hello, Reverend Thornton," she said. "Yes, Maxwell's just come from New York. It—it was…quite a surprise." Her voice was unnatural and strange, as if she couldn't quite get her breath.

The man she'd called Maxwell stood then, leaving the folded newspaper in his chair, and came forward now, his arm extended. "Maxwell Peterson, Reverend. I'm Alice's fiancé. I couldn't let my little sweetheart make the Land Rush without me, could I?" He gave a jovial bark of laughter.

Elijah thought he had to have heard him wrong. He stared at Alice. "Your *fiancé?*" His own voice sounded strange to him, too. He made no move to shake the man's proffered hand, and finally, the other man lowered his outstretched arm to his side. Far from being embarrassed, though, Maxwell Peterson beamed with satisfaction.

Alice looked everywhere but at Elijah or Peterson. Elijah saw Peterson turn his gaze on Alice. The man's jaw had hardened, and a vein throbbed in his temple.

"Darling, aren't you going to tell him?" Peterson asked. "No matter, I will. You see, Reverend, she and I...well, we had a silly quarrel before she left New York about her coming here to Oklahoma, but Alice was determined to prove to me that this place is where she wants us to raise our family—far from the hustle and bustle of New York City." He chuckled. "My foolish, willful sweetheart. So of course I had to follow her and tell her I'd seen the light, didn't I?"

"I...I see," Elijah said, choking with the effort to sound normal and unmoved. "Well...Miss Alice, I just came to ask if we'd be doing our rounds around the town tonight as usual?" he asked, as if he hadn't been planning to invite her to go riding.

"Alice..." the other man said, clearly prompting her.

She looked up then, and Elijah saw none of the lively sparkle in those sky-blue eyes that had always been there. They were expressionless.

"I—I'm afraid not, Reverend. Now that Maxwell's here, I'm afraid I just won't have the time any longer...."

"There's so much to talk about before the wedding," Peterson explained in a companionable, man-to-man sort of way. "We're to be married right after we claim our homesteads, Reverend. Alice, darling," he added, as if a thought had just struck him, "we hadn't talked about it, but would you like Reverend Thornton to do the honors? Of course, I'd planned to have Prescott brought out by train—that's our man of the cloth back in New York, you see, Reverend." He grinned. "But really, Alice, if you've become friendly with the parson here…"

"We can talk about it later, Maxwell," Alice murmured, her voice brittle as leaves in November.

"I understand," Elijah managed to say, which was the first lie he'd uttered in a long, long time. He didn't understand at all. He had to get away from here. "Well, I'm sure I'll be seeing you around Boomer Town, Miss Alice. Nice to meet you, Mr. Peterson." And that was the second lie.

Elijah didn't remember walking back to his tent. Somehow he was just there, and Clint was bending over him, worry written plain on his face.

"Elijah, are you sick again? What's wrong?"

"Yeah, you're pale as a whitewashed fence," Gideon agreed. "You're not having one of those relapses Alice was so worried about, are you? Did you find Alice?"

"I'm not sick." *Only sick at heart.* "Yes, I found her." Staring straight ahead of him because he couldn't bear to see their reaction, he told them what he had found when he had returned to Alice's campsite.

Both men shook their heads when he was through.

"I wouldn't have figured her for a woman like that," Clint said.

"Me neither. Not at all," Gideon muttered.

"That makes three of us."

Silence hung in the air. He wished they'd stop staring at him as if he was a stick of dynamite about to explode.

Finally Gideon said, "I think I'll go over to Mrs.

Murphy's and see if she'll make up some plates of whatever she's serving for supper and send them with me."

"Good idea. I'll go with you, Gideon," Clint said, a little too quickly. "Help you carry things. We'll be right back, Lije."

Just like that, Elijah was by himself. He was thankful that his brothers were savvy enough to see that he needed to be alone with his misery.

How could he have let himself lose sight of his calling so far as to fall in love with Alice Hawthorne, a woman he'd met just two weeks before, a woman he'd never really known at all, apparently? From the devoted way she'd nursed the sick and tended the wounded, he'd convinced himself Alice could be content with the simple life as a preacher's wife, but evidently, it had all been an act. Just something to pass the time until she saw if she could bring her rich beau to heel. She'd certainly fooled him.

What if he'd married her, and then Peterson had shown up? After looking into those lifeless eyes of hers, he had no doubt Alice would have left him without a qualm.

He remembered the day of Marybelle's funeral. Mercifully he hadn't had to conduct the service; another preacher in the same town had done it. He'd walked away from her grave that day and vowed never to fall in love again and open himself up to such hurt. Serving the Lord and His church would be enough for him. Well, heartbreak was the least of what he deserved for forgetting a promise to God.

Chapter Eighteen

"Horst, the Chateaubriand was superb. You're a master at Béarnaise sauce," Maxwell praised, and the little Bavarian man beamed.

How Horst had obtained the prime cuts of beef in the middle of Oklahoma, much less made Béarnaise sauce, Alice didn't know, but she had no appetite.

"Alice, dear, you're just picking at your food," Maxwell chided. "Even if you aren't going to have to race with the rabble this coming Monday, you're going to need your strength as we start our wedded life together."

Remarks such as that made her feel as if he was playing with her like a cat played with a mouse. Didn't he notice that she'd expressed no enthusiasm whatsoever at the prospect of marrying him? Or did nothing matter but what he wanted?

Elijah, why was I such a fool?

There could not be two more different men than Elijah Thornton and Maxwell Peterson, she mused. One, kind and selfless, honorable, serving the Lord; the other only out for himself. If she married Maxwell, he'd treat her as just another possession—a prized possession, maybe, but a possession nonetheless.

"Alice..." Maxwell prompted, and she realized she hadn't answered him.

"I'm not that hungry, Maxwell." She motioned for Horst to take her plate away. Maxwell had played cat-with-a-mouse with Elijah, too, when he'd suggested Elijah officiate at their wedding. That had been so cruel of him. The pain in Elijah's eyes would haunt her dreams.

"Perhaps you would like dessert, raspberries and blackberries with fresh cream, Miss Hawthorne?" Horst asked, seemingly oblivious to the tension inside the pavilion, as Maxwell persisted in calling it.

"All right."

"Yes, it's the beginning of a whole new life for us, come Monday," Maxwell said with satisfaction.

Alice wasn't convinced Maxwell and she were going to be allowed to waltz across the borderline at dawn on the day of the Land Rush, no matter how much money he had or who owed him favors. The army officers so far had been incorruptible, from all reports. Even if they were susceptible to a bribe, they wouldn't want to face the outcry that would arise if they were seen granting early entry to homesteaders.

Maxwell would find out one way or the other sooner or later, Alice supposed. She wouldn't be surprised if his high-handed manner got him placed under arrest until the run was over. That might be a way for her to evade him—if he didn't somehow manage to pull her into trouble with him. But maybe she could throw herself on the mercy of the army and rely on them to save her from Maxwell....

She was desperate to find a way to speak with Elijah alone—if only to apologize for Maxwell's cruel taunt, if nothing else. Even if she didn't dare confess her true feelings for him, she couldn't leave him with the thought that she approved of what Maxwell had said.

"Darling, you're very quiet," Maxwell murmured silkily. "If I didn't know better, I'd think you were unhappy."

Something in the cold watchfulness of his eyes roused her from her daydreams of escaping him.

"I'm just tired, Maxwell." She tried to smile. "That was a long ride we went for, wasn't it? It was so warm..."

"Well, you chose this hot place," he muttered, his face sulky. "It's only April, and it's already hot as blue blazes. We could have stayed in New York, where we could summer at the shore or in the Adirondacks, but, no..."

"I'm sorry, Maxwell. I'll be more chipper tomorrow, I promise." But how on earth would she get through tomorrow and the next day and the next—and the rest of her life?

He laid a hand on her wrist. "That's my good girl. I wouldn't want to have to tell your mother you've become melancholy."

There it was, the threat implicit in the velvet words. "Good night, Maxwell. I think I just need a little sleep."

"I suppose you've just learned to keep country hours," he mocked. "Up with the sun, early to bed.

That won't do in the future when we're the social leaders of Oklahoma, you know." He turned to his servant. "Horst, walk Miss Hawthorne to her tent, and stay outside it for a while in case she needs anything."

Alice only just managed not to scream at Maxwell—or to beg for Horst's help after they left the tent. Horst was Maxwell's creature, through and through, and like the army, incorruptible.

"Brother, you look like something the cat drug in after dragging it through a bramble patch," Gideon commented the next morning when Elijah sat up and threw his legs over the side of his cot.

"You're awfully ready with the colorful comparisons these days," Elijah growled, rubbing his jaw wearily. "Maybe you should be a writer rather than a rancher."

Gideon rolled his eyes, grinning. "Not hardly. But seriously, Lije, did you get any sleep? I heard you tossing and turning half the night."

Clint chimed in with his agreement.

"Some. Sorry if I disturbed you both." He'd wrestled with what he should do about Alice until the wee hours, and he was still undecided. But one thing was clear. He had to speak to her again and give her the chance to tell him if what Peterson was saying was true—that they'd been sweethearts who'd had a quarrel but had mended their differences. The Alice Hawthorne who'd faced him yesterday had been so different from the Alice he'd known these past two weeks that he could almost believe she'd been drugged—or threatened.

Yesterday, when he'd come upon them, Alice

hadn't glowed with happiness, as a woman reunited with her love should be. Could this rich New Yorker have some dark hold over her?

If he went to see her early—as soon as he could dress and down some coffee—might he be able to speak to her alone? Or would he find them together, in circumstances that would proclaim her a different sort of woman altogether than what he'd thought she was?

Either way, his stubborn heart compelled him to make the effort. He had to know, to intervene if she was with Maxwell Peterson against her will.

Lord, help me learn the truth.

Then the scriptural promise echoed in his heart. *And ye shall know the truth, and the truth shall make you free.*

Elijah found Alice sitting on a camp chair in front of her tent, sipping from a cup of tea. Peterson was nowhere in sight, but the short, dark-haired servant who'd been hovering yesterday stood between her tent and the New Yorker's absurdly fancy one, present if she wished anything but unobtrusive. And ready to summon his master if Alice tried to go anywhere alone, he surmised.

She was dressed—not in the simple, pretty calico dresses he'd always seen her in, but in a fussy creation with an overskirt caught back on the sides with ribbons and an abundance of lace trim and flounces. There were ribbon bows on her shoulders, too. Was this how Peterson liked her to dress? The Alice he knew would have shunned this dress as pretty but impractical in this setting.

As had happened yesterday, she didn't see Elijah at

first, for she was staring into her cup, her eyes unfocused, her slender shoulders slumped as if they held the weight of the world.

"Miss Alice, may I speak to you?" he said softly.

Her head jerked up. "Elijah," she whispered, and then he saw her dart a glance over her shoulder at the servant behind her.

Sure enough, the servant was already turning on his heel and heading into the big tent. Elijah would have to talk fast, he knew.

When Alice turned back to him, her face was stricken, and her blue eyes had the look of a hunted creature.

"Alice, you don't look happy," he said quickly. "Tell me the truth. Is this—is *he*—what you want? Just say the word, and I'll help you, no matter what he tries to do."

"Elijah, I— You can't be here," she said in an urgent, hushed voice. "Go away, before—"

He bent low, so he could speak as softly as she had. "Before what, Alice? Is he intimidating you in some way? Hurting you? I won't let him. Alice—"

She closed her eyes as the sound of footsteps rapidly approaching behind her reached both their ears.

Elijah already knew what he would see when he looked up—Maxwell Peterson bustling toward them, straightening his vest.

"Ah, Reverend Thornton, good morning to you. Is there something I can help you with? A donation for your good works, perhaps?"

Elijah straightened. "No," he said evenly. "I—I wanted to ask Miss Hawthorne to invite you to our daily prayer service in the chapel," he said, thinking fast. "She's been a regular attendee, and I thought perhaps she'd like to introduce you to the friends she's made there. Since you're here, I just want to say you'd be very welcome. We meet at ten o'clock. Miss Hawthorne can show you the way."

Peterson *would* be welcome if he wanted to attend, Elijah resolved. He could resign himself to Alice's being with the fellow if he thought she was happy with a godly man, even if he wasn't the sort of man he thought Alice should have picked. But he doubted Maxwell had darkened the door of a church in years, if ever.

A glance at Alice revealed her face had become the same unreadable mask it had been yesterday, and his heart sank.

Peterson's face hardened. "Prayer service?" he echoed, in the same tone one might use to refer to a grown woman making mud pies. "I think not."

His supercilious tone had Elijah stiffening, and struggling not to clench his fists and plant one of them squarely in the New Yorker's face. *Lord, help me control myself, for Alice's sake.*

"Parson, you've no need to concern yourself with my fiancée anymore," Peterson went on. "I appreciate you and your congregation befriending her when she arrived alone in this place, but I'm here now, and I'll look after her from this point on. Miss Hawthorne is a naturally friendly person—friendly to a fault, in fact—and not one to put on airs, but you have to realize the kind of folk that need the crutch of prayer meetings are not the sort of society she's become accustomed to. I'm going to have to ask you not to bother her again." Even while his tone stayed courteous but condescending, his eyes glared at Elijah.

"It's not my intention to offend you, Mr. Maxwell," Elijah said, keeping his eyes on the New Yorker, "or impose myself where I'm not wanted, but I'm afraid I need to hear it from Miss Hawthorne herself. She's been such a vital part of our congregation, you see." He turned his gaze to Alice. "Miss Hawthorne?"

Please, Alice, his soul cried within him. *Let me help you.* He waited for endless seconds, willing her to find the courage, despite the way Peterson's intense gaze burned a hole in her back.

She took a deep breath. "I'm sorry, Reverend, but it's as Maxwell says. I—I'll be spending my time with him from now on. Please understand—and give my best regards to the congregation. They were indeed very kind to me."

Elijah thought for a moment he spotted a split-second pleading look and the gleam of tears in her eyes when she'd said, "Please understand," but it might have been a trick of the light.

"I'll do that," Elijah managed to say. "Good day, Miss Hawthorne, Mr. Peterson." But he couldn't will his feet to move from the spot, not yet.

Peterson shifted his gaze to Alice, with the air of a man who'd put a troublesome task behind him. "Darling, if we're to make that meeting with the colonel I've set up, you'll have to hurry and change into your riding habit. Horst, please see that the horses are saddled."

The Bavarian bowed. "*Jawohl, mein Herr.* Right away."

Elijah found the strength to walk away then. There

was nothing else he could do. But even as his heart broke for what might have been, he couldn't help wondering what Peterson had meant by "a meeting with the colonel." What was the man up to?

Alice watched him go, wishing the ground might open up beneath her and swallow her. She would have rather died than send Elijah away with a hurtful lie as she had. But she'd done what she had to do, knowing she might well be saving Elijah's life.

She was under no illusions as to why Maxwell was taking her with him when he went to see the army officer. He knew he didn't dare leave her here alone that long, even with Horst to guard her. Maxwell held the Bavarian's allegiance, but Horst was only a little taller than Alice herself and slightly built. He could tie her up and gag her, but she would scream bloody murder before she let that happen. And while Maxwell was gone, if anyone demanded to see her, it would declare his assertions to Elijah this morning nothing but lies.

There had to be a way to escape the destiny Maxwell had in mind for her, a way that would not endanger any of the people she loved. *Lord, show me the way.*

"Elijah, Winona asked you a question," Lars prompted Thursday afternoon during the daily session in which he helped the preacher teach English to Winona and Dakota.

Elijah realized he'd been inattentive again, his mind wandering off on rabbit trails when he should be encouraging Winona. The Cheyenne woman had made amazing progress in the short time they had been working with her, as had her nephew.

If only he could stop thinking of how he could help Alice. Elijah had seen the pain in her eyes yesterday morning when he'd gone to see her, before that blank indifference had descended over her lovely features.

Stop it. Pull yourself together and pay attention to what you're doing now. Winona and Dakota deserve better than this.

"I'm sorry, Winona. I didn't mean to be woolgathering. What was your question?"

Winona looked around her in confusion. "I see no sheep," she said slowly. "What means this 'wool-gathering'?"

"Me, I see no sheep, too," Dakota chimed in, his brow furrowed.

Her question made Elijah chuckle in spite of the sadness that sucked at his soul. "It's a saying that means being distracted," he explained. "Lars said you had a question?"

Dakota had lost interest in the conversation. He had brought the kitten from the Gilberts' campsite with him and now was dangling a strip of rawhide along the floor, giggling as the kitten chased it.

"Yes—this word in the Bible verse, 'For God so loved the world, He gave His only begotten Son.' What is *begotten?*"

"It means God is the father of Jesus," Elijah said.

She considered that. "The Great Spirit had a Son?"

Elijah nodded. "Do you know the rest of the verse?"

"That whoever believes in Him has life that lasts forever."

"Very good, Winona." It wasn't word-perfect, but she'd gotten to the heart of the matter. Had this truth reached her heart?

"A believer in Jesus will never die?" Now she looked completely skeptical. "But even the Black Robe who visit our village long ago died. He was old."

"We will die when it is our time, Winona. But our souls—that central part of us that is our spirits—will go to live with God in Heaven forever."

She thought about that. "How you know?"

Even with her limited English, Winona managed to ask some complex theological questions.

"I have faith, Winona. I believe." He spread his palm over his heart. "I believe inside me it is true."

She laid a hand over her own heart. "I do not have this 'believe' inside me. But I listen and think about it."

"That's very good, Winona. Your English is improving very rapidly."

She smiled. "Thank you, Reverend Elijah," she said in her careful way. "I make long talk soon, yes?"

"I'm sure of it." It felt good to lay aside his sadness for a time and concentrate on someone else's needs. "Now, Dakota," he said, determined to draw the boy back into the lesson, "what can you tell me about the cat—in English?" He pointed at the kitten, which had just pounced on the rawhide strip.

Dakota looked puzzled and looked to Lars, who translated Elijah's question.

"The...kitty...play—plays—and jumps. The kitty... gray stripes—*has* gray stripes," he said, then grinned. "It is good, my words, yes, Preechah 'Lijah?"

"Yes. I think we've done enough for today," Elijah

said, knowing that the boy, if not Winona, was getting restless. "Will both of you practice your letters? We will work on them tomorrow."

"We will do this," Winona said and rose gracefully, motioning to the boy. Then she looked back at Lars.

"I will see you both later, Winona," he said. "Maybe I can help you work on your letters."

Lars waited until Winona and Dakota were gone, then turned to Elijah.

"There is great heaviness on your mind, *ja?*"

"Yes." There was no arguing with those perceptive blue eyes. Elijah prayed the Dane would leave it at that, but he knew there wasn't really a chance of that happening.

"Miss Alice has not come to chapel for—" Lars counted on his fingers "—three days. And I have seen her with a strange man in city clothes riding out of Boomer Town."

"Did my brothers put you up to this?" Elijah asked, fighting irritation. Gideon and Clint had been tiptoeing around him as if he was a porcupine rolled up the wrong way. Had they shared their worries with Lars?

"*Ikke.* No. You don't truly believe your brothers talk about your private matters?" Lars's tone was gently disapproving. "But I have eyes, Elijah. I can see you are sad, and I see this man unknown to me with Miss Alice, and I—what is that saying?—I put two and two together. Who is this man, Elijah? Why does Miss Alice not come to chapel?"

Elijah sighed. He wondered about the wisdom of sharing his concerns about Alice and her supposed fiancé, but perhaps it was best to tell the truth. If Lars had seen Alice with Peterson, chances were others had, too. The truth might be better than the rumors that could start.

"It's like this, Lars..." he began, and the story came pouring out.

Chapter Nineteen

Lars was thoughtful after Elijah finished his recital of what had happened with Alice.

"Do you think if I sent my sister to speak to her, this Peterson fellow would allow it?" Lars suggested. "Surely no man could refuse my sweet, innocent sister the chance to speak with her friend?"

It meant a lot to Elijah that Lars thought Katrine would be willing to risk the rudeness that the New Yorker might offer her.

"I don't think Peterson would risk letting Katrine speak to her alone," he said.

"Then what should we do, Elijah? Call a meeting of the church to pray for her?"

Elijah rubbed his chin. "I don't know, Lars. It's risky," he said. "If this got back to Alice and she *wants* to be with Maxwell Peterson for whatever reason, she might be offended. And we've had a lot of new folks come in the last few days, folks I haven't had a chance to get to know very well yet."

And that's your own fault, he accused himself. *You've been mooning about Alice and not tending*

to your calling, the shepherding of souls. No more!
He'd make some pastoral visits this very afternoon
and try to get better acquainted with some of the more
recent attenders.

Or was it pride speaking? Was he merely unwilling to show his weakness, his humanness, to his entire church, when they looked to him for guidance?
Pride goeth before a fall...

Lord, show me what to do.

Lars was studying him, waiting for him to come
up with an alternate suggestion.

"What about if we had a prayer meeting later tonight at the Gilberts', after Dakota has gone to sleep?"
Elijah said. "You, me, Katrine, Keith and Cassie Gilbert? Winona can attend if she wants, of course—it
might be well for her to see how Christians rely on
prayer to solve a problem," he said.

"*Ja,* that is a very good idea," Lars said, brighten-
ing. "I will let them know."

Elijah only wished that he could count on Gideon
and Clint to be part of that number. He knew they
wished him well, of course. But if his brothers didn't
believe that the Lord cared about His people, why
would they think that group prayer would accom-
plish anything?

Alice watched Maxwell warily as Horst prepared
another gourmet meal. He'd been in a foul mood ever
since they'd left the office of Colonel Amboys.

She hadn't told Maxwell about her other expedition
to speak to an army officer, and in any case, there was
no reason for her to think that they would be speak-

ing to the same officers she and Elijah had spoken to when they were inquiring about Dakota's father.

But they were directed to the same guard station to the same Major Bliss who had forwarded Elijah and her to Colonel Amboys, and sure enough, he referred Maxwell to Colonel Amboys again. Bliss looked hard at Alice before giving them directions, but Alice wasn't sure if he recognized her or not. In fancier clothing, she knew she looked vastly different.

Colonel Amboys definitely did remember her, however, and that fact was helping to fuel Maxwell's temper now. Maxwell had introduced himself, and was about to present Alice when the colonel interrupted him.

"Miss Hawthorne and I have met," he said. "Nice to see you again, ma'am."

Maxwell's eyebrows had risen nearly to his hairline. "Oh? And how did you happen to meet my fiancée?" he asked.

Colonel Amboys narrowed his gaze at Maxwell, clearly disliking the other man's high-handed tone. "Miss Hawthorne and Reverend Thornton were making inquiries about a certain officer in the army, on behalf of his son," the colonel said stiffly. "Now if you would state your business, Mr. Peterson?"

Just as Alice thought, the colonel had indeed scorned Maxwell's suggestion that any officer of the U.S. Army had promised Maxwell early entry into the Unassigned Territories, even when Maxwell waved a letter purporting to be from the officer who'd made the promise.

"I'll take that," Colonel Amboys said, neatly snatching the letter by one corner. "Army headquarters will be interested to learn that one of our officers feels free to grant such…favors."

But Maxwell hadn't smelled defeat yet. "Colonel, we're reasonable men," he said, reaching into his pocket and pulling out a roll of bills. "I never meant that you wouldn't *benefit* from helping me and my lady," he said, with a meaningful glance toward Alice.

Colonel Amboys's face went purple. "You'd try to *bribe* an officer in the United States Army? Listen, you self-important windbag! The only reason I'm not clapping you in irons is the presence of Miss Hawthorne—though I also deplore her unfortunate choice of friends, in this instance," he added, aiming a sour glance at Alice herself. "Now get out of here and take your chances with the rest at noon on the twenty-second if you want—though I think Oklahoma would be better off if you never lived there."

Now, hours later, Maxwell hadn't gotten over his humiliation in front of her, and that made him dangerous, Alice thought. It was probably in her best interest to say as little as possible until Maxwell's temper cooled.

He'd been this way since they were growing up together in the same farming community in upstate New York. He had tried to court her, but she had always kept him at arm's length, liking neither his possessive attitude nor the rudeness and disdain with which he treated others.

"The gall of the fellow, to suggest I should have to run with the rabble, as if I were one of them," Maxwell muttered now.

Alice didn't know what to say to that, but Horst, hovering nearby as always, did. "If I might take the liberty to point something out, *mein Herr?* Your horses are vastly superior to any the rabble are likely to have. You will leave them all in the dust."

"True," Maxwell said, grudgingly mollified. Horst set their meals in front of them then, and Alice hoped that, with his hunger satisfied, Maxwell would mellow. And he might have, if he had not drunk so deeply of the wine. She had refused it, as always.

"Don't think I've forgotten that you lied when you left me in New York, Alice," Maxwell said suddenly. "You told me that you were just going home to settle your affairs, and then you vanished. I finally had to track you down in Oklahoma."

"But, Maxwell, if I'd told you where I was going it would have spoiled the surprise, remember?" she said, hoping to appease him with his own words.

"Well, you shouldn't have worried me like that," he groused. "We could have planned it together—or better yet, I might've talked you out of such a harebrained scheme."

"It'll be all right after next Monday, you'll see," she said. "As Horst said, you have the best horses. We're bound to get excellent homesteads." *Dear Heavens, am I in for a lifetime of this pacifying?*

For a moment, she thought her words had satisfied him, but in a lightning change of subject, he snarled, "So before I came, you'd been out gallivanting with that Bible-thumping parson, according to that pompous fool of a colonel."

Lord, give me the right words to calm him. Don't let me somehow say something that endangers Elijah.

"The preacher and I were making an official inquiry," she said with a calmness she didn't feel, "on behalf of a boy named Dakota, who had shown up here looking for his father, a captain in the army. We were trying to assist—"

"'Dakota?' What kind of outlandish name is that for a boy?"

"Dakota's half Cheyenne," she explained, knowing that would only make things worse.

"So you were out traipsing around on behalf of some half-breed kid, some captain's by-blow with a squaw? How cozy."

In spite of her resolve to soothe him rather than exacerbate the situation, Alice felt her own anger kindling at his unfair insinuations and his cruel words about Dakota.

"We weren't *traipsing,* and Dakota is a nice boy who doesn't deserve to be called such names—"

She never saw the slap coming.

"I won't have my future wife compromising her reputation by going off alone with any man, reverend or not!" he roared, as she cringed on her chair.

All at once Horst was there, interposing himself smoothly between them, facing Maxwell as if he was the same size as his employer and had done this before.

"Go to your tent, Miss Hawthorne," he said without turning around. "I will handle this. He won't even remember it in the morning."

"Yes, I will!" Maxwell shouted, his face infused with blood, his eyes red as a stampeding bull's. "Don't think I can't send word to New York and make your mother pay the price!"

Alice fled.

"Lord, help us to remember that where two or three are gathered in Your name, there are You in the midst of them," Keith Gilbert prayed to begin their meeting.

"You have said also that if we agree here on earth on something within Your will, it will happen."

"Amen," Elijah murmured.

They were gathered in a circle around the Gilberts' campfire—Keith, Lars and Elijah sitting on hay bales; Cassie and Winona on camp chairs. Dakota had gone to sleep an hour ago in the wagon.

"Reverend, Lars told us you had a weighty matter bothering you, and you needed prayer, but he said you would explain," his deacon prompted.

As concisely as possible, Elijah explained about Maxwell Peterson, and how the man had caused Alice to stop coming to the chapel or making calls on the sick with him.

"Now, if this man is her choice and Alice truly wants to absent herself from us, I can accept that," Elijah concluded several minutes later. "But she didn't look happy, and I can't help feeling like this man has some hold over her somehow, and it's not right that she be forced into a situation against her will."

"That's awful. That sweet girl," Cassie murmured.

"I agree. Something isn't right here, Reverend. We have to think of a way to help her."

"But how can we do this, if this man will not allow anyone to speak to her?" Katrine asked. "Such things should not happen in this free country, America."

"The reverend's heart is wounded, too," Winona said. "You care much for Alice Hawthorne, yes? I see it in your eyes, Reverend Elijah."

Elijah blinked. He had made no mention of how Alice's apparent rejection had hurt him personally. Was it so obvious that even a relative newcomer from another culture could see it? Looking around the circle, he saw heads nodding in agreement at the Cheyenne woman's words. They all knew it.

"I'd begun to believe that Alice might come to care for me as I do for her," Elijah said carefully. "But I've gone back to believing that the Lord means for me to be single to serve Him. And how I feel isn't important, anyway. I just want to make sure Alice isn't being compelled to do something she doesn't want to do."

No one looked convinced at his assertion about his own lack of a stake in this, especially not the women.

"Reverend, why don't you bring it up for prayer at chapel tomorrow?"

As he had with Lars, Elijah told them why he hesitated to do that, because of the possible repercussions.

Keith rubbed a hand over his balding head. "Seems to me you could ask for prayer for a situation, saying that the Lord knows all about it, but it's a private matter that you don't feel free to divulge—something like that."

Elijah stared at his deacon. That could work. God knew what they needed before they asked for it in any case, and he could gain the prayers of everyone without revealing details that weren't his to reveal.

"All right, I'll do that," he said. "Thanks, Deacon."

"Tomorrow bein' Friday, it's the last regular prayer meeting, you know, before the big day," Cassie observed. "There'll be just one more service on Sunday, and the next day will be the Land Rush."

It was a startling thought.

"So the time is short," Keith said. "But we can spend the next few days praying and trusting God for a solution."

* * *

Alice lay on her cot, staring into the darkness. Her cheek still stung, and when she had looked in her hand mirror, she could see the red imprint of it. By tomorrow's light there might very well be a bruise there.

She had seen abused women before at Bellevue. They had crept into the dispensary where the poor were treated, casting furtive glances behind them, their faces full of shame and decorated with black eyes, split-open cheeks and worse. Some had whispered about liquored-up spouses, out-of-work husbands taking out their frustrations on their wives, men insisting their women knew where the last coins were hidden so they could go gambling. Some women even insisted the beatings were their own fault for arguing.

Was she about to become one of those women? Horst had saved her tonight, but he couldn't be with them at all times, and Maxwell was his employer. He couldn't intervene in every situation.

No, she couldn't live like this. She had to run!

But she could hear Maxwell's last words before she'd run from the tent, mocking her desire to escape. *Don't think I can't send word to New York and make your mother pay the price.*

She could see no way out of the situation, no solution but to stay with Maxwell and marry him after the Land Rush. She would remain until she heard of her mother's death, and then she would find a way to disappear so completely that he'd never find her.

Chapter Twenty

The response to Elijah's request for prayer for "a matter known to the Lord" was everything he could have hoped for. Every one of his long-term attendees came up to assure him that they'd be praying and most of the newer ones, too.

"You've been praying for us and our dreams, Reverend," Cordelia Ferguson said, pumping his hand fervently. "The least we can do is pray for you."

"Well, it's not for me exactly," Elijah told her carefully, "but thank you. I know your prayers will be heard."

He couldn't help but hear her sister, Carrie's, overloud whisper as the two siblings walked away, though. "*I* think it's a matter of the heart, don't you? Think it has something to do with Miss Alice no longer coming to chapel?"

He winced inwardly and fretted over his transparency all the way to his campsite. There he found his brothers checking saddle cinches for signs of wear, part of their preparations for Monday. It could be fatal to have a cinch break as one of them was galloping along in the midst of other racing horses and careering wagons. He'd be thrown down into the path of the stampede.

"Find any problems?" Elijah asked Gideon when he saw his brother set aside his saddle.

"No, it should get you there all right," Gideon said. "Your bay's legs and hooves are fine, too, no problems."

"Appreciate you checking."

Clint looked up from the saddle he was looking over. "Lars was just here. He thought we ought to know what all of you have been praying for."

Even if we're not exactly praying men ourselves was the unspoken finish to that sentence.

"We just wanted you to know we're behind you all the way, brother," Clint added. "If you can think of anything we can do to help Alice, we'll do it."

"We sure will," Gideon put in. "Though I think the simplest solution would be to go over to that Eastern dude's tent, knock the stuffing out of him and tie his ears into a bowknot."

"Don't worry, Lije, we know you wouldn't want us doing that," Clint assured him.

Elijah couldn't help but smile at the image, however. "That's just the trouble," he said. "I want to do exactly that myself and let you two mop up what's left." He was quiet for a moment. "All I need from Alice is the slightest hint that this man isn't what she wants. Any little sign would be enough…"

He decided he'd ride out onto the prairie tomorrow, when there was nothing going on at the chapel, and pray until he couldn't pray anymore. Jesus had always retreated into a solitary place when He'd needed to seek His Father, hadn't He?

Maxwell had been on his best behavior in the past two days since he'd slapped her. He couldn't have been more attentive or more thoughtful. Last night he'd presented her with an engagement ring, an ornate ruby set in a gold band. Alice could barely repress a shudder when he'd slipped it over her finger. To her the stone looked too much like blood.

"Beautiful, isn't it?" he enthused, beaming at her.

"Thank you, Maxwell," she said automatically, glad that he didn't notice she was gazing anywhere but at the jewel.

"If you think that's something, just wait till you see your wedding ring I had commissioned to go with it," he boasted. "Solid gold, wide, engraved on the inside."

With what? she wanted to ask. *Property of Maxwell Peterson?*

She was too well aware, after treating the injuries of scores of abused women, that such sweet behavior didn't presage a permanent change of character. The monster inside Maxwell was still lurking, to return again someday soon.

"So what would you like to do today, my sweet? Shall we go for a ride? Horst found a fellow willing to rent out his surrey and pair—that would be different. Better protection for that lovely peaches-and-cream complexion of yours, eh?"

"I believe it's too hot," she murmured. She'd happened to look out of Maxwell's tent just in time to see Elijah riding past, clearly headed for the prairie.

The last thing she wanted to happen was to run into him out there. Then she thought of something she *did* want to do. Did she dare ask? Was he still contrite enough after hitting her?

"Maxwell, there's something I *would* like to do tomorrow, however," she said.

"Oh? What's that, my dear? You have but to name it," he proclaimed in his grand manner.

"Tomorrow's Sunday, and it's the last service at the chapel. I'd really love to go and see my friends one last time. I'm sure it's not likely I'll ever see them again after the Land Rush on Monday. Come with me, Maxwell," she added, and saw the expansive, genial expression fade.

"No. Anything but that."

She knew he didn't mean "anything" literally. In fact, he wasn't liable to agree to anything now.

"All right," she said, as if it didn't matter. "I think I'll go lie down for a bit. I didn't sleep very well last night."

She knew Horst would be stationed outside her tent "in case she needed anything"—or tried to walk away.

It had been a full day, beginning with the final Sunday chapel service, in which there had been much laughter and not a few tears. Despite Elijah's inner turmoil about Alice, he'd kept the sermon light, encouraging and brief, and had ended it with an invitation for anyone who wished to help him and his brothers found a new town and a new church to head for the south bank of the Cimarron near a boulder that jutted out of the river. Whether they ultimately settled there or elsewhere, he thanked the entire congregation for their support and fellowship.

In his benediction, Elijah blessed them, praying for safety on the morrow during the Land Rush, and prosperity and happiness to all those who would become new homesteaders in the former Unassigned Territories.

After the service, the men of the congregation—joined by Gideon and Clint—took down the big tent that had served as the walls and roof for this body of faithful Christians and folded it up. It would be packed away on the Thornton brothers' wagon, to serve as the temporary new church until one could be built. While the men worked, the women readied a potluck lunch, and the children played.

Before the meal, they gathered in a circle over the bare patch of earth that had been the floor of their chapel and joined hands while Elijah said grace.

Elijah had just said "Amen" when Cordelia Ferguson spoke up. "Reverend, you didn't mention it in the service, but did you get an answer yet to that matter we prayed about?"

"Not yet, Sister Cordelia," he had to admit. "I spent several hours yesterday sitting amid the tall grass of the prairie, praying about that very same matter and listening for the Lord's voice. I don't have an answer yet, but I will tell you He sent His peace flooding over my heart."

"That's good, Reverend," her sister, Carrie, piped up, "but I don't s'pose it would hurt any to pray about it once more, while we're all still in a prayer circle."

Gratitude and other churning emotions made his throat feel thick and his eyes sting with unshed tears.

"I think that would be fine, Sister Carrie. Why don't you start the prayer? And anyone who feels led can join in." He didn't trust his voice not to break.

When would the Lord answer his pleas regarding Alice? he wondered as Carrie began to pray. As he'd said, he had felt the Lord's peace yesterday, yes, but was it a peace that came in spite of painful circumstances or the peace that heralded the promise of an answer? Answers always came, he knew, but sometimes the answer was "No" and sometimes "Not yet."

Lord, please give me patience while I wait on Your perfect timing.

While folks picnicked, they talked of the homes they planned to build. Some would erect temporary "soddies"—small dwellings built out of blocks of sod cut from the prairie—to be lived in until a more permanent frame or log cabin could be built; others would continue to live in tents and start building their houses right away. Those who planned to farm rather than dwell in the new town and start businesses had the added need to quickly plow up the sod on part of their 160 acres and start crops. They were getting a late start, so they had to plant crops that would grow quickly and provide food for themselves and their livestock through the first winter.

Elijah knew the new church would be started only when its members had built their own dwellings, so services were likely to be held under the tent for quite a while. Fortunately, however, Oklahoma had later and usually milder winters than many of those who had come to settle it were used to.

Those with big families had a distinct advantage in building their homes and "sodding off" their land to plant crops, but those who weren't married or were just starting their families promised to pitch in and help each other. Farming veterans freely offered to advise those who were new at it. Cane and sorghum were the crops to plant, they said, as well as a kitchen garden to feed the family, of course.

"You're planning to farm and raise livestock, too, aren't you, Lars?" Elijah asked the big Dane, who was sitting next to him. "Near us, if it's possible?"

"*Ja,* of course. And someday I hope to have a wife and children to help. Meanwhile, I am glad my sister is with me for now."

"And Katrine? What are her plans?" Elijah inquired. He couldn't picture the beautiful Katrine living with her brother and his family forever.

Lars shrugged. "She has not said. But of course I would wish for her that she finds a good man and has a blessed, happy life with him and the children they will have. But my sister's husband must be a godly man, *ja?* It is something we both value."

Elijah nodded. "Yes, the Bible does indicate Christians should marry those of their faith."

Was there a veiled message in Lars's words? Elijah had thought Katrine might suit Clint at one time, but if Clint never returned to faith, it sounded as if there'd be no blessing from Katrine's brother for such a match. What Clint did was up to him. Elijah knew he could only serve as an example.

And where would Alice settle? The question bubbled up in his head like a wellspring. Or would the pushy New Yorker who'd come to claim her talk her into going back East?

He didn't have long to ponder before someone posed another question.

"What will you call this new town, Reverend?" The question came from Winona, who was sitting with the Gilberts nearby, as were Gideon and Clint.

The question took him by surprise. "I confess I hadn't given it any thought, Winona. I guess I figured some name would occur to us when we got there, right, brothers?"

They nodded. Elijah turned back to the Cheyenne woman. "Are you familiar with the area, as Lars is? Do you have any suggestions?" He wouldn't be averse to a Cheyenne place-name, he thought, to reflect the Indian heritage of their part of Oklahoma. The red man had been here long before the white settlers.

She nodded. "Yes, I have been to this place of which Lars speaks. We call it by Cheyenne words that mean 'Brave Rock,' for this boulder stands tall at the edge of the river, never changing, no matter if the river is full with the rains of spring or its level drops in heat of summer."

"Brave Rock," Clint murmured. "I like the sound of that."

Gideon nodded his agreement. "I think we've got a town name, Lije."

Later, when the congregation had dispersed to their campsites to complete their packing and anticipate tomorrow, Clint turned to Elijah. "Feel up to a little more work, Lije? Mrs. Murphy promised us food for our suppers if we helped them take down their tent. *And* one of her ginger cakes. You're not getting over-tired, are you?"

"I think it's been long enough that you can stop

coddling me, with—" He stopped, realizing he'd been about to say, "with Alice's blessing." He'd always assumed Alice would be present during this final day's events, and on the next day when everyone lined up at the border and awaited the noon rifle shot signal.

Alice...

"Sure, if she's offering ginger cake, I'm in," he said. The busier he stayed, the better.

"Is that everything?" Elijah asked, as Clint loaded one more rope-bound parcel inside the wagon that evening after supper.

"Yep, everything we can pack before morning, anyway," Gideon said. "Since the Land Rush isn't starting till noon, we'll have plenty of time to get dressed, have breakfast and strike our tent in the morning."

It sounded like way too much time to kill to Elijah. He wished the rifle shot was to sound at dawn. He felt like a bedspring with a hundred-pound weight on it, anticipating being released to its full height. There was entirely too much time to keep him from impulsively going to Alice and trying once more to get the truth of whether or not she was with Peterson against her will. He still couldn't believe she had actually *chosen* to put herself under his thumb. This was 1889 America, not medieval Europe. Women were not chattel. Why, in Wyoming, they could even vote.

Dusk was rapidly deepening into night. Lantern-light dotted Boomer Town here and there, and the shouts of children at play had ceased.

"Reckon we better turn in early," Gideon muttered,

after throwing the last of his coffee onto the fire. "Going to need a good rest to get through tomorrow."

"I reckon you're right, brother," Clint said. "Coming, Lije?"

"In a minute." Long after his brothers had let the tent flap fall behind them, Elijah stood at the dying campfire, staring as far as he could see at Boomer Town. Many of the tents had already been taken down, especially those that had sheltered businesses. By an order from the army, the whiskey tents had closed by evening—the last thing they wanted to contend with during the run were tempers fueled by liquor. There were bare patches of earth where the mercantile and hardware tents had been, too. Before long the dirt roads would grow grass again and what had been Boomer Town would revert to prairie. There would be no sign that this place had ever been packed with tents, wagons, livestock and hundreds of folks all wanting the same thing—a piece of ground to call their own.

Elijah supposed he should follow his brothers' examples and try to get some shut-eye. But he knew it'd be of no use. After an hour of listening to his brothers' soft snores, he set out on a walk through Boomer Town. For one last time.

Chapter Twenty-One

Alice couldn't sleep.

Everything in the two tents was in readiness for the next day, thanks to Horst's efficient packing, and yet they had eaten a gourmet meal tonight as always— steaks worthy of Delmonico's, roast potatoes, a crisp salad and chocolate cake for dessert. Maxwell had drunk deeply of port wine and retired early, much to her relief. He had remained on his good behavior, but she had learned that when Maxwell imbibed, there was no telling what could set him off.

"Sleep well, Miss Hawthorne," the ever-courteous Horst said after he had escorted her to her tent. "By this time tomorrow night everything will be different, *ja?*"

"Yes…good night, Horst." *Same captivity, different location,* she thought ironically. For tonight, though, Horst would take up his position at her door as always, she supposed. She couldn't imagine when the little Bavarian man ever slept. He was always present, ever ready to serve his master's slightest whim— or hers. He would remain in Boomer Town with the wagon Maxwell had purchased until his master and Alice had staked their claims and sent word as to their location; then he would follow. Alice knew Maxwell wouldn't go back to Horst himself—he wouldn't be willing to leave her and his claim. She wondered idly how he expected to send word. Did he assume the prairie would be thronging with messenger boys, just hoping to take his missive in exchange for a generous tip?

Maxwell had announced they would head due north to where he had heard a town called Guthrie was being planned. It was probably best that she and Maxwell were headed to a different location than the Thorntons. It would surely be torture to see Elijah marry someone else and live happily with another woman, knowing all along she could have been his wife if she had not been so foolish. She knew he had originally said he was going to remain single and devote himself to building his church, but somehow she couldn't picture the handsome preacher forever without a wife, sons and daughters at his side. He was too kind, generous, and, yes, handsome a man to remain a bachelor.

It was airless in this tent. She was never going to get any sleep, especially if she didn't stop thinking about Elijah and wondering how his last services at the tent chapel had gone. Could he be lying in his tent, awake as she was, and wondering what she was doing? Most of her hoped not. She wanted him to be happy, even if that meant being happy without her.

She should think of something else. Would Clint become sheriff of the Thornton brothers' new town? She supposed they might well call the town "Thornton." Whom would Clint marry? How about Gideon? Would he always be content to be alone? She could picture Gideon raising the finest horses and beef cattle in the territory and, later, the state of Oklahoma.

How were Dakota and Winona progressing with their English? How were Lars and Katrine? She'd enjoyed the pretty Danish girl's delicious cooking and pleasant company. Would Mrs. Murphy still make those delicious ginger cakes wherever she built her new café?

What had happened to Cheyenne, the pretty Appaloosa mare Lars had sold to her? Had the Thorntons given the mare back to him, since she would not be riding her tomorrow? The matching liver-colored chestnut saddlebred geldings that Maxwell had brought for both of them to ride wouldn't be nearly as fast as the agile Appaloosa, she thought. Ah, well, it didn't matter to her whether she and Maxwell ended up with claims or not.

She'd gotten another letter from her mother just yesterday. Realizing the temporary post office would be closing at the end of business on Saturday, she'd sent Horst to check one last time for any letters, and there had been one for her with a New York postmark. He'd brought it to her just after she'd finished dressing for dinner.

The seal hadn't been broken, so Horst had either brought it directly to her or Maxell had figured there was no way, with the Land Rush taking place tomorrow, that a letter from her mother could affect the outcome anyway. Alice opened it eagerly, poring over the lines of familiar script until she found these words:

I should tell you Maxwell Peterson was here shortly after you left inquiring as to your whereabouts. I didn't tell him anything, but he said he has ways of finding out. I never did like that man, and I didn't think you did either, my sweet girl, so I hope he's not as smart as he thinks he is.

Alice had chuckled at that. She'd gotten much of her shrewd judgment of people from her mother. She read on.

You'd be better off alone the rest of your life than with that bully. Well, I'll close here and send this off. I'll wait to hear from you once you are settled. Best of luck to you and be well. Know that you are in my prayers, my darling daughter.
Your loving mother

After reading it, Alice removed the globe from the lamp and held the letter up to the flame, then dropped it to the dirt floor of the tent and watched it fade into ashes. She'd have liked to keep the letter to reread later, but she dared not, not with what her mother had said about Maxwell. She didn't trust him not to search her things.

Alice wondered if Maxwell would permit her mother to come and live with them, once they were settled. She longed to see her and didn't want her mother to spend her final years alone, but would it be better or worse with her mother there, witnessing Maxwell's controlling ways and temper?

She sighed, the sound echoing in the empty, dark tent. Fortunately she didn't have to decide anything about the future tonight. She was just borrowing trouble to try to plan so far ahead. She had to survive tomorrow first.

Commit your way unto the Lord, and He shall bring it to pass.

Where had that verse come from? Once Maxwell had come and forbidden her to attend any more chapel services, she'd felt as if she was living in a vacuum, cut apart from fellowship with other Christians.

She couldn't sleep; she might as well take her lamp outside and read from her Bible. Horst wouldn't bother her if he saw that she had just come out to read. Maybe she could find that verse, if she looked hard enough.

Putting on a wrapper, she picked up her Bible, her lantern and a box of matches, and stepped outside.

Horst wasn't there.

For a moment, she couldn't believe her eyes and rubbed them before looking again. There was no figure sitting in his usual camp chair by the entrance flap of her tent, nor was he sitting by the embers of the campfire, nor could she make out his figure hovering between the campfire and Maxwell's pavilion.

Was it a trick? Was the little Bavarian man lurking somewhere in the shadows, ready to sound the alarm if she stepped one foot away from the campsite?

She stepped as close as she dared to the side of her tent in both directions, but no Horst emerged from the shadows. Perhaps Maxwell's servant had decided it was high time *he* got a good night's rest, too. Or maybe Maxwell had told him that there was little chance now of Alice slipping away—not so close to the race.

For one crazy moment, she contemplated sneaking away, stealthily setting first one foot, then the other onto the dirt road that led between the rows of tents and wagons, until she was able to run the rest of the way to the Thorntons' tent.

But no—it was still too late, she reminded herself bitterly. After his second attempt to speak to her, Elijah had made no further attempts. He didn't need her, now that the inhabitants of Boomer Town were about to disperse in myriad different directions tomorrow. She had saved his life, yes, but he'd always said that he had never planned to marry. Perhaps if Maxwell hadn't come, Elijah might have changed his mind, but she had seen the bitter hurt in Elijah's eyes. He'd taken her refusal to stand up for herself as a final no. He didn't need such a spineless woman, and if she went to him now, way past time for a decent woman to be paying a call, she'd only embarrass herself—and put Elijah and his brothers in danger if Maxwell figured out where she'd gone.

Maxwell had shown her the matching pistols he'd brought from New York—pistols he planned to carry during the race tomorrow, he'd confided slyly. She knew he'd think nothing of using them against any man—or woman—who crossed him, then find a way to cover it up. And Maxwell still had a long arm that could reach clear to upstate New York, where her mother lived.

It was better she remain right here and do what she

had planned to do—read her Bible and pray. Prayer was always the best option, wasn't it? And it was her only option.

Elijah hadn't been able to prevent his feet from carrying him to Alice's campsite. He had resolved to walk in every direction around Boomer Town but the one that would take him past the tent in which Alice slept—and the larger tent of Maxwell Peterson. But he'd walked all over the partly dismantled tent city, praying for those he passed, and felt no drowsier than before.

A half-moon shed fitful light over the two tents as he drew near, and— What was that? In the circle of light cast by a lamp, a slight figure stood in a loose-fitting garment tied at the waist, facing the fire that had burned down to a few glowing coals.

As he studied the figure closer, he saw that it was Alice. Her eyes were turned to the starry sky above. Tears silvered her cheeks. Her hands were clasped in prayer.

"Alice?" he called, keeping his tone soft, wanting neither to startle her nor have his voice carry to the big tent behind hers.

"Elijah? Can that possibly be you?" Her face glowed with astonished joy in the reflected light, a joy that reignited hope within him.

Did she care about him after all?

Alice took a step toward him, then stopped. He realized that since he wasn't carrying a lantern, he was swathed in darkness. "Yes, it's me. Alice. Please, what are you crying about? Can I help in any way?"

"Oh, Elijah…I'm so miserable," she said, keeping her voice low, also. "I don't want to marry Maxwell Peterson. I never did."

"You don't have to marry anyone you don't want to," he told her. "We'll see to that. Gideon, Clint and I—the whole community. We'll see that you're not forced into anything against your will."

Her face had taken on a tentative hope, but now she looked anxious and frightened again. "But you don't know what Maxwell Peterson is capable of! I've *seen* what he can do, Elijah! I was afraid for you and your brothers…and my mother, back in New York. He threatened to hurt my mother, Elijah!" She crumpled then, folding at her waist as if she'd taken a blow. Her sobs came in earnest now.

He came forward then and gently raised her to her feet and pulled her into his embrace, patting her back as if she was a disconsolate child.

"Alice, you have to trust God and me and all of us to make sure that doesn't happen. I promise we *won't* let him do this to you. And we'll have the Lord's help. Remember that verse in Romans, *If God is for us, who can be against us?*"

She raised tear-filled eyes to him, eyes lit with the merest spark of hope. But it was enough.

"But what am I to do?" she asked, stepping back from his arms with obvious reluctance. "If I tell him I won't stay with him, I'm afraid of what he'll do, Elijah."

"Let me think a moment…. Give me an hour," he said. "One hour to prepare, and then I'll return and we'll tell Peterson together, all right?" He took both her hands in his. "Trust me, Alice. Trust God, okay?"

"But it's late, Elijah. Everyone is sleeping, getting ready for tomorrow…"

"It doesn't matter, Alice. We'll help you."

"All right, Elijah." Her voice shook, but her gaze was steady. Trusting. "One hour. I'll be waiting."

She took that hour to change her clothing from the wrapper to one of her simplest calico dresses. No matter what happened, she'd never wear those fussy beribboned and flounced dresses Maxwell had brought her ever again.

What would Elijah do? Did he dare stand against all the power that Maxwell Peterson could wield, even if Elijah brought Gideon and Clint with him?

A verse from Proverbs echoed in her head. *Trust in the Lord with all thy heart, and lean not to thine own understanding.*

She sat down on the camp chair by her bed, and prayed harder than she ever had in her whole life.

"Alice?" came a whisper from just beyond the tent flap. It was Elijah. A glance at the watch pinned to the bodice of her dress showed her he'd been as good as his word.

Shaking with mingled fear and hope, she lifted the tent flap and went out into the night. Elijah stood there, the very essence of a preacher in his black frock coat and immaculate white shirt.

"Are you ready?" he asked, nodding his head toward Maxwell's pavilion.

A lantern's glow suddenly lit one end of the big tent, sending a frisson of fear snaking down her spine. She shivered in spite of the determination she felt, the resolve Elijah had given her with his steady voice, earnest gaze and trustworthy manner.

"I'm ready."

Chapter Twenty-Two

Horst was there, silently lifting the tent flap before Alice could even call out. Eyes unreadable, he gestured both of them inside, then left the tent. Tucked under one arm she saw the ornate presentation box that held the matched pistols Maxwell had shown her only hours ago.

Max lumbered out from behind the screen that hid his large camp bed, shoving his arms into a dark red dressing gown with black velvet collar and cuffs. His hair stood out at all angles. His red-rimmed, glaring eyes were still clouded by sleep. "What is the meaning of this?"

It was like facing down a big rabid brown bear. Alice shook in her shoes, more frightened than she had ever been, but she knew Elijah was right behind her, and the Lord was there, too. That knowledge gave her the courage to speak.

"Maxwell, I—I'm sorry," she said in a voice that shook only slightly. "I need to tell you that I don't want to go with you tomorrow. I want to stake my claim alone. I can't marry you."

His forehead furrowed, he stared at her as if she had spoken in Hindustani. "What? What are you saying, Alice? Of course you're going to marry me. Everything is all set. The Land Rush is just hours away. You're wearing my ring, for—" Then he seemed to notice her ring finger was bare. "Where's the ring I gave you, Alice?"

With trembling hands, she took the heavy gold-and-ruby ring out of the pocket of her skirt and held it out to him.

He took it, staring at it as if he wasn't quite sure what it was. He raised disbelieving eyes to Alice; then, when her gaze didn't waver, he seemed to see Elijah behind her for the first time.

His face a mask of fury, he threw the ring into the corner of the tent, where Alice heard it *ping* off the trunk that sat there.

"This is *your* doing!" he roared at Elijah. Then, teeth bared in a snarl, fists clenched, he lunged at Elijah with his head lowered like a charging bull.

Elijah neatly sidestepped his charge, which sent Maxwell crashing into the table that had been set with luxurious china, crystal and silverware only hours ago. While the maddened man picked himself up, Elijah pulled Alice gently out of the tent.

As her eyes readjusted to the darkness, she saw what Elijah had done while he had been absent from her for an hour.

The entire population of Boomer Town appeared to be present. Every settler who had ever attended the chapel, everyone whom she had ever helped with her nursing skills stood there in the darkness, many carrying lanterns. Gideon and Clint, Lars and Katrina,

Winona and Dakota, Keith and Cassie Gilbert stood in the forefront of the throng.

Elijah put a steadying arm around her shoulder.

"See, no one will let any harm come to you, Alice."

Now she began to believe it was true.

Maxwell Peterson stumbled out of the tent. Straightening, he stared at the assembled crowd, then back at Alice and Elijah. He shifted his gaze to Clint as Elijah's brother came forward.

"Maxwell Peterson, I'm Clint Thornton, and as the *de facto* sheriff of this community, and the future sheriff of Brave Rock, Oklahoma Territory, I have to inform you that we take any threats to the community very seriously. No such threats will be tolerated against Miss Alice Hawthorne or anyone else, do you understand?"

"You gonna arrest me, Mr. Lawman-Without-a-Tin-Star?" Maxwell jeered. "Do you even have a jail?"

"Not yet, Peterson, but it'll be one of the first things we build," Clint replied, clearly unfazed by the other man's scorn. "Don't you ever come back to Oklahoma, or you'll be its first resident."

In a motion too smooth for Maxwell to react, Clint reached for a pair of come-alongs from the back of his waistband. Gideon came forward then to help hold Maxwell, along with Elijah, as Clint efficiently bound the New Yorker's arms.

"I demand you release me!" Maxwell bellowed, his face purpling. "Horst! Where are you, you worthless German traitor?"

No short Bavarian man appeared, Alice saw with amusement. She could almost feel sorry for Maxwell.

"You'll be sleeping in your own tent tonight," Clint informed the furious Maxwell. "Whatever sleep you can get with your arms bound, that is. My brother and I will be standing guard," he added, nodding toward Gideon, who met Peterson's gaze unperturbed.

Elijah stepped away from Alice and approached Peterson then. "At first light," he went on, "my brothers and I, and some of the good people you see out there, will be escorting you to the army, who'll see that you get on the first train out of here. You're never going to bother Miss Alice or anyone she knows ever again. I know the army will take a dim view of your threats toward her mother back in New York, too. I'm thinking you'd better forget you ever uttered any such thing, because the army—and the law enforcement officials they will notify—has a longer reach than you do."

As Alice watched, Maxwell seemed to shrink inside himself, seeming to lose inches of height and breadth as his bluster evaporated, leaving him like a deflated balloon. Without any further direction from Clint or Gideon, he turned and shambled back inside his big tent, ignoring the spontaneous cheer that went up from the eyewitnesses to his defeat.

"Thank you, Elijah," Alice said, beaming through tears of joy as the tent flap closed behind Maxwell. "And Gideon and Clint. And all of you," she said, calling to the throng, who couldn't seem to stop cheering.

"Alice, do you want to sleep here?" Elijah said, nodding toward her tent, as the crowd began to scatter to their campsites. "You'll be safe enough, with Clint and Gideon standing guard in the other tent. Or,

if you'd rather not sleep here with Peterson so close
by, you could come down and sleep in the Thornton
tent, and I'll sleep outside under the stars."

Alice doubted she'd sleep tonight. She was too
full of joy and relief. "I'll stay here," she said, indicating her tent, which loomed in the darkness like
an old friend.

Elijah smiled, a smile that sent warmth rocketing
through her like wildfire.

"That's the spirit," he said approvingly. "I'll see
you in the morning, then. Gideon and Clint and
some of those here will escort that scoundrel to the
army and make sure he'll be on that train out of here.
There'll be plenty of time to get ready for the opening
shot, and I'll make sure you can stake your claim."

Having bid Alice good-night, Elijah sighed as he
walked down to the Thornton campsite and lay down
on his cot in the otherwise empty tent.

He had wanted to remain with Alice awhile. Once
they were alone, he would have asked her if, now
that Maxwell Peterson could no longer come between
them, she could ever care for him the way he cared
for her.

But a little voice inside Elijah told him to wait.
Alice was too vulnerable now. Minutes ago, she'd
been saved from a life no woman should have to contemplate. As the one who had first come to her aid,
Elijah had too much of an advantage.

The Land Rush would start in twelve hours. As
he had promised, he would see that she staked her
claim, so that when—*if*—she agreed to his court-

ship, it would be from a position of strength and independence, not need.

The man lying trussed in his big tent had thought to dominate her, impose his bullying will on her in every facet of her life. But Elijah wanted Alice to *choose* him, and if she agreed to be his wife, he would offer her a life of faithful partnership in serving the Lord—he as a preacher, she as a nurse. He would seek her benefit before his own, always. And if she chose him, he would love her all the days of her life.

They would send for her mother to join them, just as soon as the elderly lady chose to journey here from New York. He didn't know if Mrs. Hawthorne would want to live with them or near them, but she was welcome either way. He hoped he and his future mother-in-law would enjoy a close relationship. He and his brothers had lost their mother when Clint had been born, so it had been a lifetime since he had had a mother.

Elijah grew drowsy picturing the sons and daughters he and Alice would have, daughters with her lively dark red hair and sky-blue eyes, sons with his dark hair and hazel eyes. Or maybe vice versa. Would one of them choose to follow in his father's footsteps and become a preacher?

He was getting way ahead of himself, wasn't he? Children and a mother-in-law—when he didn't even know if Alice wanted him in her life. But somehow, on this night before the great Land Rush, life seemed rife with possibilities.

The sun hadn't even fully risen and Alice was getting dressed when she heard the commotion outside.

She opened the tent flap just enough to see out, and was in time to spot Gideon and Clint strong-arming a disheveled-looking Maxwell, his arms bound behind him, out of the big tent and onto a wagon piled high with the trunks that Horst had placed there yesterday. As Elijah had promised, at least a score of those who had stood outside to support her last night stood waiting to help the brothers and escort her former fiancé to the army and the train they would put him on.

"But what about the tent? And where are my matched pair of saddlebreds?" Maxwell roared at Clint. "That's expensive horseflesh, not that *you'd* know it! What about the ruby-and-gold ring? It's somewhere in that tent, I tell you!" His tone turned wheedling as he looked to Gideon. "It's worth a lot of money. Find it and it's yours, if you'll just untie me."

"Thanks, but I can't picture me wearing some lady's ring," she heard Gideon tell him. Alice saw a wry smile curve his lips. "And anyway, Peterson, you know we looked high and low for that bauble last night and didn't find it."

"But it's got to be there!" Peterson whined. "And my pistols—"

"We didn't see any pistols, either," Clint told him. "Now be quiet. It's too early in the morning to be caterwauling like that."

"I have the right to free speech!" shouted Maxwell. He was still ranting when Clint took a clean strip of white cloth—likely part of the monogrammed tablecloth she and Maxwell had dined on last night—and gagged him with it.

Of course they hadn't found the pistols, Alice thought, remembering how she had seen Horst walking away with the box that contained them. She had a notion he'd made off with the ring, too, taking advantage of his employer's confrontation with the Thornton brothers last night to sneak back into the tent and find it.

She wished Horst luck. If he hadn't abandoned his post last night... Had he done it on purpose, tired of Maxwell's tyrannical ways and disapproving of the way his employer treated her? She liked to think so. If he was smart, he'd get away from here on one of the saddlebreds, maybe using the other as a packhorse.

Poor Maxwell, she thought, as they loaded him, willy-nilly, onto his own wagon and drove slowly away. He had been gifted with financial ability and business acumen, but he had wasted his gifts, and spent his time abusing and dominating those he saw as beneath him. She wondered what he'd do the rest of his life. She felt sorry for him but not sorry that Maxwell's life would go on without her. She let the tent flap close and finished braiding her hair into a coil at the back of her head.

When Alice stepped outside, the wagon and its escort were gone. Elijah waited at the campfire, holding a steaming cup of coffee out to her. She spotted a covered skillet sitting on the big, flat stones at the edge of the fire and thought she smelled the delicious odor of bacon.

This would be the very last time she sat and ate food cooked at this campfire, she realized with a start. All around her she heard the sounds of Boomer Town being disassembled—people calling out to each other, horses whinnying as they were readied to carry riders or pull wagons, axles and leather creaking. So many people had already struck their tents that she could see clear down the dirt road now.

"Ready for the big day?" Elijah asked, smiling. "Looks like you've dressed well for it."

She'd donned her divided skirt and the riding boots and the lightest long-sleeved shirt she owned. Her sunbonnet dangled from its strings down her back. She'd need that soon enough—it was going to be a hot one today. Elijah was ready to ride, too. Gone were his ministerial frock coat, black trousers and immaculate white shirt. In their place he wore rough denims, a striped shirt and a bandanna at his neck. His own wide-brimmed hat sat waiting on a hay bale.

"I *hope* I'm ready," she said, taking a seat on a hay bale at his side. "I can't help wishing it was all over already."

"We'll be fine," he said, as if he sensed her nerves. "I'll be riding beside you, remember? The Lord hasn't brought us this far to abandon us now."

Alice smiled, warmed by his encouragement. She couldn't imagine facing this race by herself now, a woman alone, as she had been just three short weeks ago. How naive she had been, to think she needed no one.

She needed this man, she realized, but knew this wasn't the time or the place to say so. Afterward, perhaps, if she saw any hint that the feelings that had been building before Maxwell's arrival could be rebuilt.

He'd cared about her; she knew that as sure as she was sitting here. But perhaps Elijah had thought better of it and would remain the unmarried preacher of the Brave Rock Church. She told herself she would be content with that, as long as she lived near him and could help him serve the people of the town they would all build together.

She straightened her skirts, overly aware of him beside her. By unspoken consent, she noticed they did not speak of Maxwell Peterson. Instead, they focused their thoughts on the Rush.

"As soon as we're done eating, we'll collect the horses and load up your belongings on your wagon and mine, then take them to Katrine," Elijah said. "Got your stake to mark your claim?"

"Already packed in my saddlebag and inscribed with my name," Alice told him. "Will Katrine be all right, guarding everything for your brothers and us, Elijah?" She didn't like the thought of the sweet Danish girl being responsible for so much. There would be others left behind to guard wagons and belongings, she knew. What if someone thought to take advantage of them?

"That's what the Security Patrol is for," he reminded her. Then, as if he read her mind, he added, "I know they haven't accomplished very much in regards to Boomer Town's safety before, but at least Katrine will be armed. Lars tells me that she's not a bad shot. Cassie and Dakota will be staying behind, too—Cassie didn't want the boy in the midst of all that confusion. Winona's going to ride her horse alongside Keith's wagon in case he needs any help."

"That's good," Alice murmured. Mr. Gilbert was no longer young.

"Those who've been left behind with wagons will be sticking together," Elijah went on. "In addition to the Security Patrol, contingents of the army will be patrolling what's left of the tent cities to prevent any mischief."

"We'll owe Katrine a debt of gratitude for being willing to do this," she said, and Elijah nodded his agreement.

"After everyone's staked their claims, Winona will ride back here to guide Katrine and Cassie to the homesteads in their wagons. She'll drive the Thornton wagon. She knows the area thoroughly where Lars is heading."

It sounded as if they'd thought of everything while she was still sitting with Maxwell, trying to tolerate his company. But that was over now.

Her mind shifted to other matters. "I'm glad Winona and Dakota have stayed with us," she mused aloud.

"I am, too," Elijah said. "It will be good to watch the boy grow up. I pray that he and Winona will come to faith soon. I have a feeling Dakota could become quite a warrior for the Lord."

Alice smiled at the image of a grown-up Dakota, preaching the Word. She prayed that Indians like Winona, and those of mixed blood such as Dakota, would be able to live in harmony with their white neighbors. This Oklahoma, with its red clay and ever-blowing wind, should belong to everyone.

By eleven, everyone was milling around near the borderline. The army officials wouldn't let them come forward and arrange themselves along it for another half hour, and the uniformed men had already made it clear that anyone who stepped foot over the line before the rifle shot at noon would be unceremoniously escorted to the back of the crowd and forced to wait till everyone else had taken off. Folks had already lined up just behind that demarcation, however, and had only to move forward when permission to advance was granted at last.

Just visible down the line was a wooden tower on which a trio of soldiers sat. From there would come the rifle shot that would signal the beginning of the run into the new territory.

Gideon and Clint had returned from their expedition, and joined Elijah and Alice at the border. They grinned as they reported that Peterson had still been protesting his fate when they'd turned him over to the army, but Colonel Amboys, who'd assumed custody, was having none of it. He'd put Peterson on the same train the last group of would-be homesteaders had come in on just this morning, so he could be its first passenger on the return trip East. A pair of soldiers had been ordered to make sure their charge made it all the way to the end of the line.

It had been a happy reunion between Alice and her Appaloosa mare when she and Elijah had gone to the corral to collect their mounts. Cheyenne had arched her neck and trotted over to the rail as soon as Alice called her, then lipped the sugar lumps Alice held in an outstretched hand. Cheyenne had stretched her neck across the rail and snuffled Alice's face as if greeting a long-lost friend. Now, saddled and bridled and carrying the bedroll Alice would need tonight, Cheyenne pawed the buffalo grass beneath her hooves as if eager to be galloping over the prairie.

A bugle call pierced the cacophony of neighing horses, braying mules and buzzing conversations.

"All right, move up to the border!" cried an officer. "Everyone's to be orderly—no pushing, no shoving. A wagon has just as much right to the front of the line as anyone on horseback. But those of you on foot and on those confounded bicycles—and I've got to say I think you're all insane—would be smart to let the horses and wagons take off first. A wagon driver or a rider might not see you for all the dust, and you'd get trampled."

A cloud of red dust rose above the shouts of those driving wagons. Elijah was glad that Alice was staying close. Gideon and Clint were on his other side, and Lars just beyond them. At Lars's other side was Keith, driving his wagon, with Winona riding alongside it. Farther down the line, Elijah could see Molly Murphy and Sean in their wagon, and the two Ferguson sisters, driving a buckboard.

Far down the line in the other direction, he thought he spotted a rider who looked like Theo Chaucer. There was another rider with him who might have been Theo's brother Brett, but he hadn't turned his head in Elijah's direction, so he couldn't be sure. There was a third rider just beyond him, but Elijah didn't recognize him. A wagon sat beside the third rider, with a man and woman sitting on the driver's perch. The woman held a small child in her arms. The man might be Reid, the third Chaucer brother, but he couldn't see the woman well. He remembered Reid had a twin, Evelyn—was she here with her brothers?

He saw that Clint had raised a spyglass and was looking in their direction, too. "Yeah, it's the Chaucers. Of all the luck. We can't get away from them even today of all days."

"It's not likely they'll head in the same direction we do," Gideon said, before Elijah could. "I don't reckon we'll ever need to see them again."

"Everyone who's planning to go with us to Brave Rock, listen to me," Lars called out then. "Try to stick with me. I'll be heading northwest from where we are now. The spot I told you about, where Brave Rock sticks out in the Cimarron River, is just about thirty-one miles from here as the crow flies—but of course, we are not riding flying crows."

They all chuckled.

"So stay with me if at all possible. I know the best, easiest ground to travel."

Gideon spoke up then. "We'll all set out at a gallop, of course, but after that we need to pace our horses. They'll tire fast if we try to run them the whole way. So slow your horses when I slow mine, and take advantage of streams we pass to let them drink. With any luck, they'll all last the distance without injury. It'll probably take us till sometime in the afternoon to get there."

It was a long speech for Gideon to make, Elijah thought, but who better to make it? He was the expert horseman, after all.

"I would like to pray for us all," Elijah said, and everyone—even Gideon and Clint—bowed their heads. "Lord," he prayed aloud, "thank You for this opportunity to come into a new land where we hope to live our lives for Your glory. Please give us safety as we run this race, keeping our eyes on You. Bless our mounts and give them swiftness and sureness of foot and endurance, and give us strength this day and in the days to come as we start our new lives. We ask these things in Your name. Amen."

Alice looked at her watch. "It's nearly time," she said and reached for her canteen to take a drink.

Elijah did likewise. Then, after replacing their canteens in their saddlebags, they each took up their reins and sat forward in their saddles. Elijah felt his bay's shoulders bunch as the gelding sensed he would soon get to run.

"Good luck, Elijah," Alice said in a voice just loud enough for him to hear it. "God bless you and thank you for all you and your brothers did."

"Good luck to you, Alice, and God keep you safe."

This was it. The soldiers in the tower were standing now, two of them aiming a spyglass in either direction, no doubt to see soldiers up and down the line. The soldier carrying the rifle had aimed it at the sky.

"Get ready!" bawled the mounted cavalryman nearby.

Elijah thought he heard a distant report down the line, and a second later, the nearby soldier shot his round, too.

Hundreds of cries and the thunder of hundreds of hooves echoed around him as their mounts surged forward. The Land Rush was on!

Chapter Twenty-Three

Alice had never known a more terrifying, more exhilarating time in her whole life as the first few minutes after the rifle shot had sounded. Immediately she and Elijah were swept up in a sea of galloping riders and dust. It was a wall of noise—the thunder of hooves, the pounding of wagon wheels, the crack of whips and shouts echoing all around them. Alice heard a resounding crack as, somewhere in the thickly packed galloping horses and jolting wagons, an axle snapped. Some fifty yards to her side, she saw a canvas wagon top waver and fall as the wagon with the broken axle went down. She said a quick prayer for those inside it, hoping they weren't injured by the crash or trampled by those behind them.

Was it Keith Gilbert's wagon? she wondered furiously. No, there it was, behind them, with Gilbert flapping the reins, urging his team onward. Winona clung to her galloping horse as if she was one with it.

She saw Elijah bent low over his mount's neck, his bay running neck and neck with her Appaloosa. As if feeling her eyes on him, he took one hand from the reins and pointed his thumb up. She nodded. They could not have heard each other over the din if they'd shouted at the tops of their lungs.

She turned her eyes to the prairie ahead of them, keeping Lars's buckskin in sight, and reminded herself to scan the ground just ahead of them continually. Cheyenne was a plenty savvy horse, but a gopher hole in their path could spell disaster for both of them.

They rode at a full gallop for at least a half hour, then, at Lars's signal, slowed slightly to a lope, a fast canter that ate up the ground beneath them and that the horses could keep up for a long while. The crowd had thinned around them as riders and wagons split off to the south, north and due west of them. Here and there she'd seen some even jumping off their horses and wagons, unwilling to take their chances farther on, shoving stakes with white banners attached to them into the ground.

Half an hour after that, Lars signaled them to trot. "We're coming to a stream soon. We'll stop there and refresh ourselves, *ja?*"

"What's that up ahead?" Elijah called to Lars in midafternoon, pointing off to his left. "Between the trees. It's shining. Can that be the Cimarron?"

"*Ja,* it's the Cimarron!" Lars called back, his face creased in a grin as broad as Oklahoma. "As soon as we get closer, we'll turn west and follow it to the Brave Rock."

"Hallelujah!" cried Elijah.

"Thank God," Alice said. She knew now how the ancient tribes of Israel must have felt upon reaching the Promised Land.

It still felt like an eternity till they spotted it—the black boulder sticking up out of the curving brownish-green water, just beyond its red clay bank.

"Brave Rock, there it is!" Clint cried. "Yee-haa!"

Even the horses seemed to gain a second wind, speeding once more into a gallop. When the group came to it, they stopped for a moment, letting their horses rest. Here would be their town.

Gideon looked over his shoulder then. "There's a rider coming way back there. Don't know if he's one of your flock or not, Lije, but we'd better get going and stake our claims."

Alice looked back and saw the distant speck. Gideon had to have the eyes of a hawk to identify it as a man on horseback, but it *was* coming fast in this direction.

Lars said he was heading just south of where the town would be situated, and spurred off. Then Clint and Gideon headed off in one direction, she and Elijah in the other.

Alice followed him on a deer track that headed more southwesterly than Clint and Gideon had gone, not far from the rock and the river it jutted out of.

She knew from Elijah's smile when they reached the ideal spot—a wide meadow dotted here and there with trees. In the distance just to the east, she spotted a twin line of trees that probably flanked one of the many streams that meandered into the Cimarron.

By tacit agreement, they reined in their mounts.

"How does this place suit you?" Elijah asked.

"It looks just right," she said. There was no sign of anyone else's stake planted anywhere, and they had spotted no one behind them. Whoever had been coming behind them must have gone another way.

"How about if I plant my stake over yonder?" She pointed to where a walnut tree stood.

"All right by me," Elijah agreed. "I'll plant mine there." He pointed to a slight rise to the west of it. "Two parcels, side by side."

They galloped in each direction and, in a minute, had each stuck their stakes into the red Oklahoma clay.

She had done it! She was the proud possessor of a homestead of 160 acres of Oklahoma soil, Alice thought, hugging herself from sheer happiness. No matter what happened, this was *hers*. No one could take it away from her.

And then she realized the one thing—the one *person*—who could complete her joy. Her mare, cropping the lush grass, had strayed a few feet while Alice had planted her stake, but now Alice mounted again, nudging the Appaloosa into a lope toward where she could see Elijah pacing off a rectangle of land—no doubt where he would place his church.

He looked up as she approached and waited with a half smile on his lips, a smile that grew broader as she skidded to a stop.

"Are you happy with your land, Alice? Where are you going to place your infirmary?"

Intent on what she had been about to tell him, she said absently, "Oh, probably in the shade of that walnut tree... Elijah, I came to tell you something."

Elijah looked at her intently. "And what is that, Alice?"

She knew she was risking everything now. He

might tell her that he was standing firm in not marrying again, but something in his face told her there was nothing to fear.

She jumped off her horse and into his waiting arms. "I came to tell you that I love you, Elijah Thornton. My life will only be complete if it's lived with you."

It must have been just what he had been waiting to hear, for he lowered his mouth to hers and kissed her for a long, sweet time. "And I love you, Alice Hawthorne. Let's get married just as soon as we can, all right?"

"More than all right," she said, and kissed him again to show him how much more.

Suddenly the sound of a horse coming fast had them jumping apart. Both of them tensed.

It was Gideon. Elijah relaxed and Alice saw a broad smile replace the wary look he had worn a moment before. Gideon would be the first to hear their good news, Alice thought.

And then she saw the shocked, haggard look on Gideon's face.

Gideon reined his mount to a skidding stop. "You've got to come quick, Alice, Lije…"

"What's happened?" Elijah demanded. "Is Clint hurt?"

"No, he's all right, far as I know…. I saw him galloping off to the land he wanted." Gideon was breathless, and his words tumbled out between gasps. "But there was this other fellow—the one that was comin' behind us, I think—he seemed to be following me… heading straight for the claim I was aiming for…"

"Slow down, Gideon, take a drink," Elijah said, offering him his canteen.

Gideon took a long, shaky draft. "The last stretch before the land I'd picked out is a little tricky—Lars had warned me of it. The path is narrow and climbs steeply, but it's the quickest way there. I took it, and this fellow tried to follow. Then I saw out of the corner of my eye when his horse stumbled and went down.... I—I figured I'd go back just as soon as I planted my stake, so I did, and...he's hurt bad, Alice. The horse fell on him, best I can figure. You've got to hurry...see if there's anything you can do for him. He's pale as paper, Alice..."

Elijah and Alice exchanged a look. "I don't have my medical kit—I packed it in the wagon," she said. "There are just a few bandages in the saddlebag..." But she knew she had to try to do what she could. She grabbed Cheyenne's reins again.

Elijah had already unsaddled his horse, so he jumped on behind Alice, and they took off, following Gideon's galloping mount.

It felt like an eternity until Gideon reined in again. "There he is!" he cried, pointing as he jumped off and ran to the sprawled figure in the grass. Alice noted a riderless horse grazing nearby, its reins trailing, saddle still on its back.

As soon as Gideon got close to the man, he recoiled and turned away, shuddering.

Alice walked past Gideon and looked down at the injured man. She knew as soon as she caught sight of the wide staring eyes in the man's unfamiliar, bloodless face that they were too late. She hoped he hadn't suffered for long, whoever he was.

"He's gone, Gideon. I'm sorry," she murmured.

Elijah had come up behind her, and now bent and shut the man's eyes.

"What if I'd stopped and gone back right away?" Gideon asked, stricken. "I should have gone back..."

"No, Gideon," she reassured him. "The horse probably did fall on him, causing internal injuries. No one could have saved him."

Gideon took a deep breath. "You're sure?"

"I'm sure."

Clint had arrived on the scene, no doubt alerted of trouble by some brotherly sixth sense. Elijah quickly informed him of what had happened.

"Any idea who he is?" Elijah asked his brothers and Alice. "I've never seen him before."

Gideon stepped over and looked at the man again. "Me neither." Clint said the same.

Alice shrugged. "He's no one I've treated in Boomer Town."

"I'm going to say a prayer for him, and then we'd better contact the authorities," Elijah said.

Alice felt a tear slide down her cheek for the unfortunate man. She wondered if he had a wife and a family. Were they even now waiting back in one of the tent cities for him?

"I'll take him with me and find the authorities," Clint said to Elijah. "Gideon, help me catch that stray horse over there, and we'll tie the man on him. You and Lije stay here, and watch over Alice and our claims."

It was a sobering reminder of how quickly tragedy could strike in the midst of joy, Alice thought, as Elijah put a comforting arm around her. This accident could have happened to any one of them during the perilous race, she realized, and she said her own prayer of thanksgiving for the way the Lord had kept all of them safe—and for the strong arms around her now. She leaned her head against Elijah.

They slept on their bedrolls that night, Alice under the walnut tree that would soon shade her infirmary, Elijah across the meadow on his adjoining land— when he wasn't taking his turn standing watch so Gideon could rest.

She didn't mind sleeping under the open sky, for Oklahoma had brought all the stars out this night to display God's glory.

Two wagons arrived about noon the next day, bringing the Thornton brothers' and Alice's tents and belongings. Keith Gilbert drove the Thornton wagon. He had left an exhausted Winona at their claim, for the Cheyenne woman had ridden through the night back to Boomer Town to lead Katrine and Cassie Gilbert to Brave Rock. Alice's wagon was driven by Lars. Katrine was resting with Winona. Lars had brought Dakota with him, for the boy had gotten a good night's rest, and Lars was afraid he would plague his aunt and Katrine while they tried to sleep.

For a few minutes they each told about their experiences in the Land Rush, and of seeing members of the congregation who'd staked homesteads nearby— the Ferguson sisters, the Lamberts and—especially heartening to Elijah—the LeMasters. Polly and Felix Fairhaven had staked a town lot next to Molly Murphy's, so it seemed the future mercantile would be next to the future café.

"You have a—how do you say it?—a long face, Gideon," Lars commented. "What's wrong?"

Gideon told him about the man who'd been crushed by his horse while trying to beat Gideon to his claim.

"*Ja*, that's a bad business," Lars agreed.

"I saw several cracked-up wagons and carriages on the way here," Keith Gilbert said. "Any idea who he was?"

Gideon, Clint, Elijah and Alice shook their heads. "The cavalry contingent I met didn't have any ideas, either, but they're going to make inquiries."

"Well, I say we are all very lucky, to arrive on our claims in one piece, *ja?*"

"Blessed," Keith Gilbert said.

"There's something I want to get off our wagon right now," Elijah told them. Going to it, he reached into a place just behind the driver's seat and came out with a burlap-wrapped rectangle.

"What's that?" Clint asked.

Elijah grinned as he unwrapped the parcel and let the burlap fall. It was a light red brick. He enjoyed watching everyone's baffled expressions. Finally he saw the light dawning in Gideon's eyes.

"Is that—?"

"It *is*, brother. A brick from our very own kiln on our plantation, Thornton Hall. I took it that last day we were there, planning to use it someday when we built a church. It'll be our cornerstone."

The Thornton brothers smiled at each other. A piece of their past, forming a piece of the future church.

"And I'd guess you and Alice have good news to tell, don't you, Reverend Elijah?" Cassie asked.

Elijah grinned. "Is it that obvious?" He put his arm proudly around Alice, who leaned into him, blushing. "I'm proud to tell you that Alice has consented to become my wife."

"Oh, my goodness!" Cassie cried, and rushed to give Alice a hug.

"That's fine, mighty fine," her husband agreed. "Congratulations, Reverend."

"Brave Rock's first wedding, *ja?*" Lars said, clapping Elijah on the back. "When is it to be?"

They had told Gideon and Clint about it earlier, of course, but now they were happy to share their plans again.

"Saturday, the first of June," Alice said.

"Yes, we figured it would give folks time to build their houses and start their crops," Elijah said.

"Wait—who's going to marry you two?" Keith asked. "You can't perform your own wedding, can you?"

Elijah smiled. "I'm hoping in the coming weeks to hear of another nearby preacher who'd do it."

"Well, I don't think there'll be a happier couple in Oklahoma," Keith said. "We're all overjoyed for you, aren't we?"

There was a chorus of agreement.

"It'll be right handy, having a nurse in the family, as often as one or the other of us gets banged up," Clint said with a chuckle.

Elijah gazed down at his bride-to-be, lost in Alice's loving sky-blue gaze, and gave her shoulder a squeeze. "The Lord has been amazingly good to us." He'd once loved Marybelle, but now he had been given a new love and a new life. *Thank You, Lord.*

He looked back on how far God had brought the two of them in just three short weeks, from strangers with secret wounds to a loving couple who would soon wed. There would be trials and troubles ahead of them in this new land, but he could go through it all with a smile, with Alice by his side.

"I was reading my Bible this morning when I woke up under the tree where the infirmary will be built," Alice said. "And I found this wonderful passage in Luke—'Ask, and it shall be given you; seek, and ye shall find; knock and it shall be opened unto you.'" She gestured all around her, at the grassy meadow with its wildflowers, and on beyond that, in the direction of the Cimarron River, at the Brave Rock that rose up out of it, at their friends. "I think He's done that, don't you?"

"Spoken like a true preacher's wife," Elijah said and kissed the top of her head.

* * * * *

Dear Reader,

This is the first time I have been asked to participate in an author continuity series, and I found it an enormously challenging and enjoyable process, working with two other authors to make sure our plots and characterizations mesh to form an enjoyable three-book series. I'm grateful to the editors of Love Inspired Historicals for their confidence in me and to fellow continuity authors Karen Kirst and Allie Pleiter, who wrote the second and third book in this series respectively.

Alice Hawthorne is dear to my heart because she, like me, is a nurse. In my "other job" I have spent many years in emergency nursing, which gave me an added understanding in the challenges she would have faced nursing the sick and injured on the Oklahoma prairie. Who knew all those classes in nursing history would come in so handy? And I sympathize with Elijah, for it's often difficult to know if the vows one makes in the midst of turmoil are really the Lord's will or not.

I would love for you to visit me at my website at LaurieKingery.com to learn about future releases and past books. I also participate in a blog at ChristianFictionHistoricalSociety.blogspot.com. My blog date is always the nineteenth of the month. And for the fans of my Brides of Simpson Creek series, I'll be returning to Simpson Creek with my next book. The publication date will be posted on my website.

Blessings,
Laurie Kingery

Discussion Questions

1. Elijah Thornton is a minister, yet his brothers have lost their faith. Do you think he feels this is a bad reflection on him as a minister? Why or why not?

2. Alice Hawthorne is fleeing an abusive relationship in an era when women's options were much fewer. Have you ever been in this position? How did you handle it?

3. Alice initially wants to leave her profession, nursing, behind. Have you ever felt that way about your profession or job? How did you handle it?

4. Gideon and Clint Thornton have both lost their faith during a period of loss, but Alice has not, even though she lost her father and is suffering adversity. Why do you suppose Gideon and Clint did, but not Alice?

5. Can you imagine yourself taking part in a land rush such as those that took place in Oklahoma Territory? Why or why not?

6. The Thornton brothers are the targets of bad feelings from the Chaucer family. Have you ever been in a situation like this? Were you able to work it out?

7. Alice makes a number of friends in the tent city of Boomer Town, who essentially become part

of her new family. Do you have friends like this who are as close as family?

8. Alice was afraid of loving Elijah because she thought that he would try to control her, like most men, as she sees it. Besides Maxwell Peterson, who might have been responsible for her feeling this way?

9. When Elijah lost his fiancée, he thought this was a sign that God only wanted him to serve the church from that point on. Have you ever mistaken God's will for you? What did you do about it?

10. The U.S. government opened lands to settlers that had formerly been set aside as Indian territory. Should the government have done that? Why or why not?

11. What character in this story did you most connect with? Why?

12. Elijah seeks to handle the enmity from the Chaucer brothers in a way that glorifies God. How does he show by his actions in this matter that he is a Christian?

13. At the beginning of this story, Elijah is publicly denounced by Horace LeMaster, an ally of the Chaucers. Have you ever been publically criticized and embarrassed as Elijah was? How did you deal with it?

14. Winona Eaglefeather and her nephew, Dakota, choose to adapt to a new culture. Have you ever had to do that?

15. Alice had parents who supported her early dream of being a nurse, even if it meant she left the farm. Did your parents support your goals as you were growing up, and if so, how did their support help you achieve your goals?